SHU WEI'S REVENGE

A NOVEL

JACKSON FAHNESTOCK

Bayside Press
San Francisco, California

Printed in the United States of America

ISBN 978-0-9988034-1-8 (softcover)

Bayside Press
330 Mission Bay Blvd. North, #302
San Francisco, CA 94158
fahnestk@sbcglobal.net
www.jacksonfahnestock.com

cover design by www.ebooklaunch.com

character sketches and map by the author

To my family

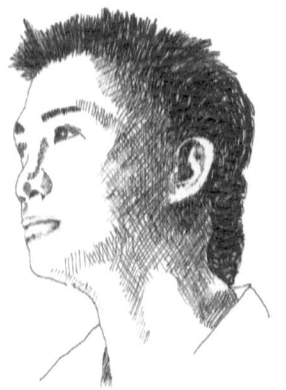

Shu Wei

Shu Lan-lan

Grace Caldwell

Bo Cai

Chun Dai with a
young Shu Wei

A Character Sampling

Lin Feng

Mei Huang

Girls from the orphanage

Jun Min

Yong Qiang

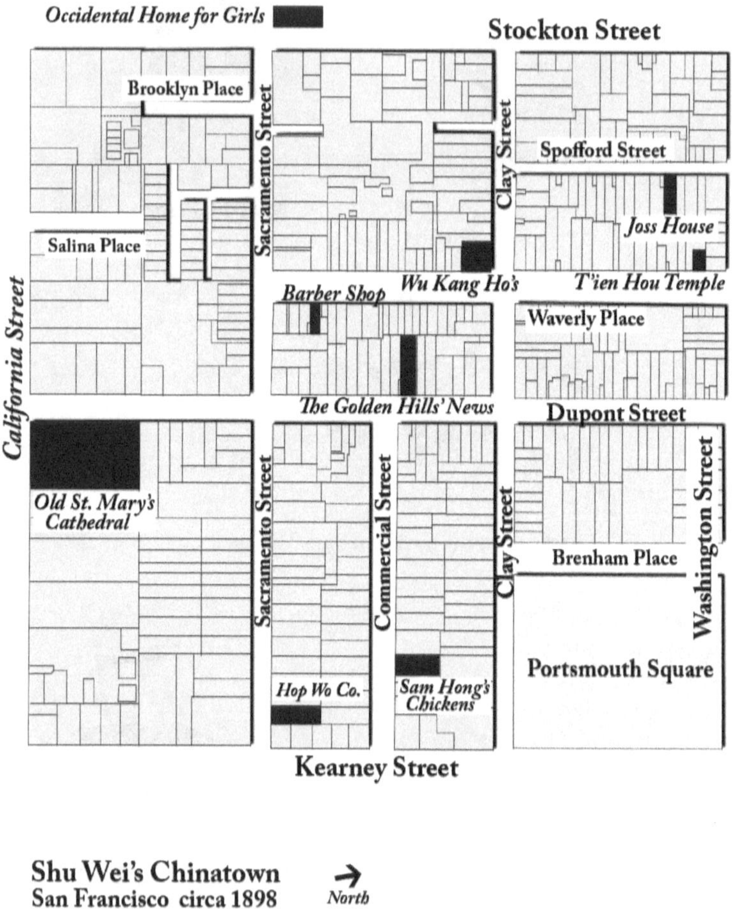

Occidental Home for Girls

Stockton Street

Brooklyn Place

Sacramento Street

Clay Street

Spofford Street

Salina Place

Joss House

California Street

Barber Shop Wu Kang Ho's T'ien Hou Temple

The Golden Hills' News

Waverly Place

Dupont Street

Old St. Mary's Cathedral

Sacramento Street

Commercial Street

Clay Street

Brenham Place

Washington Street

Portsmouth Square

Hop Wo Co.

Sam Hong's Chickens

Kearney Street

Shu Wei's Chinatown
San Francisco circa 1898

→
North

Stockton Street

Church Court

Bo Cai's
Rescue

Stark Street

Pacific Alley

Stout's Alley (Ross St.)

Sullivan's Alley

Cigar
Factory

Court

St Louis Alley

Jackson Street

Pacific Place

Pacific Street

Silver Dragon Rest.

Dupont Street

Hap Tran
Tong

Globe Hotel

Adler Street

Broadway Street

Washington Pl.

Bartlett Alley

Hong Lu's

Pawn
Shop

Montgomery Avenue

Kearney Street

CHAPTER ONE

Fire

Sanhou, China 1898

Dusk had just made its transition to an inky lampblack when seventeen-year-old Shu Wei first smelled the sulphuric odor of smoke. He strained to get a clearer view from the small bedroom window at the front of the house. He already suspected the source. It had to be his father's shop, two blocks away. The wood-snapping fire already had sent red-hot embers skyward in a swirling mass. His bony frame shaking and heart pounding, he gave a frantic shove against the heavy wood front door. As he began running down the street his long fingers tugged at the high collar of his white cotton tunic. Nearly tripping on the rutted dirt road, he frantically grasped at the untied drawstring of his trousers.

Another figure was sprinting just ahead of him toward the blaze, shouting, "No! No! My store . . . my—my life!" His father was half running, half stumbling.

As Shu Wei drew nearer, his eyes strained to penetrate the boiling inferno. A figure with a smoldering stick limped away from the shop. His fear turned into a gut-wrenching panic. His feet were like lead. "Father, father," he yelled in a panicky voice. Gasping for air, he staggered after Lin Feng, the fifty-six-year-old village patriarch of the Tang Chung Ling clan. Too late.

The older man had already launched himself into the burning building. The structure was now fully engulfed in angry flames and acrid smoke.

"Father, please come back! You will burn yourself!" Shu Wei called out in a gravelly voice, the caustic air constricting his throat. But Lin Feng continued unfazed. His delirium made him unaware that his right sleeve and pant leg were already on fire. In desperation, Shu Wei grabbed his father and pulled him away from the fire and quickly wrapped his own heavy tunic around him. Wispy bursts of smoke sprouted from beneath this makeshift shroud. The nauseating odor of burned flesh assaulted Shu Wei's nostrils and his father collapsed into a ball on the ground, shrieking.

"The most evil gods have wreaked eternal havoc," he wailed. "My entire life's work is gone. And . . . and, I could not save . . ."

Shu Wei held his father to his chest, trying to dampen the old man's convulsive sobbing. He ripped shreds from his father's work shirt and tied them around the burns.

"Could not save what, Father? Tell me," Shu Wei pleaded. Lin Feng could only spew hysterics. "I . . . I could not save my apprentice, Yong Loo. I saw him in there, but the flames were too much . . . I could not reach him."

Shu Wei gently cradled his father's head. The patriarch's cropped hair now reeked of charred rosewood and kerosene. Then, something caught Shu Wei's attention. A figure in the shadows of a nearby storefront pulled a scarf around his face. From what Shu Wei could make out, he had a bent frame with a cape-like garment hanging loosely from his slumped shoulders. Rays of light from a kerosene street lamp momentarily gave clarity. A large ring shimmered on his right hand and an angular pin anchored his headpiece of layered cloth.

The over-sized ring and the stooped appearance looked familiar to Shu Wei. *Where have I seen this person before?* In his mind, he moved through a gallery of faces he'd seen, even conversed with on occasion in his role as Town Scribe. A few minutes later, his trance was broken by the clanging of a fire wagon bell. It rang harsh and metallic to his ears, almost like the wind gongs he played at school. *Why such a delay in reaching us?* By now the building had caved in on itself, leaving a festering pile of glowing timbers. The firemen let loose a paltry spray of water that merely dampened the forest of dancing flames.

Shu Wei watched with glazed eyes as the fire warden applied an ointment to Lin Feng's burns—an act that he felt would hardly be adequate. Wrapping a wool blanket around Lin Feng's trembling body the warden began, "How did this disaster . . .?"

Lin Feng broke in, "I'm afraid there will be a b-body in this pile. They must have tied my . . . my apprentice to . . . to a chair and set him afire. I saw him but couldn't reach him." The words had barely cleared his parched lips when his body convulsed into violent spasms. Delicately enfolding him, Shu Wei felt his father's wildly racing heart through the old man's thin hemp work-shirt.

Turning from Shu Wei and his father, the warden signaled to one of his men to begin hacking through the debris. Shortly, two of the men hauled out a blackened shape, wrapped it mummy-like, and laid it next to the fire wagon. Shu Wei drew back, a bout of nausea overcoming him. His father slumped numb and bewildered. Olive-colored eyes looked down to his lap, absently studying his gnarled, soot-stained hands, his thumbs weaving endless circles.

Shu Wei heard muffled gasps and excited chatter behind him. Voices from a growing cluster of townspeople rose and fell, words scattered in the wind: "What happened?" "Disaster!" "Is that the boy who . . .?" "The God of Thunder has visited our town!"

Someone tapped Shu Wei on the shoulder. His rigid body reacted with a start. *What now?* He glanced backward. A furled document was thrust into his hand and the messenger quickly retreated. Still stunned, Shu Wei finally peeled back its ribboned sheath. His eyes strained to gain focus. Slowly he made out a Chinese calligraphic script in dark brown ink on a mottled sepia papyrus sheet. It began, *'The Magistrates of the Honorable Court of Sanhou'*... A sharp pain raced up the back of his tensed neck. Drops of his perspiration partially smudged the lettering. He read on: ... *'requires the presence of Lin Feng and Shu Wei to appear before the Town Tribunal to answer charges related to their various misdeeds. The hearing is to commence on the fourth hour from sunrise of the day hereafter.'*

Lin Feng sat, numbly staring at the ground, head propped by a hand dusted with ash. His eyes were glazed, unseeing. Shu Wei thought better of showing his father the document. *The poor man needs medicine and care,* he thought, his anger rising. *These fools are incapable of giving a helping hand to their own fellow being.*

He gently took his father's good arm and draped it over his shoulder. The two straggled up the street, Lin Feng's limp feet carving winding furrows in the dirt. The curious townspeople followed a short distance, muttering indistinctly before turning back. A mangy black dog yapped at their heels until finally turning back to rejoin its owner.

Once inside their home, Shu Wei laid his limp cargo on their upholstered couch against one wall of the sitting room. For the first time, he could see the true condition of his father. He blamed himself. *What agony have I brought to you, dear father?* he wondered.

Lin Feng shuddered, eyes fixed on the beamed ceiling, murmuring incoherently. The burns on his arm and leg were already starting to blister into a galaxy of white pustules, like fields of white plum blossoms. Blood was spreading in vein-like threads throughout the crude bandages. His dry lips squeezed out a desperate moan.

Shu Wei's sixteen-year-old sister, Shu Lan-lan, and an older woman burst through the front door. "What in the name of the immortals has happened here?" asked their *amah*, "Auntie" Chun Dai. "We were tending our plot of mulberry trees at the town's edge when we heard the fire bells and saw the smoke. Curiosity got the best of us. We had no idea that we would find this!"

Shu Lan-lan was a foot shorter than her brother. Her long neck was encircled by a multi-colored cloth necklace—the lucky one that she wore even as she slept. Her sturdy braids splayed slightly outward. Deep-set chestnut eyes finally caught sight of her father lying motionless. She bent to his forehead and brushed away crumbs of powdery residue. "Dear father, tell me what has happened to you."

Shu Wei broke in, "Our father's store has burned to the ground. His talented apprentice is dead as well."

A torrent of tears streamed down Shu Lan-lan's face as she attacked a nearby table with her clenched fists. A pair of ceramic urns rattled in protest. Chun Dai began to tremble and then collapsed into a nearby chair. At seventy, her skin was a wrinkled bronze from her outdoor labors. Several white mulberry blossoms were still nested in her thinning blue-gray hair. Lips aquiver, she attempted to speak. Nothing came out. Suddenly she hurried to Lin Feng's limp body and gushed, "We must treat his wounds before infection takes hold. Shu Lan-lan, go fetch a wet cloth and a tray of ointments and salves. Shu Wei, get the herbal basket from the cabinet beneath the sink."

In the kitchen, Shu Wei braced his hands against the upper cabinet. His mind racing, he had to keep his head, he had to proceed with caution. *I need to keep my story to myself* he reasoned. *No need to make this devilish mess worse. I never thought it could come to this. I will look for the right time to tell father how this came about.*

Shu Wei felt his throat contract as Chun Dai carefully peeled back the matted pieces of cloth on his father's burned arm and leg. Some of the singed skin had already bonded to the fabric, exposing an oozing scarlet pulp beneath. She applied a dressing of jujube tree bark and gingerly applied new dressings. Chun Dai became a blur as she raced to the sink just in time to cough up bile, the only contents in her empty stomach.

Shu Lan-lan covered her father with a blanket and noticed that he had closed his eyes, trying to ignore the pain. Turning to Shu Wei, she said, "Brother, have you any idea what brought this misery on us?"

Shu Wei had been lost in thought, but his head swung abruptly toward his sister. Nervously fingering a raised childhood scar on his right arm, he said, "No sister. I can only say that the town elders have been in dark moods lately."

Chun Dai returned, dabbing her face and neck with a damp towel. "What do you mean by 'dark moods'?" she asked.

"I . . . I can't say exactly. The other day they were staring at me and muttering things I could not make out. Their hands covered their mouths as I approached." As he spoke, tiny globes of moisture formed on his upper lip. *I think I'm getting myself in deeper. Hopefully they won't ask more questions.* "They have told father and me to appear before a tribunal at the town square tomorrow morning."

"What could be the reason for . . ." Shu Lan-lan paused when she heard her father moan as he shifted stiffly on the couch. His tightly-woven hair had become a mass of damp, ashy flakes. Dried blood streaked one cheek.

"We must get your father into his own bed. He will need all the energy he can muster for tomorrow the way it sounds," said Chun Dai.

Shu Wei was aware of a steady glare from his sister as they struggled with Lin Feng's limp body. *I'm certain that when my story comes out they will all understand.*

When Lin Feng was stabilized, Shu Wei and Shu Lan-lan each retreated to their rooms and collapsed on their beds. Chun Dai gave chants to Buddha at the family shrine in the main hall. Hands trembling, she lit two joss sticks anchored in a porcelain urn that sat on a lacquered rosewood bench.

That evening, sheer emotional exhaustion allowed only fitful sleep for everyone. Shu Wei sat upright in bed. His head drooped, only to snap upward each time. He felt a tautness developing in his muscles. A leg cramp caused him to abruptly crawl out of bed. He curled up in a fetal position on the heavy plank flooring in the corner of his room, folding his long arms around his bent knees, pulling them tight to his chest.

CHAPTER TWO

A Tribunal

The next morning, Shu Wei was unconsciously covering his ears, trying to escape the ceaseless pounding noise. Curling even tighter into a ball in the corner of his room he yanked his sweat-soaked tunic around his head as a fortification against the intrusive knocking.

"Shu Wei! Shu Wei!" Chun Dai burst into the room. "What are you doing on the floor? You must come quickly. The man is here from the town. He said you must come now."

"Where is father? Have they taken him?" He attempted to rise but his right arm collapsed, sending him against the wall with a thud. Regaining his stability, he rose and rubbed his bloodshot eyes.

"He is waiting in the entry. The man is angry. Hurry."

His father stood, shakily clutching his burned arm with one hand and leaning into the entry door frame with the other for balance. A man with a bent nose, a permanent scowl, and a wrinkled black mole on one cheek had a vice grip on Lin Feng's shoulder. Shu Wei was still trying to shake his sleepless fog. "Let us live our lives in peace," said Shu Wei. "We have done nothing to bring this grief on our family."

Shu Lan-lan stood nearby, unspeaking, her reddened face buried in her hands. Abruptly, the man loosened his grip on

Lin Feng and charged Shu Wei, grabbing a handful of skin on the back of his neck. Shu Wei grimaced, letting out a gurgled protest.

"You will join us now in our little ceremony!" ordered the man. "And you will not utter another word. Is that understood?"

Chun Dai screamed her protests as she watched the trio head toward the town square. "Criminals! You will hear from our most beloved god, *Chu-Jung*. He will bring us justice and serve revenge on your filthy souls." She pulled her apron to her face in despair as the man turned his head and spat in her direction.

As the three arrived at the town square, Shu Wei's legs were rubbery. Their overseer brought Shu Wei and his father to either side of him. Lin Feng's face was drained of all color and his knees were trembling under the strain. The man abruptly lifted him under the armpits and said, "Stand like a man, you old fool!"

The five town elders were seated on a two-level wooden platform in the center of the cobbled square. The town was governed by *jia gui*, village rules and regulations that reflected the dual lineage of the dominant Tang and Liao clans. A magistrate from a northern province sent forth his edicts to be enforced by these officials. It was commonly known that infighting between the two clans had recently strained the integrity and balance of governance.

The platform seemed purposely placed so that it was directly across from the heavy-timbered structure that housed the Writers Guild. It was here, not all that long ago, that Shu Wei was awarded the prestigious tan and white robe of the Town Scribe.

Shu Wei had hoped that that day was to be the beginning of a grand future for him. He reflected on how fleeting and tenuous optimism can be.

Out of the corner of one eye Shu Wei caught a blurred impression of the milling crowd of townspeople gathering to observe the spectacle. He could occasionally hear fragments of their mutterings, some born of curiosity, some of hostility.

The five town elders were seated, three on the lower level, two on the upper. They sat on padded velvet cushions with gold-colored trim. Shu Wei felt their eyes staring icily beneath long flowing shags of hair. Their black beards reached almost to their waist-bound sabers. Elaborate splashes of color covered their lavish gowns—the only softening elements in the stygian cluster. Crude serpentine medallions in hammered brass impaled their beaded headdresses. Shu Wei had never encountered that kind of display of pomposity and self-importance.

The taller figure on the top right spoke first. His shaggy mock beard had drifted lazily off his upper lip. It reminded Shu Wei of a comic in a Chinese opera. His cape sported an image of a fire-breathing Chinese Dragon. The animal's sharp taloned feet were poised for attack. Fire gushed from a mouth rigid with sinister intensity. Several pronged horns grew from a head with angry bulging eyes. Flames licked outward from his tail. An oversized ring consumed an entire finger on the man's right hand. *That ring! I know that ring!* Shu Wei knew instantly that this had to be the man in the shadows at the fire. Shu Wei named him Huǒlóng, Fiery Dragon. How appropriate he thought. His pulse quickened as he realized that this man must also be the leader of the heinous group.

"You, Shu Wei, and you, Lin Feng, are before us today to address your criminal and immoral acts," said a squatty man with a tinny voice from the lower riser. His eyes curved downward toward a misshapen nose.

Shu Wei drew back in shock. Do his ears deceive him? *Criminal? Immoral?* These words, he felt, had to be uttered by a fool if they were aimed at his hard-working father and him.

The squatty man continued, "First, it is the opinion of this body that you, Shu Wei, have forsaken the trust of this town by abusing your position as Town Scribe. You will be banned from any such future activities and discharged from this town."

"Your most honored elder, I find your charges without merit and . . .," challenged Shu Wei.

"Silence!" yelled a figure with a tangled beard projecting goat-like from his chin. "You will cease your blather instantly. We are not gathered to hear the ramblings of a crazed scribe. Your skills brought you a trusted role in this town, but you have misused them in a most dangerous way. You will remain silent from here on!"

Huŏlóng spoke next. "Lin Feng, you are charged with setting fire to your store to avoid your obligations to the treasury. It is clear to all that your intentions were to stage this event, even to the point of burning yourself to enhance your disillusioned sense of innocence. Even more villainous and despicable, you bound up your poor unsuspecting apprentice, Yong Loo, doused him in kerosene, and lit the fire. Very simply, you caused his incineration. We also know that you have been unable to comply with your obligations to compensate him properly, leading you to employ this contemptible remedy. As if all of this weren't enough, you failed to submit, for the past three years, proper taxes to this township. Your acts are deceitful and beneath the morality of a *yáng*, a rice weevil. You will be punished accordingly." A wave of anxious chatter swept the crowd of onlookers like the flapping of so many birds taking flight.

Shu Wei leaned out far enough to catch a glimpse of his father. He looked as though he would collapse into a heap onto the cobblestones at any moment. Just then, his father seemed to find a hidden resolve and he held himself erect in a surge of pride and resistance.

Lin Feng boomed out, "Your charges are beyond slanderous! The charges you speak of are without foundation and . . .

and are designed to conceal the dirty misdeeds of certain townspeople. I built my furniture and woodworking shop from sweat and goodwill over the past twenty-four years. People gathered here will give good testament to all of this. Besides, I am a descendent of the Tang Chung Ling clan. We have proud beginnings. Our people . . ."

"Quiet, you old goat!" the long-necked one in the top row hissed. "You will be carved up and spread like manure in a farmer's field if you insist on continuing your outbursts."

But Lin Feng only raised his voice more defiantly. "I carried on even after the tragic death of my wife ten years ago. And you know that my son has been a faithful contributor to the arts and writings in this town. He . . ."

Huǒlóng had had enough. "Stop, you imbecile! You are only making a grander fool of yourself. The charges brought before this tribunal are incontestable. It has been hereby decreed by this body that, starting three days hence, your family will cease to reside or transact business in this town. Further, you will all forgo the benefit of your properties and other assets; they will be reassigned to the town and village of Sanhou. You should consider yourselves highly fortunate. This body has chosen not to invoke the death penalty only after the Chief Magistrate levied a more lenient order. You may now remove your shameful selves from this square."

Shu Wei stood, frozen in place, still trying to imagine how his life could change so dramatically, so quickly. All at once he was aware of a light-headedness. The next thing he knew, he was collapsing onto to his knees. Dumbfounded, he rose unsteadily looking around at a spinning collage of tree limbs, sky, and faces.

As he regained his equilibrium, a fuzzy outline of a figure came into focus. A man from the crowed grabbed him around the waist and steadied him. He discreetly placed a wadded-up piece of paper in Shu Wei's hand and whispered, "Keep this from sight!" Before he could thank the man for aiding him, he had disappeared into the crowd. The townspeople were edging their way backward, most still trying to digest the meaning of what they had witnessed.

When Shu Wei finally glanced over at his father, he saw him perilously hunched over. Gently, Shu Wei pulled his father upright and the two wobbled back up the street to their home, unspeaking. Lin Feng was now limping badly as he clutched at his bandaged leg.

Shu Lan-lan and Chun Dai stood, hands clasped, waiting expectantly at the front door. Shu Lan-lan ran and embraced her brother, then, more gingerly, held her father. Expressions of anguish took the place of words. Finally, Chun Dai said, "Come in and let us know what happened, however dark the news."

Shu Wei brushed her aside as he guided his father back to the lattice-back couch in the main hall and placed a pillow behind him. "The town elder judges are fiends!" he shouted. "Their version of justice speaks to their evil intent and corrupt ways. We were to never have a fair hearing. They have managed to draw the very life force from our souls."

Lin Feng, eyes locked on an insect winding an erratic route over a bowl of aging fruit, said, "We cannot remake the minds of a few who are set on destroying others for the sake of their own gain. Shu Wei, their references to your 'abuse of your position as Town Scribe' puzzles me. Perhaps you can tell us more."

Shu Wei silently wandered the room with its family heirlooms and idols, pausing to stare at a faded photo in a tarnished frame. Just a day after his fifth birthday his Auntie had hold of his hand as they made their way to the market, both carrying folded bamboo-ribbed umbrellas. Shu Wei had a glow of pride on his face. Auntie, with her life-hardened visage, gave off an air of certainty, protection. His heart suddenly ached for a return to those bucolic times.

Haltingly, Shu Wei said, "Father . . . I—I am at as big a loss as you. My—my mind is turned upside down. There is no reason . . ."

Shu Lan-lan broke in, her voice building in intensity, "Dearest brother, you must not deceive your own family. This is no time to pull away from us."

Pivoting away from the group, as if to shield himself from the pain of answering, Shu Wei's eyes were drawn to another picture in a frame with brass corner-holds sitting on a mahogany table. He and Shu Lan-lan sat cross-legged, arms splayed backward against warm grassy ground as they listened intently to the lively telling of one of Auntie's many Chinese folk tales at the base of their sacred mulberry tree.

"I am deceiving no one!" Shu Wei barked. "What of the charges against our father? Is he less guilty than I? Their vile pronouncements spared neither of us. I have no more reason to feel their slander is better placed against one or the other of us."

"Please! Please!" said Lin Feng. "The devil has taken up residency in our fine town and invades our home. I have lately become aware of other townspeople having their property raided under imaginary claims. Their monies are now owed to the treasury for life. They endure their lives robbed of fairness and justice. These villains that perpetrate these acts are said to have come from the north under orders from Empress Dowager Cixi. They were to extinguish the foreign devils but are now catching smaller fish in their nets for their own gain. I do not want their lawless and deceitful ways to tear this family apart. We have worked too hard making something of our lives to . . ." He suddenly let out a cry of anguish as he grabbed his leg.

Calming, he continued, "I should tell you all something that I've been meaning to say for a while now. The prospect of leaving our little village and home is something none of us can imagine. But, in my case, it may offer relief. The ghost of my beloved wife inhabits every splinter of every stout timber in this home. I have no means of escape from that. I know you all miss her dearly and are feeling this painful sadness as well; but mine has become intolerable."

Shu Lan-lan whimpered, "Father, I had no idea that . . ."

"Please, allow me to finish. My furniture and woodworking business has suffered, mainly I believe due to my despondency. But there are other things that I can't share with you at this time. It has to do with my business as well. In time, I will give all of you a full accounting of these matters. So, these worries have brought me to this point."

Shu Wei's stomach tightened as he considered his own reason for desperately wanting to stay in Sanhou—his writing. But when he had mentioned this long-term goal to his father before, Lin Feng cautioned that the pen would only get him in trouble. 'You should get a proper skill, like woodworking. I make products that give satisfaction and that also fill a need.' Shu Wei had told his father that he had no interest in standing in sawdust all day and that writing, while not resulting in something three-dimensional, gives satisfaction and has its own merits. His father had glared at him and had turned back to his workbench, saying nothing. Shu Wei still marked that day in his fourteenth year as a turning point in his relationship with his father. The father-son link had become more tenuous. He wasn't quite sure of the source of this wedge: his own need for a clear path to the future? A fear of restrictive subservience, even though it was his own father? Or maybe just because it *was* his own father?

The air in the room suddenly felt to Shu Wei like there were fewer breaths left in it. Heavy, damp. He nervously loosened the upturned collar of his tunic; it now showed dark gray-brown perspiration patches as testament to the frenzied emotions of the last two days.

Auntie stroked her furrowed brow and tried her best to head off the trickle of tears that soon became a cascade. Shu Wei reached his long arm around her broad shoulders and held her. She buried her head deep into his chest.

Lin Feng continued, "I feel we have no choice but to take the threats of our tormentors seriously. We must look after our own welfare, even if it means severing deep roots. My own concerns over the past few weeks led me to correspond with my dear friends, Li Po Tun, the doctor, and Wu Kang Ho, the merchant who has been a loyal part of my trading business. They have arranged passage for us to San Francisco by way of Hong Kong. We will leave early in the morning two days hence."

Out of the corner of his eye, Shu Wei saw something float to the floor. He suddenly remembered the mystery man who handed him a crumpled piece of paper at the end of the tribunal session. He must have been clenching it in his fist until now. Retrieving it he saw that it was a hand-written note; written in handsome Chinese seal characters with the name of a merchant known to Shu Wei at the top. The words read, *I can help you!* The signature of one Wei Zhang appeared at the bottom.

CHAPTER THREE

Memories and Madness

The next morning Shu Wei awoke with a spasm of pain in his lower back. "*Āi yōu*," he muttered, uncurling his aching body. He straightened his stained gown and, with curled knuckles, vigorously rubbed his tousled hair. His clothing was still layered with a sooty residue; he hadn't changed in two days. Gradually sitting up he felt the pinch of the floor bed's straw stuffing. Every movement taxed his joints. Standing up was a struggle. Tense shoulder muscles still carried the weight of yesterday's debacle. He ran his tongue over chapped lips. After gargling stale water from a ceramic ewer, he spat the frothy residue on the floor.

He stared at a photo of himself on his dresser. At the age of seven he was intently strumming a honey-colored Chinese *yáng pí pá*, a mandolin. In a sudden impulse, Shu Wei knocked it violently from its stand. Glass shards and frame fragments scattered about the floor.

He stood transfixed, staring at the shiny bits on the floor. Then his eyes swept the room. It suddenly came to him. He would no longer see this home again. A home that had meant the world to him. Built thirty years ago, it was still considered a *xīn jū*, a new house, in this year of 1898. Based on the *sze-hop-yuen* style, it was square in shape. All rooms surrounded a central courtyard where the sun spilled into the adjacent rooms. The entry, courtyard, and main hall, were aligned along a north-south axis according to *feng shui* principles. Most of the family's celebrations and ceremonies took place around the grand elm table in the main hall. A modest shrine for the worship of deities and ancestors stood along the north wall nearby.

Even though the village of Sanhou consisted of only twelve hundred inhabitants, Lin Feng enjoyed the status of a respected merchant. His home's details spoke of the importance and relative wealth of this family. Outside, a richly-decorated roof ridge and wall frieze added to the character. Inside, mouldings of floral motifs adorned some walls. Two pilastered columns were capped by elaborate serpent-fish. Ceilings of hand-cut wooden beams rested on a regular grid of lacquered posts.

A hard knock on the bedroom door broke Shu Wei's reverie. Shu Lan-lan peeked in at the debris, stared at him, and said, "You must keep your wits. As father says, 'nothing is to be gained by allowing rage to consume you.' Please come downstairs. Auntie has prepared a hearty congee with *rousong* and *zha cai.*"

"My rage is my only outlet," shouted Shu Wei. "Our lives have been ruined by this black madness."

Collapsing into her brother's side and sliding an arm around his waist, Shu Lan-lan whispered, "Forgive me, brother, but we must spend our emotions wisely. We have long and difficult days ahead." Together they crossed the courtyard to the high-ceilinged main hall.

Idle thoughts again filled Shu Wei's head. He remembered times when he and his sister would play happily in their father's workshop in the town, even joining him for tea at his workbench on occasion. The smells were intoxicating: oils, oozing saps, mahogany and sandalwood scents, and the scorched smell of wood being cut or sanded. They rescued small wood shapes from the cutting room and made them into fantastical constructs: towers, temples, even bridges. The sawdust leavings were scraped away to provide roads and paths. A small village sprang up in one corner. Sometimes he taunted his younger sister by scooping up some of these shavings and sprinkling them on her head like caramel-colored snowflakes. It always ended the same way—Shu Lan-lan running to her father crying and her father giving them each a broom and a small cloud of Dragon's Beard Candy, quickly followed by orders to clean the shop. Those were good times.

Now he was picking up the pungent aroma of Auntie's special rice porridge. It normally delighted Shu Wei, but not today. The gauzy curtains across the dining room's opening to the corridor let in random sprays of sunlight, but things seemed darker, gloomier. The creaking of the floorboards seemed to be more invasive. Even the shadows had menacing forms. He wondered if this was the new reality. Even his head felt heavier, his mind disoriented. Misery had engulfed him gradually, but now thoroughly. Shu Wei lowered himself into a lotus-like position on a long wool floor runner. Chun Dai handed him a bowl giving off waves of steam. He toyed with the flossy pork topping on the porridge.

"Break from your trance, Shu Wei, and eat," implored Chun Dai. "We still have many things to do. Our precious hours here are already slipping by. I have sent an urgent notice by courier to Lin Po Tun and Wu Kang Ho in Hong Kong that the three of you should be met at the main dock in the Central District."

"Father, will you please join us!" Shu Lan-lan pleaded as she leaned through the doorway to the library just adjacent. Lin Feng sat rooted to his favorite purple sandalwood chair in his reading corner. On one side of him a small brass tub held a few faded red joss sticks with their soft spinning entrails of smoke. On his other side, a woven bamboo basket, lid up, held several antique Chinese woodworking tools, including files, corner jigs, chops, sharpening stones, and a mortise chisel. Lin Feng waved off her comment and languidly contemplated his favorite tool, a plane, like the one claimed by Chinese mythology to have been invented by Lu Ban, a scholar turned woodworker. He kept turning and stroking it over and over, his face betraying resignation.

Shu Wei sensed that his father had slipped into a kind of mental fog. *I have lost him,* he thought. *Very little of him is with us now.* Lin Feng's reddened eyes had grown dusky. His shoulders folded inward toward his chest as he fondled the tools. But most disturbingly, his wound dressings now showed the ominous glaze of infection.

"Come, children," interjected Auntie. "When we've finished I would like to make a final visit to our favorite mulberry tree. We will collect healing fruit and bring them back to Lin Feng to revitalize his blood."

The dishes were washed and the three headed to the mulberry grove at the edge of town. Shu Wei's melancholy made him oblivious to the damp sweet scent of the narcissus and citron flowers lining the path. The family had tended the lot as long as they had lived in Sanhou. Their sacred white mulberry tree loomed just ahead, the site of many happy rendezvous and folk stories read by Chun Dai, like the *Dream of the Red Chamber.* It stood proudly in a grove of thirty others. The threesome settled on an old wedding quilt.

Craggy and wrapped in twisted sinewy black bark, the tree's trunk proudly bore its age of seventy-two years. A web of gnarly branches supported a dense network of bright green leaves that still held a scattering of small over-ripe puffy fruit. A semicircle of rocks that was arranged at its base served as an open air chapel—a place to entreat spirits, particularly troubled ones. Shu Wei's eyes were locked on the stones. He suddenly scrambled to his feet. Without a word he bolted down the path that led home. A trail of swirling dust marked his flight.

Shu Lan-lan and Auntie sat open-mouthed. It happened so quickly. Had he gone mad or snapped? Or worse—was he suddenly bent on revenge on the elders? They rolled up the quilt and hurried back home, Shu Lan-lan having to wait now-and-again for Auntie whose aged limbs were less limber these days.

Shu Wei, reaching the house long before his sister and Auntie, flew at the front door. "Father!! Father!!" he screamed, as he ran inside. Lin Feng stood on his favorite chair in the library, attempting to hang himself. He had just tossed the loose end of the rope over a crossbeam above, preparing to secure it in place. The other end was wound in several tight convolutions around his neck. Shu Wei snatched the loose end from his father and, surprised at his own strength, folded him over his shoulder and lowered him to the floor. Another few minutes, Shu Wei knew, would have meant having to bear the loss of another parent—a parent to whom he already owed a great deal. He intended, more than ever now, to forge a greater bond. He would find a way to ease the pain. *There must be a way.*

Shu Wei and Lin Feng both lay prone, side by side, the younger man's chest heaving. For a time, Shu Wei's thoughts were ephemeral, forming and evaporating like a kettle's steam. He was incapable of bringing shape to words. Sometimes it's best to hide in the silence for now.

The two still had not moved when Shu Lan-lan and Auntie burst in. "Great Son of Heaven, what has happened here?" wailed Auntie as Shu Lan-lan pried the rope from Shu Wei's clenched fist. She then loosened the coiled portion from around her father's neck and held his head in her hands. "Why? Why father?" Her eyes bore into his as if, deep in those dark orbs, reasons would be found.

"Shu Wei, is this why you left us so unexpectedly? Did you sense something?" Auntie asked.

Dazed and facing his amah he said, "I must have had a sign of some kind. But I really don't believe in that sort of thing.

Looking at the rocks around the mulberry tree I was remembering our celebrations of the spirits we used to have and then. . . ." his voice trailed off. "Thinking about our deceased ancestors may have triggered my next thought. This morning father had pulled out his farming rope that he uses to haul stumps from the fields. I didn't give it much thought at the time but I'm glad it stayed with me."

"Shu Wei, I need you to be at your father's side at all times before we leave," demanded Auntie. "I will prepare a bed beside him. And please take that rope and carry it to the ends of the canal and bury it. I will also remove all sharp implements from the kitchen. Your father needs to be closely watched. You'll need to confer with his friends in Hong Kong about all this."

Later that night Shu Wei lay facing his father in bed, in a dazed, semiconscious state. Every twitch his father made brought him upright. Finally, leaning back against the wall, he listened to Lin Feng's labored exhalations until his own exhaustion took over. The young man fell asleep next to the elder, two heartbeats searching for a common rhythm.

CHAPTER FOUR

Leaving Home

Two days later, a third quarter moon still showed its muted profile early in the morning as Shu Wei's family gathered next to the canal. Auntie Chun Dai had convinced Ho Tan Dheng, their neighbor, to ferry the three eastward from Sanhou to their rendezvous with a larger river steamer at the Denjiang Channel. They would then travel downstream to Hong Kong. Auntie stood on the grassy sloped bank of the canal clutching a well-used hankie in one fist as she gave tearful embraces to Shu Wei, Shu Lan-lan, and Lin Feng. She had carefully wrapped a seedling from their prized mulberry tree in a mixture of moist soil, manure, straw, and tea leaves. Handing it to Shu Wei, she ordered, "Take good care of this. Plant it when you get to San Francisco. This will be our keepsake that will nurture memories and bind our souls."

Auntie had dressed Lin Feng's burn wounds with a new coating of *guan cao*, an ointment made from local aquatic weeds. She told them both, "You will need to have the doctor Li Po Tun examine your poor father's condition when you get to Hong Kong. I don't like the way his wounds look."

A pyramid of oranges and a basketful of red envelopes stuffed with money had been stashed nearby—secret gifts from the few townspeople that still cared. The rest were too frightened to venture near. "What will you do with yourself?" Shu Lan-lan asked Auntie. In a voice barely audible, Chun Dai replied, "I will go back and live with my older sister on her chicken farm just outside Shanghai. But it will not be the same—not without all of you. I will write to you when you are settled. I can't bear . . ." Her composure gave out just as Ho Tan Dheng told them the sun had risen above the horizon.

The boat had the scaled-down lines of a junk with a modest cabin and an arched canvas covering on one end. A generous port-side space was given over to Lin Feng where he was lowered into a mattress of straw-filled feed bags. His temporary sanctuary. Shu Wei and Shu Lan-lan sat on the starboard side with feet propped up on suitcases. Provisions that Auntie had prepared for them were stored next to them. A warm breeze sent a malodorous blend of decaying fish and teak varnish from the boat toward Shu Wei. He hoped it would not be a long trip.

Finally settled in the boat, the three waved to Auntie in unison as the boat pulled away from the shore. Shu Wei felt a sudden tug in his belly. This couldn't be happening. He had never left his hometown of Sanhou. Surely things would settle down and they'd return to make new lives, better lives. Another tug in the belly, this one a little sharper. That thick-headed feeling he felt the other morning had returned.

The trip along the canal was familiar and yet hostile, warming and yet chilling. He peered down the network of tight residential lanes that dove and weaved among pitched gray tile roofs and mossy verandas adorned with paper lanterns. He and his sister had traversed one of these historic stone-slab walkways many times on the way to the home of Ban-Wo-Kang for their English lessons. This scholar proudly told them he brought his version of the King's English there from Hong Kong. With a half-smile he told them that, because some nineteen imperial and thirty-one first-degree scholars had settled in the area, his wisdom had surely been enhanced by their lasting spirits. He boasted, "Of course, now I am endowing you both with that knowledge."

Colonnades, small bridges, balconies, piers, wooden eaves, and lush plantings, once welcoming, now seemed to close in around Shu Wei, their dark shadows haunting him, burying him. Out of the corner of his eye he was aware that his sister had waved at a former classmate on the old stone arch bridge, the one dating from the Song Dynasty. How could she be so lighthearted? So seeing? So aware? *She is surely made of different stuff than I,* he thought.

They reached the edge of Sanhou and were approaching the beginnings of the larger settlement of Denjiang. Water scorpions took leave of the shore reeds to interrogate their visitors. Frogs weighed in with guttural croaks. Here, the flatness of the land stood in dramatic contrast to distant mountains that resembled a caravan of camels, their silhouetted humps dressed in coral and puce. Fisherman flung their nets into water that was now a gritty nut-brown color. The current had picked up. Small eddies began to appear. The ribbon-like tail fins of swamp eels carved soft channels in the water.

Being on the river with a warming sun brought back childhood memories. He pictured himself as a young boy sitting along the banks of the Little Denjiang River watching the colorfully decorated timber junks as they bobbed along with their sails of bamboo matting, their great cargoes of poles lashed to the sides. When school was out in the summer he worked in one of the many ice shacks that lined the river. Hard but rewarding work, he lifted large blocks of ice onto boats that cooled the loads of fish heading to the markets.

When the day's work was done he often sat against the side of one of these shacks, casting his hemp line into the swirling waters. His constant companion was his imaginary four-legged snake-like dragon. A mythical Chinese symbol of power, strength, and good luck, it had powers to tame the waters and offer up baskets of exotic fish from the deep, cold depths.

As a younger boy, he and his friends were attracted to an island a few hundred yards upstream from the ice shacks and their docks. They were drawn to its musty and seductive collection of three old Buddhist temples. A blue-and-gray-veined marble bridge arched over a rock-filled stream that threaded its way among a series of hillocks perfumed with azalea, mango, and fig. They launched all manner of toy watercraft at a modest waterfall at one end. Hours were spent playing games imitating famous Chinese warriors battling each other from behind shrubbery, or from the webbed windowsills and porches of the temples.

A sudden lurch of the boat and a frantic cry brought Shu Wei upright. Lin Feng had awakened in a heightened state of agitation, ripping clothes from his body, nearly capsizing the boat. Shu Lan-lan had the presence of mind to grab him around his ankles and stabilize him. A high fever had taken hold; his father's shirt was saturated with sweat and his face had turned a vivid crimson. Shu Lan-lan ladled what fresh water was left over his face and torso while Lin Feng babbled incoherently.

Shu Wei joined his sister in toweling their father down and repositioning him beneath the canvas covering. They forced him to drink a mixture that Auntie pleaded they take. An old family recipe, it consisted of Chinese box thorn, mung beans, lotus leaves, and peppermint.

"You are poisoning me!" the old man yelled.

"Father, we are doing no such thing," soothed Shu Wei. "We are trying to bring your *fashaw* down. Drink it, he urged."

Giving in, Lin Feng tilted his head back and reluctantly, slowly, drank the mixture. Chills racked his body. Shu Lan-lan removed her quilted jacket, laid it on him, and held him until, finally, the convulsions subsided, his body relaxed and he slept once again.

Leaning against one of the boat's center braces Shu Lan-lan sat cross-legged, picking her teeth with a dried reed stem. Staring off into the distance she noticed that the horizon held a greater variety of structures. The fields held more workers. The river carried a bigger variety of boats. They were approaching the harbor of Denjiang.

"What will become of us brother?" she asked.

Shu Wei, experiencing one of his headaches, didn't respond. His head felt as though his brain were filling with turbulent water and someone was beating on a *tang gu* drum. Or was he only hearing the rush of the river and the steady thud-thud of the boat's steam engine.

He felt a pinch on his left elbow. Swinging around abruptly, his arm struck one of the awning supports. Shu Lan-lan couldn't suppress a crooked smile. She stifled a giggle. Shu Wei's taut face muscles quickly softened. He realized that this was the first light moment they had shared since the time of the town tribunal debacle.

"I asked you a question. What will become of us?" Shu Lan-lan repeated. "Our father's condition scares me. I don't know if he'll even make it to this so-called 'promised land' of San Francisco."

Shu Wei smacked his parched lips and said, "As you know, my sign under the Chinese Zodiac is the Earth Rabbit. The rabbit is endowed with ambition and many talents. People trust this animal. But he's also a gossip and a bad gambler. So I will not make a bet on our future. Our father is a tough old lizard. He will survive us all."

Shu Lan-lan pondered the word 'gossip.' "Your words are not very encouraging. In fact, your behavior has worried me these past few days. We all need to pull together. We—you and me especially—are left to shape our family's destiny, our *yuán fēn*."

Shu Wei gazed over the side into the water. He thought the brackish copper-colored water that showed his swirling reflection suited his mood. Maybe he could join the sea life in this waterway—if they'd have him. Just then a Japanese sea bass poked his silvery head from the waters as if to extend an invitation. "You are lucky, I am without net my friend," he murmured.

"Shu Wei, can you at least give me some idea of how we find ourselves caught up in this mess, this *zá luàn*. I think you know a lot more than you are telling me."

"Sister, I cannot tell you what I . . ."

The jarring blast of a high-pitched whistle came from a large steamship pulling away from the dock. They looked behind them at a large sign announcing *City of Denjiang*. Ho Tan Dheng, their neighbor and pilot, maneuvered his craft into a slip. "Well, this is as far as I go," he announced. "You need to catch that steamship over there to Hong Kong, the one with the green-and-red banner on the dock posts. I'll help you transfer your things."

As he was being loaded onto a three-wheeled contraption, more often used to carry baggage, Lin Feng swatted at his matted hair as if mosquitoes had nested there. He pulled at his shirt, almost tipping himself onto the wooden-planked jetty. Shu Wei and his sister adjusted their grip and jockeyed their cargo over to a passenger waiting area with stacks of luggage, whining children, and a mulling mass of people. Shu Wei had never seen such a diverse assortment of humanity in his life. It looked like a traveling acrobatic troupe with their colorful outfits and varied skin tones. Even their manner of speech seemed exotic. The inflections took different routes to get to familiar words.

With some confusion, the threesome boarded the steamship. The boat had a large wood-paneled cabin and cushioned bench seating along the walls, accommodating fifty or more passengers. Globed lighting hung from the coffered ceiling. Outside, lounge chairs and a scattering of cushions on the deck were already occupied by those versed in a more aggressive style of boarding. Shu Wei and Shu Lan-lan barely secured a spot against a cabinet housing a fire hose as they looked at each other while the hordes whizzed by, some bumping Lin Feng's cart without any sense of regret. Lin Feng raised his good hand in protest. "I guess we're in the big city now," Shu Wei observed.

"Yes, and I hear that Hong Kong is even bigger—more than 200,000 people now," said Shu Lan-lan. "And the newspaper I saw back there said the British just leased the New Territories from China, whatever those are. The map showed huge pieces of land and islands that will be more than eighty per cent of Hong Kong's territory."

Pulling his legs beneath him, Shu Wei drew a thin blanket over the two of them. "You were always the student of geography and history, weren't you. Your whole wall at home was filled with maps. I was surprised you didn't cover up your windows too—as well as yourself."

"You had your books—you and your Confucius," replied Shu Lan-lan. "I seem to remember your floor was covered with dusty volumes. I guess that was a way to keep me out. It wasn't safe to go in. And, I wonder how many you actually opened."

"My Confucius! *Our* Confucius you mean! I studied, as you did, the Five Classics and the Four Books—the very heart of our education system. What our great teacher in Sanhou, Wei Zhang, taught us about the Zhou Dynasty is still of great interest to me. Not just because that dynasty lasted longer than any in the whole world but because they had this instinct to communicate by writing on bronze or bamboo strips. But, to me, I was inspired by the writings done during the Qin Dynasty in the second century BC. It helped to give the people a standard language that they could communicate with people all over the country. In my own way I am—or, I guess, was—trying to do that in our town with my writing as Town Scribe."

"Yes, well, you have to admit that some of your prose over-stirred the passions of some of the townspeople. Please tell me that this desire to communicate was not the flame that started the fire at father's store."

Shu Wei tucked his chin into the collar of his tunic and rolled his eyes. "I have enough grief to last a lifetime and you shower me with more doubts and distrust. I have told you to have faith in your older brother. As you say, we need to stick together."

Shu Lan-lan pinned her glance on him for some time before going over to secure the blanket around Lin Feng. He was sprawled on a cluster of cushions in one corner, wheezing out words that appeared close to gibberish. She kissed him lightly on his cheek, and he pawed the air randomly as though he were searching for some phantom spirit.

Finally, lulled by the thump-thump-thump of the engine, brother and sister collapsed against one another. Exhausted from the last few days of traumatic events they at last fell into a deep sleep. Shu Wei's subconscious was now owned by these events. Disturbing images came to him of his father drawing a woven-reed raft to the shore of the mighty Tien-ho River. An enormous four-headed dragon appeared, expelling a fiery wall of noxious odors. His mass blocked all but the smallest rays of the sun. The scaly creature used his immense webbed wings to send giant waves crashing over the shore, overwhelming poor Lin Feng. Shu Wei was frozen in place. He could neither reach out to his father nor could he make his shouts heard. The monster finally backed away, water cascading in bloody sheets from a mouth full of jagged fangs. As he slowly sank back into the river, his snout twisted into a sneer. Lin Feng's plaintive cries gradually ebbed as pea-green foamy mists covered any trace of the colossus.

CHAPTER FIVE

Hong Kong

As they approached Hong Kong harbor from the west the cadence of the boat's engine changed dramatically. A deep growling below decks signified a slowing of their speed. The boat shuddered with the throttling-down. Shu Wei and Shu Lan-lan awoke to a light drizzle that settled on their blankets. Ribbons of scarlet-infused clouds now stretched low in the early evening sky. When Shu Wei stood up, his eyes widened as he caught sight of the spectacle before them. Towering hills loomed in the background. In the foreground, a sprawling waterfront was lined with impressive commercial structures. All manner of craft filled the harbor—a veritable carpet of insects with elaborate mast-like feelers, steamers large and small, junks with corrugated sails, flat-bottomed scows, massive sailing ships.

The new Central *Praya*, or esplanade, offered a prominent setting for a string of three-story buildings with elaborate arched colonnades and balconies at all levels. These were muscular buildings, clothed in Victorian and Edwardian motifs that upstaged the more delicate Chinese buildings toward the hills. The prominent six-storied Hong Kong Hotel heralded the city's first luxury accommodations.

The seaside bulkhead of the Praya served as anchorage for the smaller sampans and junks that were still servicing this historic *entrepôt*. Teeming with traders' boats often lashed together six-deep, it stood in counterpoint to the modern cityscape behind, served by two-wheeled polished carriages and rickshaws. Aromas of spices, oiled timbers, fish, horse leavings, and the malodorous river water wafted on a gusty evening wind.

Lin Feng had not yet awakened. Shu Wei nudged him and said, "Father, you must see this amazing place!" Not responding, Shu Lan-lan gave a gentle slap to his cheek. His eyes fluttered as if this would reveal only as much reality as he could tolerate. "What . . . what is it?" As his words formed, bit by bit, they realized that this was the first phrase he had uttered since leaving their village of Sanhou.

"We are in Victoria father," said Shu Lan-lan. "We get off here and meet up with your friends Wu Kang Ho and Li Po Tun before our journey to San Francisco."

Shu Wei knew that Wu Kang Ho, the wealthy merchant, and Li Po Tun, the doctor, were respected in China. Their long friendship and business dealings with Lin Feng, had been of great benefit in securing the immigration papers for the three travelers. This had been a difficult task; The Chinese Exclusion Act had been passed sixteen years before to limit the threat of immigrants to American workers. The two had also arranged to cover, through a Benevolent Association in San Francisco's Chinatown, the standard steerage fare of $200 for each passenger.

As the steamship nosed into a berth the deckhands swung into action pitching ropes and shouting commands. Just as the boat was secured at the dock cleats they spotted a pair of hands waving in their direction. Lin Feng was filled with new energy as he raised himself awkwardly and, standing shakily, gave a wave of recognition to his old friends.

Li Po Tun was elegantly tall. His narrow olive-skinned face was punctuated by prominent cheekbones and deep-set dark brown eyes. British-Malay ancestry afforded him the luxury of idiosyncrasy in this global crossroads of ethnic groups. A flattened fez and a bejeweled walking stick fitted this man of gentle but important bearing. His short silk flared brocade jacket was anchored with a wide checkered sash. A pair of creased ivory pants partially revealed sequined slippers at the cuff.

Wu Kang Ho, on the other hand, stood a foot shorter, with sparkling eyes and a broad girth. Clearly, he had enjoyed the good life of a successful career in trading. His gray tailored pants ended just above a pair of elegant full-grain leather boots embossed with his initials, characteristic of his native India. He spoke in a lively staccato, oozing a vapor of cigars and brandy. A dark maroon bowler hat accentuated the fullness of his face, his reddish-brown skin vibrating as he spoke.

When he spotted Lin Feng disembarking down the ship's ramp limping badly, Wu Kang Ho blurted out, "What on this hallowed earth has happened to all of you? You poor souls look bedraggled," he exclaimed as he wrapped his long arms around Shu Wei's and Shu Lan-lan's shoulders. Shu Wei pinched his eyes together, fighting back tears, thinking these were the first friendly faces he had seen since being cast out of Sanhou.

CHAPTER SIX

Another Encounter

"I'm afraid it's a sorry tale of misfortune," said Shu Wei. "We will tell you more this evening."

"We have had a brief explanation of these affairs from the message delivered by your courier a few days back," said Li Po Tun. "Our ship leaves tomorrow afternoon so that will give you all time to have an evening of peace at the hotel before the arduous ocean journey begins. Lin Feng, I shall have my assistant go over your condition. From what I can see from here, your bandaged wounds show signs of infection."

Shu Wei felt the warmth of these caring individuals give him a temporary sense of relief from his melancholy. Even his headache's intensity eased. But what should he say happened? They would want to have all the details. How should he handle that?

The group walked along Wellington Street, near the Central Market to the north. Shu Wei and Shu Lan were intrigued by the lively mix of Chinese and British enterprises in tall, balconied buildings. A few coolies carried their passengers in litters, semi-enclosed cabins supported by stout bamboo poles resting on the calloused shoulders of the carriers. Rickshaws and goods carts were everywhere. Signage advertising tailors, shoemakers, dry goods, the China Mail offices, and dress and hat makers, fought for attention with banners and laundry fluttering on balconies like oversized butterflies.

Li Po Tun's assistant registered Lin Feng at a nearby hospital for tests and observation before the others settled into their rooms at the New Horizons Hotel a few blocks away. Shu Wei and Shu Lan-lan marveled at the claw-foot tubs. Brass kerosene wall sconces glowed with their feathery flames casting shadows over beds covered in colorful damask. When Wu Kang Ho came to accompany them to the dining hall they were still peering from windows and admiring the tiny masses of twinkling lights of the harbor. Shu Wei was reminded of fireflies and the story of Che Yin in the Jin Dynasty. Che Yin's family was destitute and had no money to buy lamp oil for him to study by. He caught as many fireflies as he could in a white silk bag to allow him to read. He later became a senior scholar under Emperor Wu.

In the first-floor dining hall men in starched linen jackets and black bow ties carried in large trays with domed coverings and glass goblets. The waiters brought sets of chopsticks and placed them beside settings of silverware.

As they enjoyed their dinners of braised partridge with bok choy and lotus-seed soup, Li Po Tun asked, "Now, who can tell me what caused this calamity to befall your family? The only thing we know so far is that your father's store was burned, his apprentice Yong Loo died, and some kind of tribunal was held that ordered your family from the town."

"I believe Shu Wei has the most to offer," said Shu Lan-lan. "All I know is that I have a father now that is in bad straits and a brother that is acting mysteriously."

All heads swiveled toward Shu Wei.

"I will tell you what I know. It all began when . . ." Shu Wei stopped mid-sentence when, out of the corner of his eye, he caught something very disturbing across the room. *It couldn't be. But it was!* The limping man from Sanhou with the black cape and large ring on his right hand sat down just five tables over. His head spinning out of control once again, bile rose in the back of Shu Wei's throat. A fine film of sweat formed on his forehead.

"Shu Wei!" said Shu Lan-lan. "Are you okay? You have turned pale."

Shu Wei got up and, in his hurry, almost knocked a tray from a waiter's hand on the way to the bathroom. He barely made it before he expelled most of his dinner. He hung over the sink for minutes. A man came in and quickly retreated.

Shu Wei returned to the doorway of the dining room and motioned for Shu Lan-lan to come to him. She gave him a puzzled look from across the room but reluctantly rose and excused herself. As she neared her brother, she could see he was distressed.

"The man is in there," said Shu Wei.

"What man? What are you talking about?"

"The man from our town who was at the tribunal."

"Are you sure?"

"Yes! Yes! I'm positive. I can't stay down here. I am going to my room."

"Our hosts are still finishing their dinner. They will wonder what happened to you."

"Just tell them I was not feeling well and went back to my room."

"You keep finding new ways to mystify me."

"Apologize for me. I have to get going."

Returning to the table, Shu Lan-lan glanced quickly around the room. She had a sinking feeling as she noticed the man with the cape looking her way.

Later that evening Li Po Tun knocked on the door to their room.

"How are you feeling Shu Wei?" he asked kindly.

"I am better. It must have been the madness of the past few days."

"Shu Wei and Shu Lan-lan, I'm afraid I have some bad news. Your father's arm has contracted a very serious infection that has spread. He told me your Auntie applied *guan cao* to the wound. Had I been there, I would have advised against it. It may have accelerated a surge of toxins in his body. The doctors at the hospital have recommended amputation of the arm. Your father was very upset of course. He didn't want to hear of it. He wants to keep his arm."

"You hun ye gui," moaned Shu Wei. "The wandering ghosts are following us. We must keep father's spirits up. Li Po Tun, is there no cure for our father?"

"We can administer medications to control pain and, to some extent, decrease infection. He has told us he would rather die than lose an arm. Our only hope is that the ship's doctor can keep him stable until we reach San Francisco. I have given word to the *City of Peking's* medical staff. They will do all they can."

After Li Po Tun left, Shu Wei slumped forward, head in hands. His fingers moved violently through his scalp, his fingernail rims showing traces of blood. He pounded his fist on the bed until Shu Lan-lan grabbed his wrist. "Calm yourself brother," she said. "You and I will need our *qi*, our energies, to get our father into better health and to keep our senses."

Shu Wei asked Shu Lan-lan, "Did you see a man that looked suspicious in the dining hall?"

"I saw a strange-looking man casting glances at our table, yes."

"He has followed us here," said Shu Wei. He untied and laid out a long leather pouch on the bed. Inside was a scabbard and a pair of five-and-a-half-inch knives. Chinese inscriptions were etched on both blades. The scabbard was covered in ray skin and brass fittings. "These are part of our father's collection of antique knives—we left behind all but these. They could come in handy."

CHAPTER SEVEN

A Note

The next morning, the *SS City of Peking* steamship eased out of its dock at Central. A sturdy workhorse, it was built in 1874. She and her sister ship, the *City of Tokio,* were the largest vessels ever built in the United States. Shu Wei and Shu Lan-lan leaned over its starboard rails as squawking gulls traced intersecting arcs in the air at the stern. They were entranced with the enormity of the vessel and its ability to deftly maneuver among the many craft that seemed to crawl like fleets of dragonflies scurrying across the water, sails like gauzy wings.

Shu Wei's mind had cleared somewhat from the previous evening although tiny spasms now ran through his taut neck muscles. The ship was now on a westward tack, passing by the Hong Kong-Canton-and-Macau Ferry Pier. Hordes of people milled about the landing: British men in their white jackets, boaters, and pith helmets; bare-chested dock workers with coned hats; women in their late-fall finery flaunting their artful Chinese umbrellas; and the locals peering down on the scene from nearby deep-set balconies.

As they moved away from shore the hills became a dominant wooded backdrop with a long string of buildings, their arched colonnades resembling unending cells of honeycombs. Now heading past Victoria Peak and the Mid-Levels they turned to the south, and the two felt the first stiff sea breeze hitting their faces. It felt good. It was restorative. Their despondency over their misfortunes had consumed them. But this feeling was finally being tempered by the promise of new beginnings.

"I am going down to our quarters to organize my things," said Shu Lan-lan. "Are you coming?"

"I will be down in a few minutes. I need to feel the breezes for now."

Shu Lan-lan splayed her fingers on her brother's back and worked them in circles. She could feel taut strands of his muscles, like bundles of reeds from the harvest.

"The length of your hair would make a fine loon's nest—not sure about a queue," said Shu Lan-lan. She pulled on the inky strands and wove them, twisting and turning, into the approximation of a short braid. "Maybe more luck at the end of our trip." She drifted away toward the staircase to steerage.

Settling in on the edge of her cot in their sparse quarters she glanced at her sleeve and saw that a thread had unraveled at the cuff. She recalled the time she'd made the muslin blouse, her favorite *chèn shān*. She helped cut a large section of fabric, pins as guides, from one of the several bolts of cloth that Auntie kept in her sewing nook. Shu Lan-lan loved to explore Auntie's collection of pins, pin cushions, ribbons, cords, thimbles, and all manner of small tools and accessories. Her dexterity grew as she practiced on her own patterns made of rice paper, cutting and basting scraps together in rough stitches for fit, binding, gathering, and finishing. Just two weeks ago, Auntie had said she had become a *móshu shī*, a magician with the thread. Scraps became owl puppets and crocheted hats with ear flaps for the cold months in Sanhou.

Memories slid by like leaves on a frozen lake. The one that settled was that final visit to the mulberry tree. Shu Lan-lan felt an icy chill creep across her skin even though it was warm and musty in the overcrowded steerage cabin. A stinging tug of joy-lessness grabbed at her stomach. She wondered where all this would end. Her father was very sick and her brother was vague in his talk, even distant. She was struggling to find meaning now in the sayings of their beloved Buddhist scholar in the village: 'Hold fast to every trial and hardship, for those are the very things that shape the future self. Inner strength and courage are born of these.' *I must remember to keep these words close to my heart.* She slumped to the floor on her knees, elbows resting on the cot, hands clasped together in prayer.

Still standing at the upper deck rails, Shu Wei felt the moist air fill his lungs. He watched a cormorant dip and glide across the sea's frothy surface, beak occasionally slicing through the surface to find a suitable dinner. Being in the habit of parsing many things he encountered, he wondered, *Where have you come from? Have you strayed too far from a safe haven? Maybe you have found cozy lodgings somewhere on this ship. I would pay any sum to trade my life for yours right now.*

A sudden firm grip pinched his forearm. Before even looking around he knew. It was Huǒlóng.

"Enjoying the trip so far?" he sneered. His wardrobe had been subdued for greater anonymity. He now wore a maroon cape, hitched at the top with a jeweled clasp. A more modest dragon insignia was now appliquéd to a muffler that rode high on his neck. Like the mythical nine-tailed fox, the man's eyes were narrow and penetrating. A raised scar ran from the edge of his mouth to his left ear.

Shu Wei was incapable of speech or reaction.

"I know, you thought your little nightmare was over," the evil man continued. "Well, if you do as I say everything will work out just fine." Shu Wei felt a sharp jab in his side. When he looked down, Huǒlóng had a short knife, *My own knife! How did he get it?*

"I can see you're finding it interesting that I have one of your knives. When I approached just now you were lost in thought. A bit of advice: Don't hide your prized possessions in your pants pockets."

Shu Wei's thoughts came in a barrage of notions careening about like dice. *No time to sort this all out. I can't run, he has too tight a hold of me. Can't yell, it may be the worst thing to do.*

"You and I will get to know each other quite well from here on out. Our little show in the town square was just the beginning. Don't try to do anything clever. I will never be far away. And, one more thing . . . do not say anything about our little get-together here to your family or anyone else. If you do, you will find yourself getting all tied up and awfully wet. Let me remind you that I spared you only because I have big things in mind for you."

Huǒlóng ambled off, a remnant of the day's sun glinting off the angular pin holding his layered headpiece. A long, braided queue hung down his back to his waist, its ribbon dancing in syncopation with his crooked walk. Shu Wei rubbed his arm where Huǒlóng had held him. He watched as the man turned and winked, his lips curled into a smirk. His back muscles, newly constricted, brought pain to his shoulders. *What does he mean by "big things"?*

Meanwhile, below in steerage, Shu Lan-lan had erected a makeshift mesh sling above her bunk. From it she hung two herbal sachets to deflect any further invasive energies from the evil gods that had taken over their world. She had included bits of citron to temper the foul air in the cabin and shreds of peony to conjure thoughts of a peaceful journey. Wu Kang Ho told her that she would be one of only fifteen females in steerage, five of them Chinese. She already felt uncomfortable. As she was rolling up her pant legs slightly to wipe some grime from her gold-and-silver filigreed slippers, she looked up just as two older Chinese men smoking and gambling nearby shot her a hungry leer. One curled his tongue up around his upper lip suggestively.

She sifted through her meager possessions from home. A stuffed festival doll, a miniature flattened kite, a goldfish lantern, a tattered photo of her family standing with Auntie Chun Dai sitting cross-legged. When Shu Wei brought two bowls of noodles in steaming broth and a bread loaf her eyes brightened. "What have you been up to? Were you helping the captain steer the ship?" Trying for an upbeat tempo, she was even surprised at herself.

Shu Wei silently placed the bowls on an upturned crate that served as a table. His shaking hand caused some of the contents to spill. "Careful," said Shu Lan-lan. "This is precious. We will not see our next helping until tomorrow noon."

Sitting down on the bed beside her Shu Wei cradled his forehead in his hands. His head was bursting with things he needed to tell her. He needed more time to think. Maybe tomorrow. He couldn't let on what was happening . . . yet.

"You seem to be carrying worries for a whole village. What can I do to lessen your cares?" asked his younger sister.

"Allow me time," he replied. "A little more time. I need more time to think so that we can have a proper dialogue."

"More time. You will have nothing but time on this voyage. But I hope . . ."

Their attention was suddenly drawn toward a tall figure approaching them. Thwack. Thud. The elaborate walking stick of Li Po Tun beat out a tempo of conviction and authority. "Well, there you are, you two. I see they have given you the prime suite in steerage." His quick smile animated his bushy eyebrows. "At least you have beds. I can see that some of your neighbors aren't so lucky."

"Some of our neighbors are also lacking in respect and manners," said Shu Lan-lan.

"Please come to me if they become a problem. Now, let's go see your father. I'll also show you my cabin, in case you need to find me."

Li Po Tun guided the two through the labyrinth of the upper deck. Shu Wei and Shu Lan-lan felt out of place among the well-dressed passengers who sprawled on lounge chairs or stood chatting, fondling their long silver and jade cigarette holders like skinny musical instruments. Women swept by in long, elegant dresses with tall collars anchored with elaborate bows, and jackets with leg o'mutton sleeves. Some carried straw boaters at their sides.

Hearty conversation floated on cigar-drenched air from mahogany-lined libraries and salons, sitting bays, and dining suites. They marveled at the diversity of the passengers: a tobacco-colored woman wearing a yellow and green sarong knotted at the waist; a pasty-skinned man in a tailored double-breasted coat, a shiny top hat, and a fob dripping from his waistband pocket; a cigar toting Asian dandy, a bamboo cage with a captive bird in vivid colors resting on his shoulder. Shu Lan-lan peered longingly at a woman lost in a book, her pince-nez glasses an ornament of privilege.

The medical ward was a contrast in style: spartan, cramped, unadorned, utilitarian. Lin Feng's eyes fixed on a point on the ceiling. His color had taken on a yellowish tinge like that of the bed linens. Drooping lines disgorged various liquids into his veins.

"Lin Feng, you have visitors. You need to be on your best behavior." Li Po Tun tried to bring a lightness to the moment.

Li Po Tun sensed the two's unease and said, "The wardroom doctor said that he has been stabilized and the infection is under control. Your father has been medicated to relieve the pain and deter the instinct to harm himself."

Shu Wei brushed some loose strands of hair from Lin Feng's forehead. Puffy sacs sat like tiny earth mounds beneath his tired eyes. "I am so sorry father," he said in a hushed tone. "We will all build new lives. I am certain of it."

Lin Feng looked toward his son and nodded, moisture rimming his eyes. "Your lives far exceed mine in value. You must cherish one another and find new and rewarding paths," he whispered, his thin voice cracking.

"We will not hear of your talk of weighing one life over another," said Shu Lan-lan. "Our very fortunes depend on our bonds to each other."

Lin Feng turned to face the wall. He couldn't bear to have them see him cry, but his trembling figure beneath the covers revealed the transparent truth.

"I think it's time to let your father rest," said Li Po Tun. "He is in good hands. We must let him have his peace."

When Shu Wei and Shu Lan-lan returned to their quarters in steerage they found Shu Lan-lan's favorite silk mango-colored tunic lying in a crumpled mass on the floor. Their personal belongings were strewn about their beds. Shu Wei knew right away that the note he brought from Wei Zhang was missing—the note that Wei Zhang had stuffed into his hand at the tribunal. He was convinced that Huǒlóng had created the mess. Then he noticed a note stabbed with a large pin into Shu Lan-lan's pillow.

The note on the pillow read 'Your friend Wei Zhang is dead! Forget him.' Shu Wei's head felt like a thousand bees were implanting their stingers in his brain. Then he saw the chop. A depiction of a dragon that appeared to be smiling. *How depraved.* Fists clenched, Shu Wei's arms flew out wildly, punching the air. "Curse the six-headed serpents that have done this. Who could have such an evil heart?"

"What is it? What is that note?" Shu Lan-lan had taken hold of Shu Wei's elbow.

Holding the note tight to his chest he said, "Never mind, it is of no consequence." He folded it and tucked it into his pants' pocket.

Images of the leering men near their sleeping quarters immediately came to Shu Lan-lan. *What are they up to now.* "I need to see it. Please give it to me!" Before Shu Wei could react, she had thrust her hand into his pocket and retrieved the piece of paper. "Oh, this cannot be true! Wei Zhang was a dear associate of our father's. And what is this chop, this stamped signature, all about?"

"I am afraid I have few answers. The only thing I know is that this note was handed to me in the town square as I lay on the ground after collapsing. This villain must have found it in my bag. As for the chop, I am at a loss."

"I thought we had left our demons on shore. Clearly, this person knows you and knows that you had Wei Zhang's note," said Shu Lan-lan. "Could this be the man in the dining hall in Hong Kong?"

Shu Wei shrugged and said, "Huh . . . uh I don't know. Maybe." He stooped to gather up his small writing book, a Ju Ware lotus bowl, a folded game board, and a favorite book of folk tales. With a breathy sigh, he said, lifting up a corner of a loose floor board, "Fortunately I put what little money we have in our pouch down here along with my notebook with all my notes. We are lucky our invader wasn't overly ambitious in his search.

"I'm afraid, dear sister, that we would not have much hope in bringing this person to justice. I am told that these acts are commonplace; the officers on board are not generally inclined toward the Chinese and less so toward female Chinese. It is best we keep this to ourselves."

Shu Lan-lan all of a sudden felt a deep twinge of malaise and homesickness. She loved her brother but it seemed his attention was on his own personal burdens. This didn't leave much room for her. She missed her mother and Auntie terribly. They would have brought more compassion to her bruised soul.

CHAPTER EIGHT

A Death

Shu Lan-lan found that she couldn't keep her eyes closed for more than a few minutes at a time. To make matters worse the overhead bunk would shudder periodically. She guessed that her brother's nightmares had come back.

Indeed, Shu Wei's tortured mind was once again at work. He tossed fitfully as each vivid scene erupted. This time giant flames licked frantically toward the sky. They were rainbow-hued rivers of tremendous heat. It was like approaching the chambers of *Diyu*, the mythical Chinese purgatory. At one point, he heard his father calling to him. He tried responding. *I'm coming father. But I can't see where you are.* He tried to answer but was silenced by the deafening roar of the inferno. His father finally appeared . . . a ghost-like figure floating overhead, a rope tethered to his neck, the free end frayed and flapping. A crimson gown bulged like a giant Chinese lantern. He looked placid, almost carefree. His hands were reaching downward toward earth, flames curling from his fingertips.

Shu Wei sat bolt upright in bed feeling like he was suffocating. Grabbing at his neck, he barked out a few raspy sounds. Ignoring his sister's urgent questioning from her bed below, he promptly fell back into a dreamy torpor. This time he was haunted by reality. The setting was Sanhou. He was carrying his table to the town square where he held court every Thursday, to take the pulse of the town. As the official Town Scribe in Sanhou, he had become a trusted recorder of the townspeople's events, opinions, and news. While he generally kept his writings within the bounds of propriety, his weekly renditions could occasionally veer onto the thin ice of opinion.

This particular Thursday as he was arriving at the town center, he noticed two figures closely huddled in passionate conversation. Both men were unfamiliar to him. Bushy hair flared out from beneath a violet knitted cap and a scraggly beard sprouted from his chin. His skin was weather-beaten hinting at a more severe climate. Remembering what his father had said about the Empress sending agents from the north made his heart race.

Over time he learned that his sensitive ears could pick up "accidental information," what some would portray more accurately as eavesdropping. But he would be careful to attach anonymous sources to his ill-gotten information as if to scrub out any illegitimacy.

The two men were seated inside a latticed arbor covered in a dense tangle of a Chinese trumpet vine. He picked a spot where gaps in the vines would not reveal his presence. Turning his back to the men he pulled his wide-brimmed hat low, shadowing his face. Discretely pulling out his notepad he glanced left and right. He began to write.

His bamboo pen dug deeply into the paper as he transcribed the subversive discourse filtering through the knotted boughs: schemes of transferring revenues from the town treasury into the pockets of a few; willfully taking properties from the poorest and most feeble-minded citizens as vague penalties for "underpayment of obligations"; placing tariffs on livestock feeding on public lands; and a host of other egregious and unscrupulous activities, not the least of which is a plot to kill the Town Tax Collector. His pen tore the fibers of the paper when he heard his father's name. Lin Feng was accused of owing a large sum of money advanced to his business from the treasury. True or untrue this was beyond unsettling.

Shu Wei shakily placed his ink pen back into its casing. The shadow that was then spreading over him seemed odd— this was a crisp fall day with a bright azure sky. Just as he looked up he felt a tug on his notebook. Instinctively, he gripped it more firmly. A stinging slap on his cheek almost toppled him from his chair. The notebook went spiraling onto the ground.

"I've been watching you, you oily little snake," said a man crouched over him. As Shu Wei retrieved the notebook, the fellow kept one hand raised ready for another strike. His long face was accented by a crooked nose and half-shut eye. A stained white kerchief covered most of a scar at the base of his neck. Two leather shoulder straps crossed at the mid-point of his chest where a metal badge implied authority. Tucked at the junction of the straps was a sheathed blade.

"I am the *Dì Bǎo*, the Constable of this town. I will bring your activities to the attention of our town elders. Your underhanded ways are not befitting of the title of Town Scribe. Now be on your way. This will bring everlasting shame upon you and your family."

Just like the other man, Shu Wei had never seen this person before. His manner of dress and inflected speech were not of the village. As he walked back home Shu Wei's legs were heavy and wobbly. Things had taken a depressing turn. What to make of all this unfortunate incident? Surely no good could come of it. His dream ended as he shook himself awake, shivering.

The next morning, leaping from his upper bunk, he barely avoided Shu Lan-lan who was sitting on her bed consuming a bowl of watery oatmeal and a piece of stale bread. "How do people eat this?" she gasped. "I find it's better if I hold my nose and wash it down with tea."

"I will go upstairs to see if I can get us some noodle dishes," offered Shu Wei. "I saw some of our countrymen having a better time of it on the upper deck."

The weather had taken a turn for the worse. A fine icy spray blew horizontally in advance of an approaching storm from the starboard side. Shu Wei was resolute in his quest to find a source for more appealing food. The rain was now forcing people to seek refuge on the main deck under canvas slings or in alcoves. Footing was a challenge with the increased rocking of the ship. Spotting a Chinese family clustered beneath the bridge walkway ahead, Shu Wei made his way toward them, dodging anchor chains, rope coils, and crane mounts.

"Hey, Chink! Don't know enough ta get out a the weather do ya," snorted an inebriated figure with a soiled green woolen cap and dark green oilskin jacket. He lay in the shadow of some weather cloths that were stretched between two stanchions. That was the first time he had actually heard the term 'Chink.' He then remembered what his father would say, 'A bee stings and knows not what he does—it is small and has no wisdom of life.'

Figuring he'd had enough confrontations so far on the trip Shu Wei attempted to step over the man's feet but tripped over them instead. "Hey, Chinko! Ya jush 'bout broke my leg. You got nothin' between those ears?"

Shu Wei decided his foray for Chinese food would have to wait. Thinking that this belligerent person may somehow be connected to Huǒlóng he thought better of hanging around. He reversed course and returned to their steerage quarters empty handed. Wu Kang Ho told him later that he learned, through the captain, that the man's name was Brian O'Grady. An educated Irishman, but a man with a lightning temper, he finally got a job in the bursar's office on the ship. His drinking had prompted a fist fight with the first officer. It seemed excessive bravado had not served him well; the officer had been captain of England's National Rugby Union Team.

With a broken arm and no longer employable, O'Grady roamed the ship using his sober side to charm women. Tall and lanky with tousled rust-colored hair and a Van Dyke goatee and mustache, he tossed a scarf rakishly about his neck for a final flourish. His skill at several card games served him well. The Dublin pubs had been his source of enlightenment. Settling into first class parlors, drink in hand, he scoured the wallets of the unsuspecting. Fortunately, as O'Grady stayed on the upper decks and Shu Wei's family were below, their paths seldom crossed.

By the fifteenth day on board their lives had finally reached a more settled state. Shu Wei and Shu Lan-lan sat, heads down, each immersed in different sections of a Chinese language newspaper. They'd had no sighting of Huŏlóng for the last seven days. It was, however, an uneasy calm. A man with an official looking badge on a rumpled uniform poked at their paper and asked them to rise.

Motioning to examine Shu Wei's health inspection card, the medical officer said, "Ah, another candidate for the scurvy is it? Now open your mouth and let me see what's growin' in there." Exhaling with a cigarette-laced breath, he punched Shu Wei's card for the twelfth time on the trip. Shu Wei stood seething, barely holding back angry words.

"Now my little beauty, we'll need to look some more at that rash," the officer said to Shu Lan-lan.

Shu Lan-lan drew back in apprehension and said, "You always say I have a rash but I don't."

"All Chinese have some kind of rash. Or didn't your backwards school cover this?" the officer churlishly asked as he made more marks in his notebook.

When the man left Shu Wei offered, "It would please me to see this uncivil doctor attacked by a flock of hawks. But they would no doubt recoil at the taste of his flesh. No point in reporting him. I'm sure his behavior is well known—they want someone of his ilk to keep the lower class off guard."

They were still contemplating the rudeness of the medical officer and didn't see him approach. Nor did they recognize him. He had on a western suit, not the usual menacing cape. The pants were high-waisted charcoal gabardine with pleats that plunged to the tops of his shiny black brogues. His hand, pocketed, held open a white knee-length jacket, its gold threads shimmering in the dusty light that trickled down from the hatch above. A flat-brimmed hat had a green feather stuck jauntily in the band. A flag of caution. A glowing cigar dripped its ash onto Shu Lan-lan's bed covers, causing a flare hole.

"I'm glad to see you two are still having a good time of it," said Huǒlóng with a twisted smile. "You probably thought I had forgotten you. But, be assured, you are constantly in my thoughts. I just visited with your father and, for some reason he didn't seem too pleased to see me again. But I assured him I am taking good care of you both. I will stop back soon . . . just in case you need something."

As Huǒlóng headed back up the staircase he turned and tipped his hat. Shu Wei and Shu Lan-lan sat in stunned silence, their rage and confusion building. How were they to deal with this dangerous and devious man? What were his motives?

"That is our man again from the hotel dining room in Hong Kong, isn't it?" queried Shu Lan-lan.

"That is the man . . . but I would characterize him as a monster rather than a man. He stalks us relentlessly like the *xìn tiān wēng*, the albatross with its giant wing span that can circle the globe."

"Oh my, it's past time to visit our father in the ward," blurted Shu Lan-lan. "Our albatross has no doubt stirred him up. I will bring him some of my soothing tea."

Seeing that the ward orderly had her back turned, they went immediately to their father's bed. He lay unmoving, his arms still and emaciated beneath the parchment-like skin. Shu Wei nudged him but received no response. He nudged him harder. Still no response.

"Excuse me," said the orderly. "You must always check in with me to see patients in this ward even though you have been here before. Now, you'll need to let your father rest. He has had a difficult day. A visitor stirred him up and his blood pressure went sky high. The doctor had to increase his sedation until he quieted down. I suspect he will be able to have visitors again by tomorrow afternoon. You should know that we will not allow that troublemaker in here again."

Shu Wei felt empty inside; they were uncomfortable trying to communicate with the orderly. Since this ship was under a British flag, western medicine was the rule. Their inability to insist on traditional Chinese medicine was maddening.

"We must get our doctor friend, Li Po Tun, to help us make sense of all of this," he said to his sister. "In the meantime, let us pray for our father."

Over the next two days, Shu Wei and Shu Lan-lan were increasingly concerned about their father's condition. He had grown more delirious and anxious. New swelling was unabated on both his arm and his leg. Li Po Tun increased his dosage of pain medication.

In the middle of the night on the next day—the twentieth of the journey—Shu Wei dreamed he was being held around the neck by Huǒlóng. He kicked wildly. His arms flailed. Then a familiar voice came to him.

"Whoa son! You almost gave me a bruising." Wu Kang Ho stood beside the bed. He gently held Shu Wei's shaking shoulders. From the lower bunk, Shu Lan-lan raised her head, rubbed her eyes, and scowled up at their visitor.

"I am sorry to wake you both but I would like you to come upstairs with me. I am afraid I have some bad news."

The term "bad news" brought a sinking feeling to Shu Wei's stomach. Everything he did now was in slow motion. Putting on his shoes was like lying in a muddy pit, every movement slowed by a quagmire. His feet moved as though there were weights attached as he climbed the stairway to the main deck.

Shu Lan-lan was faring no better. She hung back, at the bottom of the stairs, as if that would stall the hearing of any bad news. She felt she had had enough of that kind of news.

Wu Kang Ho settled them into chairs in a private lounge near the entrance to his cabin suite.

"Your father has passed away. I am truly sorry. The doctor did everything he could to save him. I'm afraid things had gotten worse than anyone really knew. The toxicity in his system was too much for him to overcome."

Shu Wei sat, slumped over, one balled-up fist pulverizing the other palm. Even tears didn't seem useful. Strangely, the main sensation was one of resignation. All of a sudden, he became aware of a slackening in his body. Inevitable. It was inevitable and he knew it. He felt that this was probably something the gods had taken care of—it was beyond him and his sister to deal with. *His father's time had come. The gods willing, they will bring us comfort and guidance.* Growing up, aside from some hurtful times, he had loved his parents and assumed they would always be there for him. Now there was a chasm in the landscape of his life.

Shu Lan-lan sat there, wringing her hands as if she were washing them. Her rumpled clothing and disordered hair seemed to reflect the chaos that ripped apart her brain. Her head dropped into her lap. She pressed her palms to her ears.

"He can't leave us! He can't do this!" she shouted. "It isn't right!"

"Shh!" said Wu Kang Ho. "You'll wake the other passengers. You will both need to reach inside yourselves now to regain your balance. It is important to remember that you still have friends. Li Po Tun and I will help in any way we can."

What Wu Kang Ho didn't tell them was that Lin Feng had actually committed suicide. His despondency had gotten the better of him in the middle of the previous night. After discovering that the ward orderly was on a break, he crafted a noose out of his bed clothing. Exhausting his remaining reservoir of energy, he twisted one end around a ceiling fixture and used a guest chair to complete the act. A note left on a bedside table was scratched out in almost illegible script: "I have served my time on this earth. I could no longer find the light in the blackness. May my beloved son and daughter forgive me and may they enjoy . . ." The note ended. A signature was attempted but the pen obviously had slipped as if it too no longer had the ardor to go on.

Wu Kang Ho and Li Po Tun had jointly decided that Shu Wei and Shu Lan-lan should be spared the ugly truth—at least for now. They had already absorbed their quota of emotional blows. For now the two older friends' consciences would have to bear the weight of their decision. As for Lin Feng, he would now be judged by the gods as to his entry into the netherworld or the terrestrial.

Two days later the memorial ceremony was held in the ship's chapel which was essentially a boxy shape with an apselike appendage. Eight chairs with cranberry tufting hugged the circular wall. Since it was an interdenominational room there were no religious symbols or furnishings. Only the brass kerosene sconces on the walls gave distant hints at the spiritual. Shu Wei and Shu Lan-lan knelt on a navy blue carpet with elliptical swirls of yellow which brought a sense of vertigo to Shu Wei. They were given white robes to wear over their clothing by the ship's chaplain. Wu Kang Ho had imposed on his friend the captain to supply them with a table that held a photo of Lin Feng along with white irises in two hand-cut vases. Six jars with white candles flamed on a ledge. Not exactly Chinese but they would have to do.

As they rested their elbows on the chairs in prayer to Buddha, Shu Wei's mind was a tangle of both images of his father and of his very palpable duplicity in his death. His breathing grew heavy and the walls seemed to press in. He had a rational sensibility about putting things in a proper perspective but recent events had upended his composure, his equilibrium. Things were coming at him like a March wind, scatterings of his life being carried aloft in a giant unforgiving vortex.

Wu Kang Ho and Li Po Tun stood nearby, finger tips gently pressed together, forming fleshy pyramids. Gentle words of respect and honor floated throughout the room. Nods were made to Lin Feng's photo accompanied by quiet affirmations of reverence and, finally, wishes for a carefree afterlife.

Shu Wei and Shu Lan-lan had been told that there would be no coffin, open or closed. They were to heed their father's advance wishes. In reality, Wu Kang Ho and Li Po Tun didn't want to chance their witnessing the ugly red marks and purplish bruises encircling their father's throat. They were also given assurances that a special service and burial would be held in San Francisco at the appropriate time. Since there was no point in delivering the body back to their home town, arrangements would be made for burial in a Chinese cemetery.

As the four made their way back to their quarters, a new moon had risen on the starboard side. Shu Wei took the sighting of this tiny sliver to be an omen for a new start. Just as quickly as he spotted it, it disappeared behind a mass of dark angry clouds. It's just as well that he hadn't seen Huǒlóng sitting nearby in a deck chair, enjoying a cigarette. He may have interpreted the occluded moon as quite a different omen.

CHAPTER NINE

Immigration

As they approached San Francisco Bay the winds were mercifully mild, allowing many passengers at the bow to settle into their blanket cocoons on deck chairs and to enjoy the first views of San Francisco harbor. The morning lightened and the first tawny rays swept over the ship.

Shu Wei and Shu Lan-lan joined the gawking crowds along the rails. Their flimsy suitcases were already battered, their clothing disheveled.

Now the passing land masses became more focused. Fields quilted in ochres, limes, and faded cobalts lay luminous beneath the scrim of hazy fog. Valleys folded into more valleys. Shadows skidded along, forming and reforming as though choreographed by an unseen hand. The Bay showed its angry side, delivering unruly waves onto the shore where rocks were the final filter.

The immediate horizon was now clogged with masts and smokestacks of the various crafts entering and leaving the harbor: schooners, square-riggers, scows, steamships, and steam ferry boats. The *City of Peking* passed Fort Point, the impressive four-story brick fortification at the harbor's entrance. It was the first building the passengers had seen since leaving Hong Kong twenty-four days earlier. A few minutes later the newly-dedicated Ferry Building would appear with its impressive Beaux-Arts-style facade.

The lighthouse on Alcatraz Island burned its beam into the scudding ceiling of gray. Further on, what Shu Wei first saw as bushes on the shore morphed into animated clusters of onlookers, all having come down to watch the arrival of this giant vessel of the seas. Some came to the docks as merchants, urged on by sightings of the *City of Peking's* big funnel from the tower of the Merchants Exchange Building on Battery Street in downtown San Francisco. Others were porters, greeters, longshoremen, horse car operators, and the simply curious. Various purveyors and promoters rehearsed their best pitches for the newly landed.

"We need to keep an eye out for our hosts," cautioned Shu Lan-lan. "Have you seen them?"

Before Shu Wei could respond, Wu Kang Ho and Li Po Tun yelled their greetings as they pushed their way through the crowds on deck.

A glint in his eye, Wu Kang Ho proudly held out two packages of British tea cakes. "Here," he beamed. "These are compliments of the captain. He has been following the saga of your father and he wanted you both to know that he is deeply sorry and wishes you well."

Shu Wei stood erect, tightly pressing his shoulder blades together as if this warrior-like stance would ward off any upsurge in emotions. He felt a series of mild tremors course through his body.

A woman with a fox tail muffler and black lace veil offered her handkerchief to Shu Lan-lan as streaks of moisture coursed down her cheeks. Just as brother and sister embraced, the ship thudded against the heavy timber bumpers at the dock. Longshoremen were already fast at work lassoing the frayed ropes around the dock cleats. A sign read: *Welcome to San Francisco!*

Shu Wei held his sister tightly as the crowd pushed toward a gangway at mid-decks. "Aye, you folks now don't go sendin' your neighbors into the drink," said the second officer. "You surein' won't like the taste o' the Bay. Plenty o' time. Aunt Frannie'l still be waitin' for ya."

At the bottom of the ramp the group encountered a tall man in a dark olive wool uniform with a shiny badge indicating his role as customs officer. He first directed several returning citizens, including Li Po Tun and Wu Kang Ho, toward a holding zone and then turned his attention to Shu Wei and Shu Lan-lan. Abruptly taking hold of their suitcases he chalked a large *X* on each one. Shu Wei noticed that the non-Chinese did not have this mark. Without speaking to the two young people, the officer rifled through the suitcases, tossing items on the sidewalk. "What have we here?" he barked. "A couple of thieves?"

Shu Wei and Shu Lan-lan cast each other puzzled looks. Shu Wei attempted to respond, "What are . . ."

The man cut him off, "These pieces of silverware look to be stolen to me. They even have the initials *CoP*, our ship's insignia."

Shu Wei, stunned, tried to make sense of this interrogation. *Oh, that slimy serpent*, he thought. Huǒlóng must have slipped them into their bag after they had packed them and left to find Li Po Tun and Wu Kang Ho. "Sir," pleaded Shu Wei, someone must have put these . . ."

"Ya Chinks are always up to somethin'," snarled the officer. And half of ya are liars. I'm hangin' onto these. You'll be dealt with. This'll be put on your entry records. Now move along to that shed over there."

It stung. Not the kind of treatment he had imagined in his readings about the *Flowery Flag Nation*. His entire body was consumed with overwhelming fatigue and despondency. Was it from the newness of this foreign land or his body's delayed reaction to horrible and uncontrollable events? Or was it merely his body fighting for equilibrium after so many days at sea? He wasn't accustomed to this new feeling. Normally his mood was as stable as the furniture his father made. His mind was now a tangle of both hope and fear.

Finally, daring to glance around, Shu Wei saw wheeled carts drawn by teams of horses, straining under their burdens. Other wagons were being loaded with barrels, gunny sack packets, and latticed wooden crates by stocky men in high leather boots. A swarm of hustlers, hackmen, boardinghouse runners, and hawkers of various merchandise intercepted the weary and beleaguered passengers. Horse droppings and a grit of spilled produce, grains, and discarded packing covered the cobbled streets adjacent to the compound of pitched-roof metal sheds. The exterior of the main shed bore the words *Pacific Mail Steamship Co.* in block letters.

Wu Kang Ho and Li Po Tun rejoined Shu Wei and Shu Lan-lan after their customs and health certificates had been checked and approved. An immigration officer stood just outside a large shed. His belly tumbled over a wide black belt. Wu Kang Ho said, "We have all endured a great deal in these past days. These two have suffered the greatest; their father passed away on the ship."

The officer, mustache twitching, retorted, "So what do you want—medals? I'm here doin' my job, and I need the lot of you to move inside. I can't be gettin' involved in your life stories."

Li Po Tun's face reddened. He clenched his walking stick tighter and began to move toward the man. Wu Kang Ho, reacted quickly to restrain his friend and said, "We two are law-abiding residents of this city and engage in business pursuits and charity. Your attitude is not befitting your position. Your words are poison to our ears."

"Did I ask for your opinion?" the official growled, brusquely shoving Wu Kang Ho and Li Po Tun toward the building's main door. "Now move on before I arrest the bunch of ya."

Endless rows of cubicles lined the inside of the shed. A woman whose hawk-like nose protruded from her pock-marked face beckoned the group forward. Wire rim glasses revealed piercing amber eyes. Severely parted hair grew in frazzled clumps above each ear. Her gray woolen uniform lost some authority due to a badly rumpled collar on one side. Not looking up she ordered, "I'm takin' ya'll one by one so nobody get their knickers knotted. Who's first? I got all day."

Wu Kang Ho stepped forward, showed his re-entry certificate and said, "These two persons are seeking entry into our country. They are sponsored by the Hop Wo Company of which I and Mr. Li Po Tun are members. They will live and work at my store on Dupont Street. Their father, the late Lin Feng, passed away on board the *Peking* due to complications from a debilitating injury back in China. Mr. Li Po Tun is a well-known doctor on Waverly Place. He has treated the railroad tycoons Leland Stanford and Mark Hopkins with his miraculous cures.

"You're aware that we're still operating under the Exclusion Act, Mr. Ko?" the woman asked rhetorically.

"That's Wu Kang Ho, *not* Mr. Ko," he corrected.

Glowering at her challenger, she continued, "You, as overseers of these two foreigners' welfare and conduct, will be subject to deportation if regulations are not followed. Now, hand over your papers and your subjects. We'll see if they're fit enough to have a life here. They already have a black mark on their records—stealing from the ship's dining room." She motioned to Shu Lan-lan. "You. Sit in that chair."

Shu Lan-lan nervously fingered a loose strand of hair as she crept over to the backless stool next to the desk. "Hand over your health certificate and immigration card."

Scanning both documents with ink-blotched hands, the woman glared at Shu Lan-lan over her glasses that now sat on the lower half of her nose. "The *Peking's* medical officer has indicated that you have acted against orders to submit for examination. Why would that be?" quizzed the woman.

"I was angry. He examined me in a bad way. He kept telling me I had things I don't have," replied Shu Lan-lan.

"Well, we'll let our own medical supervisor make a determination," said the woman. "Now, let me have your immigration certificate." Motioning with a sweep of her right hand, the woman said, "Take yourself to our health station. They will bring you to your senses about how we do things in this town. Now, you! Boy! Come to this table.

"Hand over your documents!" ordered the woman who by now was becoming red in the face.

Shu Wei reached frantically into his pockets and withdrew two wadded-up pieces of paper. Then, with newfound courage, he tossed them onto the table.

"You people haven't discovered manners, have you?" blurted the woman. "I will give these back to you, and you will hand them to me in the proper way."

Shu Wei took the papers, smoothed them, glared at his shoes and then at the woman. With trembling hands and arms outstretched, he offered them as though he were a jeweler offering gems on a cushion to a customer.

"Only because we have inadequate proof of your flagrant theft of ship property, we cannot hold you. But, next time give the officer a more credible excuse—not some feeble story about a third-party plant. Even though I personally have reservations, you are passed through. Now, go join your friend before I follow my better judgment and send you both back on the next packet." The force of the stamp landing on Shu Wei's papers echoed off the trussed ceiling of the shed.

Shu Wei joined his sister in the medical examination waiting area which was a corral of metal frames wrapped with cotton fabric like canvas sails on wheels. Six chairs faced directly across from another six chairs, clearly arranged by someone with a flair for discipline. A strong chemical odor wafted throughout the space, causing many of the forlorn guests to bring hands and handkerchiefs to their noses. Nurses gowned in white bib aprons over white smocks scampered over polished linoleum. They mysteriously darted in and out of sight. Their neatly folded white caps gave them an air of officiousness. Just as Shu Wei sarcastically remarked to Shu Lan-lan that they must be *gweilo* ghosts, one abruptly loomed up from nowhere and summoned them to follow her.

Shu Wei and Shu Lan-lan were shown to separate dressing rooms. They were instructed to clothe themselves with flimsy wraps that fastened only by cords in the back. From there they were ushered into gender-separate quarters to begin a series of tests and treatments.

Shu Wei recoiled in shock as a medical aide approached with a kit containing small vials and a needle. Before he could ask a proper question, a rubber band was tied around his arm and a needle had pierced a vein, filling a vial with burgundy-colored blood. His eyes grew wide. As the needle was withdrawn he lost consciousness. Some moments later the aide offered, "Sit here a bit. You went limp on me. This is only a small test for contagions that we give all new Chinese." Shu Wei did not recognize the word 'contagions' but he was too stunned to ask. He had never seen so much blood in a tube before. They had studied ghouls in school but he hoped these people weren't connected to the Chinese *Jiangshi*, reanimated corpses.

Some minutes later a man arrived dressed in a dark blue uniform, a badge dangling from a front pocket with the initials HMS over his name: *Hector Gomez, Orderly.* "I see we've come back to life." The comment brought an ache to Shu Wei's temples.

The treatments continued. Orderly Gomez pulled out a canister of sinister-looking reddish fluid. With an implement that was part sponge and part brush he proceeded to swab the vile-smelling substance on Shu Wei's private parts. Shu Wei's whole body shivered and shook with the stinging sensation and the personal assault on his body. "There, that'll kill the worst of the germs in the tight spots. Now, we'll move on to the shower room."

Shu Wei's head was spinning. He was unable to think clearly or react. But the thought of a shower brought a degree of alertness to his foggy state. Gomez guided him to another large room that was occupied by twenty or so other Chinese immigrants and a few Europeans. There was something ominous about the makeup of the room and the overriding strong odor—the same odor that blanketed the check-in area. Fully tiled walls met a stained green tile floor that was sloped to drains at several spots. Hoses were coiled on racks on two of the walls.

The garish lighting illuminated in vivid detail the anatomical features of the naked men who awkwardly shifted from foot to foot. Shu Wei struggled to cast his eyes away from these pathetic souls, except one. His focus happened to rest momentarily on an ill-kempt red haired man with freckles covering most of his body. Shu Wei's nerve endings seemed to all come alive at once. He recognized this man, who was now glaring at Shu Wei, as the one who he encountered on the deck of the *Peking*. It was Brian O'Grady.

"All right children, listen up!" barked the orderly. "We're all gonna take a little shower. This is not the sweetest perfume but this stuff'll disinfect, sterilize, purify, fumigate, you name it. Before you folks can mingle in our world for the first time, our U.S. of A. health folks have cooked up this yummy decontaminate." He paused until the interpreter caught up with him. "Stand where you are—we'll come to you; don't come to us. One thing y'all need to do is keep your eyes and mouths shut while we're workin' on you. The stuff won't kill you, but it shore ain't fun tastin'."

Two assistants emerged from behind a screen, carrying nozzle-like devices which they proceeded to attach to the hoses. Uncoiling the hoses from the racks, they worked their way around the room, unleashing the spray of the vile smelling concoction on the stunned targets. Shu Wei stood frozen in place for minutes.

An hour later the room took on a dream-like appearance: figures moving slowly through a coral-colored fog that eventually got absorbed into the series of vents in the ceiling. Shu Wei stood motionless, trying to clear his mind enough to comprehend the nature of what was taking place. Just then, O'Grady charged across the slippery floor and caught him around the neck, screaming, "Hello, yellow-boy. Heard your old man didn't make it. Shame." Shu Wei slipped and his elbow hit the floor with a crack. O'Grady held the younger Shu Wei in a hammerlock until the orderly, Gomez, brought in two guards who pulled them apart.

Gomez shouted, "You fools! This is not a wrestling arena, it's a quarantine center. Now get into your gowns, and I will have words with you both."

Shu Wei wrapped a towel around his pained elbow as he strained to deal with the flimsy gown. A male nurse escorted him to a treatment area where he received another helping of disinfectant and a gauze wrapping. Orderly Gomez appeared and said, "If I was you, I'd stay outta that one's way. Them Irish are trouble makers. Now on your way to the next station."

"That man is a freak that was fired from his job on the *Peking* shortly after leaving Hong Kong. You can confirm this with the captain," said Shu Wei.

"Enough with details. I'm not paid to play judge and jury here. I will need to write up this incident and put it in the records."

One of the shower room attendants stood nearby. "Mr. Treadwell here will now take you to your temporary quarters," said Gomez. "You will be placed at a distance from your friend, Mr. O'Grady. In fact, you both will be under heavy scrutiny the entire time until your release."

"The entire time?" questioned Shu Wei.

"You will be under quarantine until we can determine the status of the tests and other records you have brought with you. I can't tell you how long that will be. I will notify your Chinatown friends that they will also have to remain on the premises. They have custody of you and will need to escort you to your final destination."

Shu Wei felt another ache of hopelessness and despair settle in. And yet, a surge of resolve came over him as he was guided by Treadwell to his quarters. Having focused on the pain in his elbow and the encounter with O'Grady he realized he had yet to wonder after the fate of his little sister. Hopefully she had been having an easier time of it than he had.

Shu Lan-lan was in the final stages of her "decontamination" in the women's processing shed. The questioning of the women took some time because of the greater level of specificity required than with the men. Also, the much smaller ratio of women immigrants to men gave more latitude to the aggressions of the interrogators. 'What are you intending to do and why did you come here in the first place? Do you know about the many hazards that confront young girls and women in Chinatown? Given that you no longer have a father, how will you sustain yourself? Is your brother competent?' Shu Lan-lan's head swam with the barrage of issues thrown at her. Her answers were hasty, jumbled. Things had come at her too quickly in the last several days and she had no time to come to any conclusions.

While Shu Lan-lan contemplated her predicament her body was still dripping with the same odorous drizzle. The room was consumed with a haze that seemed to go along with her mood. But something was not right. She looked down and saw that she had broken out in a splotchy rash. She felt dizzy and sensed her body temperature rising. When she collapsed, her fall was luckily broken by a girl who had been sensing her condition and called out, "Nurse, this girl has become sick. You must help!"

When Shu Lan-lan came to, she was on a cot under a layer of frayed wool blankets. Her chills had come on with a vengeance after she had been given some pills to reduce her fever. "We get some with reactions to the decontaminant," said a nurse with a blue-striped sweater over her white smock, a pale green head-wrap beneath her fluted cap, and a badge that read *Supervisor*. "You had a bad one, but we caught it in time. Now, here are some pills that will help you to sleep."

Shu Lan-lan swallowed the pills and shortly fell into a deep sleep. Memories of her childhood came to her: diaphanous figures showed themselves and then retreated. In the meadow of the white mulberry trees along the contoured slopes near their village her father was harvesting the bright green leaves. He brought them to the shed where the grubs from the moth eggs form themselves into larvae. Then he took her to a large shed where baskets filled a wall of shelving. He told her to bend close to one of the baskets and listen very closely. She heard a fizzing sound—the racket of all the silkworms furiously feasting on the leaves.

Her mother, Lin Dai-bon, came into the shed with a batch of three-inch-long silkworms that had stopped eating and lay on straw in a woven basket, ready to spin their cocoons. Shu Lan-lan was entranced with how they swiveled their tiny heads in a figure eight producing the viscous liquid that hardened in-to silk as it hit the air. The family together carried the cocoons in large baskets to the purchasing stations.

Shu Wei placed one of the cocoons down the back of his sister's dress and she screamed—half in anger, half in playfulness. Regulars to the purchasing house, they were led into the area where women reeled the silk from the cocoons. Shu Lanlan was absorbed in how the movements were very much like the moves of t'ai chi: slow and sinuous so that the strands don't break or stick.

Her father whispered in her ear, 'You can become just like the goddess of silk, the legendary empress *Leizu*, who had a co-coon fall into her tea cup and discovered the magic of weaving fabric after she unrolled the thread. Some day, I am sure, you will make your way in life from the simplest of beginnings and end up with great pleasure and contentment.' He also reminded her of the Chinese character for happiness: a combination of the symbols for white, silk, and tree.

Shu Wei's quarantine lasted for four days. On the fifth day, pinched daggers of soft sunlight fought their way through the early morning haze of the ward. As one beam of light laid a path over Shu Wei's bed, he raised himself up, shaking off the cobwebs of sleep and trying to decipher the source and meaning of a commotion. Several of his ward mates were already poised at the edges of their beds. A large-bellied man with a faded dark blue cap and a uniform with braided shoulder epaulets strode into the ward clutching a clipboard. "All right, when I call your name form a line against that wall near the yellow stripes on the floor—and be quick about it. Some of the half-witted staff here have seen fit to give you passage into this country. Lord only knows what good you all will do," grunted the officer.

When Shu Wei's name was called he joined the other boys and men who shuffled silently with their belongings toward the assigned holding zone.

"When I call your name, come forward to get your papers and go outside to the boarding area."

Shu Wei approached the officer head down. "Look at me, son! You're gettin' your ticket to leave this resort, but it carries a warning from our Bureau of Health that you were a suspected carrier of acute hepi-cranial dysfunction. Is that clear?" Shu Wei couldn't catch the words. He suspected the man purposely mumbled the specifics. Probably wasn't even a medical term. By now he was catching on that the Chinese were really not welcome in this country.

CHAPTER TEN

An Unwelcoming

Outside the Immigration Center Shu Wei stood shoulder-to-shoulder with his freed comrades, some speaking in unfamiliar languages, most still dazed from their experiences. He still smelled the fumigation odors on his body. The sun was filtered by an early morning fog. A flock of seagulls flapped in battle over soggy fish remains on the oily cobbles. Workers' shouts rose and fell, tossed here and there by swirling wind gusts.

"I was worried to the point of sickness. We have been unable to leave since I got out," blurted Shu Lan-lan. "We tried to contact someone but no one was particularly helpful." Li Po Tun and Wu Kang Ho followed close behind, with scowls of concern.

Shu Wei's melancholy was lifted in the presence of his dear sister and good friends. He couldn't remember embracing Shu Lan-lan with such fervor. He even thought he detected a small curl of a teardrop at the edge of Wu Kang Ho's eye.

"Come, let's board our coach to Chinatown," implored Li Po Tun. "New lives are waiting."

As Shu Wei grabbed the handle of his suitcase he was transfixed by the view of the impressive complex in front of him.

"Ah, you are finding that building of interest I see," said Wu Kang Ho. "That is the Oriental Warehouse. It has taken in great quantities of goods over the years. If its brick walls could speak to us they would regale us with stories of the many things that have passed through here like flour, gold, silver bars, and Mexican dollars. Parts of its generous interior held provisions headed for Americans and Europeans in the Orient like oats, barley, wheat, quicksilver, liquor, beans, and dried fish. The *Peking* just offloaded its cargo of tea, rice, and silk here for consumption in this country."

Wu Kang Ho pivoted his hand in an arc as he pointed out the rest of the compound's parts: the First Street wharf sheds and coal yards, the smaller Occidental Warehouse, and the rail tracks that spread over much of the ground like shimmering snakes. Shu Wei had not seen the likes of this kind of landscape. It both entranced and mystified him.

Wu Kang Ho's musings faded as Shu Wei struggled to deal with the sight of a nearby poster pasted onto one of the sheds. It depicted a Chinese man—his eyes lit up in lunacy—holding a lighted torch in his left hand and a smoking pistol in his right. He stood over a bloodied woman prone on the pavement. His teeth clenched a lethal-looking knife and his long queue danced crazily behind him. The caption read *The Yellow Terror in All His Glory*. Shu Wei stood staring, trying to comprehend this cartoon that seemed to be placed at the docks in a prominent position for full effect. It was unsettling to say the least.

"All aboard, those that'll be goin' to the Hop Wo Company," barked a driver who sat, legs braced against the footboard of his carriage. Two horses snorted into their feed buckets and steam drifted up from their hides—signs of recent labors. "We'll be checking your papers first. Throw your belongings on up here." The buggy head was folded back to accommodate the passengers and their eclectic cargo. Wu Kang Ho and Li Po Tun rode in a more refined carriage behind them.

Seated atop their luggage, Shu Wei and Shu Lan-lan hung on tightly to nearby railings as the lurching carriage headed west on Brannan Street toward Third Street. They numbly stared at the wood frame structures along the way that housed freight offices, blacksmiths, chandleries, warehouses, saloons, and lumber yards.

Shu Lan-lan's words came out soft and hesitant, "Our dear father has been lost, and we have little promise for a good life with so little money. Our treatment at the quarantine station was worth a lifetime of disgrace and dishonor."

"I feel we are now at the base of the great *Wutai Shan* mountain in our country," said Shu Wei. "We can reach the home of the Bodhisattva of wisdom at its pinnacle and inhabit one of those fine wooden buildings, the *Nanshan Temple*. There we will commune with the pilgrims who will give us strength and meaning for our days . . ."

"Your thinking is mysterious and bloated with myth, my brother."

Shu Wei slowly turned his back from Shu Lan-lan and said, "I am only trying to keep the ghouls from bringing us down further. My grief is the weight of five pandas upon my shoulders. Perhaps yours is like that of a kitten." At that, Shu Lan-lan folded her arms across her chest and let out a sigh of frustration. A lone teardrop found her suitcase—she quickly blotted it with her hanky.

They each had to tighten their grip as their carriage turned north up Third Street. Heading past South Park, buildings became more substantial, mostly brick and stone. Their heights rose to two and three stories. Various colored awnings thrust out over sidewalks, announcing their owners' businesses: dry goods, produce, general merchandise, cafe, grocer. The street activity grew steadily. Men wore bowler hats with dark suits. Women sported broad-brimmed floppy bonnets and full flowing dresses cinched at the waist. All manner of horse-driven carts, buggies, and carriages flowed ceaselessly while people scurried along urgently.

As they approached Market Street the impressive Call Building loomed with its baroque dome and four corner cupolas. Shu Wei and Shu Lan-lan's eyes widened and both wondered silently how such a tall building could stand. Just adjacent was the massive hulk of the Palace Hotel. Crossing Market Street, Shu Wei pointed skyward to the giant sandstone Chronicle building. Its four-story bronze clock tower stood proudly atop the structure.

Turning north along Kearny more activity and buildings came into view. A block from the California Hotel and Theatre, at the corner of Bush, the horses suddenly rose up in fright, straining at their reins. A small cluster of hooligans was lofting firecrackers at the carriage.

"Go back home, you stinkin' Chinks! We don't wantcha here. There ain't no jobs for the likes of youse!" One of the taller boys with a newsboy hat and apron launched a barrage of eggs. Shu Lan-lan was able to duck all but two; they splattered in a gooey mess on the special coat with decorative toggles she had labored over with Chun Dai last winter. Stunned, she crouched into a fetal position and held her suitcase in front of her as armor against any further assaults.

Shu Wei reached into his pocket for some peanuts he had found in a cupboard at the immigration depot. He tossed them toward the youths, but these pathetic munitions scattered harmlessly in the wind, showering him with their dusty remnants. Two boys ran after the carriage, attempting to gain a handhold on the rear mudguard. Their efforts were in vain as the driver brought the reins down hard on the horses and the carriage accelerated with a jolt. Shu Wei's face was frozen in anger and shock as he cradled his sister and rocked her gently.

"Pay these worthless tramps no mind," he said. "They are fiends and have the minds of crazed animals." Resting his face against her neck, he could feel her pulse beating wildly.

Finally approaching Chinatown, they caught familiar smells but some were unknown and mysterious. The sidewalks were alive with a diverse assortment of vendors and hawkers. Aromas of spices, fish, and roasted meats floated on the moist, dense air. Chinese women and children sporting colorful tunics, caps, and gowns glided in and out of doorways. Men clothed in black bowlers, dark wraps, and soft sandals gathered in earnest discussions at street corners and in alleyways.

"Final stop," yelled the driver. "All out here for Hop Wo. Take your belongings, you'll need 'em and more in this hellhole."

"I am terribly sorry you had an unfortunate experience back there you two," said Li Po Tun as he stepped from his carriage. "There are a class of folks in this town that have the pathetic notion that their world is the only god-given one. Someday I pray they'll come to their senses. In the meantime, be vigilant in your dealings and keep a lookout for this kind."

Wu Kang Ho helped Shu Wei and Shu Lan-lan from the step-board and gathered their two suitcases. "Yes, I pray that your future encounters will be favorable ones. We will be available as much as possible as you settle in." Shu Lan-lan was thinking back to her calmer life in Sanhou. That already seemed like a century in the past.

CHAPTER ELEVEN

A New Home

"I will introduce you to the members of our Company soon. But first, let me take both of you to my shop and your new home," said Wu Kang Ho. "It's just a few blocks to Clay and Waverly." Leading Shu Wei and Shu Lan-lan west along Sacramento Street in Chinatown, Wu Kang Ho shouted a greeting to an older man lining up long pieces of sugar cane against a wall like so many fishing poles.

Wu Kang Ho said that all the principles of *feng shui* could be found here. Having Nob Hill at Chinatown's back, the westerly winds were blocked, allowing the cosmic energy *qi*— the *yang* principle—to flow easterly toward San Francisco Bay, the *yin* body of water. Telegraph Hill offered protection on the east and Rincon Hill to the southeast. He said that this fifteen-block community faced the rising sun and nestled into an omega-shaped land form, or "dragon's lair," completing the harmony of features.

The three passed buildings of varying styles; flimsy wooden structures built from discarded ship lumber stood next to more substantial two- and three-story Victorian-style buildings built with imported brick and granite. Layers of Chinese influence had dressed up these simple facades over the years. Balconies were added, facades imitated pagodas, and storefronts displayed a variety of Chinese goods. Elements of the homeland had been transplanted, a bridge between east and west.

Shu Wei and Shu Lan-lan found themselves gawking at the sites, sounds, and smells in this exotic world: the sweet fragrance of the lilies from the curbside vendor; the pungent aroma of crabs and fish in a round woven flat, its napping seller leaning against a pair of rickety doors. A pair of wire baskets full of eggs swung in the breeze overhead. A basket mender feverishly worked his craft as he sat on a four-legged stool. Men toted large sacks of rice corded together so they looked like tied hogs. A butcher featured a skinned carcass hanging lifeless from a giant hook in his open-air shop. He chopped an order on his carving block. A man in a produce market was arranging neat stacks of bok choy, mung beans, okra, pickling melons, and burdock.

Shu Wei glanced up at a second-floor balcony, lacquered in vibrant reds and yellow. A man in a folding chair pulled plaintive sounds from a stringed instrument. Two enormous red and green Chinese lanterns swung overhead, dancing in tempo.

Their fascination rose as they passed windows filled with elegantly decorated silk embroideries, ebony-carved cabinets rich in ornamentation, bronzes, and cloisonné ware. A glance down an alleyway revealed a man smoking a large bent pipe, a cat snuggled at his feet nested into a tumble of baskets and merchandise. Cobwebbed signage and faded frescoes of another era embellished otherwise drab building facades. Winding passageways revealed flimsy wooden additions. The constant clatter of dominoes poured from windows and doors announcing the ever-present game of *pai gow*.

The variety of shops and activities settled Shu Wei. In his mind possibilities took shape. He thought, with a little effort, this all might work out after all. Maybe he could work in one of these shops, possibly even woodworking. He caught sight of a Chinese newspaper on a stand and his eyes lit up. *Or, maybe even work for that paper*, he thought.

Arriving at Wu Kang Ho's store at the corner of Clay Street and Waverly Place, they paused to admire the robust three-story facade of this brownstone structure that spoke of a former elegance. A metal awning wrapped the corner, shading a series of protruding display bays. A bracketed cornice sat below an attic floor with a roof in the mansard style and four dormers. A series of tall windows graced the second floor. Flower boxes dressed up the sills.

"Come, let me show you to your quarters," Wu Kang Ho said. He gave a mock bow and a sweep of the hand as he ushered the two new tenants in. "As you can see this is no ordinary store. We are involved in general merchandise, but we also run a bank and a post office."

A counter paneled in walnut ran most of the length of the right side of the space. The banking section toward the front was surrounded by a metal mesh cage with a hand hole. A letter box and scale stood at the counter's rear where a clerk spoke in animated terms to a patron. A low series of display cases holding pottery and other dry goods occupied most of the left side. A raised platform on spindled legs held various trinkets and baubles. Four chandeliers dripped with pendants and tassels lending a forced elegance. A plaque with the name *Wu Kang Ho Co.* in gilt lettering spread across the back wall.

Wu Kang Ho guided Shu Wei and Shu Lan-lan to the back of the store to their new living quarters. A large room held small partitioned alcoves on opposite sides, each with a draw curtain, bed, shallow closet, and lamp on a small table. A ceramic pitcher topped a three-drawer dresser along the back wall of the main room. Three chairs nested beneath a table with a lamp. A door on the opposite wall opened into a small bath. Near the door that connected to the store a hot plate and shallow kitchen sink were wedged into a wall recess.

"It's not much but enough to call home for now," said Wu Kang Ho. "We had arranged for a larger place for you both and your father, but . . ." He quickly caught himself. "I will now show you the secret access panel that leads to the second floor."

Wu Kang Ho pulled back a patterned chenille curtain that hung on a rod across most of the back wall. A wood door became visible off to one side. It led to the backyard. Pulling out a small piece of the baseboard near the door, he retrieved a pronged metal key, inserted it in a slot in the door, and turned.

As the three ascended a staircase, Wu Kang Ho continued, "I think this house was built around 1880. I bought it from the Huang family. They came into some money and moved away only three years after they bought it. I made it into a store but I kept this back area for my elderly parents but they were never able to make it out of China."

They arrived at a dimly-lit upper level that slowly revealed itself as their eyes adjusted.

"There's no bed here now, but the sink is still behind the curtain over there—not sure if it even works anymore. The Huang kids must have loved being up here—their own kingdom. Over there is the door out to the roof where they used to keep pigeons. One of the boys in the family said he would dream he was holding onto a flock of them and traveling to a far off land."

Shu Wei was envious. Even though he had his own bedroom back home, he had never had a special place like this to retreat to. His mind drifted to his favorite literary escape, *Dream of the Red Chamber,* that Chun Dai used to read to them.

"What's that thing over there?" asked Shu Lan-lan.

Twisting a knob on the wall a bright light came on and illuminated an antique puppet theatre behind a curtain on a rod. It was taller than Shu Wei and as wide as the wall itself. It had been elaborately crafted with red silk fabrics embroidered with gold, yellow, and green designs that included dragons, flowers, fish, and Chinese symbols. A proscenium stage some three feet above the floor was cut into the middle where three dusty but colorful puppets still appeared about to perform. On the floor, eight more decorated puppets stood primed for action in various styles of dress. Head coverings ran from the simple to the ornate with flower clusters or faux jewels and hats.

Returning downstairs Wu Kang Ho said, "Oh, there is one more interesting thing about this property. I understand that there was a building that stood here before this one, built around the time of the Gold Rush. Rumor has it that there was a death in the house around 1876, followed by a fire shortly after that. The property sat vacant for several years because no one wanted to touch it. But that meant that the Huang family could get a good price. To eliminate the chances of ill effects from this wandering soul, I am told there were several weeks of burning joss, spiritual money, and a paper effigy along with the laying of jade orchid blossoms.

"A monk from the local temple chanted for two more days, then declared the site safe for construction. The Huangs thought they heard ghost puppets up here but I think they were off in the mind."

The word 'ghost,' instantly hit Shu Wei. *My father. Is Lin Feng now a ghost?* he wondered. Images of his father came to him in swift succession. He collapsed onto his bed moaning. Wu Kang Ho placed his hand gently on his back but Shu Wei quickly brushed it away. Shu Lan-lan smiled meekly and quietly began to unpack her suitcase. She said, "My tears no longer run—I think I just hurt too much."

"You both need rest," said Wu Kang Ho. "You have been through a most distressing experience. Tomorrow I will introduce you to The Hop Wo Company."

The Hop Wo Company, at the corner of Kearny and Sacramento, was a sturdy three-story building—a distinctive presence in the community. Li Po Tun and Wu Kang Ho greeted Shu Wei and Shu Lan-lan beneath a green fluted canopy that sheltered the recessed doorway at street level. Gold calligraphic lettering on a marble plaque carried the name and date of an important event. Shu Wei stopped to read this inscription about the visit in 1897 by Wu Ting Fang of Xinhui, the Qing dynasty's ambassador to Washington. They had just missed it. But at least it was a connection to the homeland.

The upper floors had balconies extending the width of the structure, overhung with eaves roofed in similar green tiles. Muted red window sashes were set into aquamarine tiled walls. A pair of bronze-coated lions stood sentinel at the entry. They reminded him of the miniature bronze horse that sat on the table in the main hall of their home in Sanhou.

Shu Wei was marveling at the elaborate detailing of the building when he heard the rattling of cart wheels. Hanging over the side of a wood-slat wagon, an inebriated man yelled, "Hey, sweetie, ya can be my midnight woman!" Then, as the malcontent Brian O'Grady pointed at Shu Wei, he said, "You! Ya make me sick. You here to take my job! I come back for a longer visit." O'Grady, in the company of other disheveled broad-backed men, slobbered a last incoherent taunt as the cart careened down Kearny, leaving a trail of orange rinds, cabbage heads, and beer bottles.

Li Po Tun quizzed Shu Wei, "Is that the same monster that caused you grief on the ship?"

"The very one, and I fear he just may remain a festering sore in our lives. He came after me in the disinfecting shower as well."

"You have not told me of this last occasion, Shu Wei," Shu Lan-lan protested. "You will need to be more open with me if we are to survive in this new and hostile world."

Shu Wei felt his patience waning. He dropped to one knee and ranted, "I don't care anymore about the importance of knowing, feeling, and sharing! Leave me to my own personal ghosts."

Wu Kang Ho stooped and gently grasped Shu Wei's shoulders. "Let's go inside and meet your new friends." He led them both up the stairs to a hall on the second floor.

Paneled with highly decorative lacquered screens and portraits of elders and former emperors of China, the hall exuded a musty mix of incense and furniture polish. Shu Wei stopped before a large picture. Li Po Tun leaned in and said that this man was Dr. Sun Yat-sen, a physician who quit his medical practice a few years ago to form a group seeking to modernize China.

Li Po Tun and Wu Kang Ho turned and joined three men in silk wraps and dark burgundy jackets with pillbox hats around a large table, still showing a recent coat of varnish. Shu Wei and Shu Lan-lan stood unmoving, fearing they were facing another somber ritual with a tribunal.

"Let me introduce you to some members of our Company you two," said Li Po Tun. "This is Chin Mon Way, a respected business man and our president. Over here is Fan Ching and Woo Fong. These men were responsible for arranging papers for your travel to the U.S. and will be helping to get you both settled here."

Chin Mon Way spoke first. "Welcome to our community. It is our pleasure to see that things go well for you here. I am deeply saddened to learn of your father's passing. It is indeed a tragedy. He and I have been trading partners and friends for many years."

"We all mourn for Lin Feng and will be handling the funeral in the next few days, said Woo Fong. "Unfortunately, since your father was not a bona fide citizen of this country we are only allowed to place his remains in the paupers' cemetery. However, in time, we hope to move him to a more respectable location."

Great, thought Shu Wei, *one more dishonorable pox on our family.* He wanted to stand and voice his protest but thought against it. Better to get off on the right foot with this group.

One of the side paneled doors swiveled open. A diminutive dark-skinned man in flared white pants and a tiered turban brought out a tea service platter. Chin Mon Way said, "Please, accept our meager offer of tea and rice cakes. We will be dining at one of our member's restaurants tomorrow evening. You must be hungry after your long trip."

Shu Lan-lan glanced at Shu Wei and noticed a slight up-turn to his mouth which quickly disappeared as he saw her looking at him. "We would be most grateful and humbled to accept your offer," she said. Nods of appreciation were exchanged between the men and the newcomers. Shu Wei and Shu Lan-lan sipped their tea tentatively, taking care to steady their hands as they raised their cups, knowing that they must show strength in their emotions before these respected elders.

The next evening Sing How Min welcomed the group to his restaurant, the Silver Dragon: Shu Wei; Shu Lan-lan; Li Po Tun; Grace Caldwell, Superintendent of the Occidental Mission Home for Girls; Wu Kang Ho; Fan Ching, owner and publisher of *The Golden Hills' News*; Mei Huang, Assistant Editor of *The News*; Chin Mon Way of the Proud Cypress Furniture Company, and Woo Fong, pharmacist. They occupied the roomy ceremonial alcove in the rear with its elaborate lattice screen. Other carved panels at the rear included stylized bats, wings extended, meant to bring good fortune. Five of the guests were seated in the three-sided banquettes upholstered with bright patterned silk and metal fabric. The other four settled into handsome four-legged chairs in dark stained camphor wood with ornate carvings. Two etched glass globe lights with pendants hung over the cloth-covered table. A musician sat a short distance away, strumming his seven-stringed zither.

While an aproned elderly waiter poured each diner tea from a large brass teapot, Sing How Min began. "May our two newcomers find prosperity, health, and happiness in their new lives. And may all hardships be banished by our god, *Ehr-Lang,* who will set the hounds of heaven on any evil spirits. Let us all indulge tonight in our good bounty of food and fellowship. While this meal will not reach the heights of the Manchu Han Imperial Feast, I trust it will suffice."

Chin Mon Way interjected, "While we satisfy our appetites, I have asked members of our good company here to convey wisdom and suggest a path for you both that will help ground you. But until then we will make certain that you will become educated with the workings of our community."

Shu Wei leaned forward to get a full view of the first courses arriving. He was overwhelmed by the selection. The aromas alone were enough to sate his deep-seated hunger. Shu Lan-lan demurely raised her napkin to wipe the non-existent tea drops from her lips. She had been schooled in table etiquette by Auntie Chun Dai. Her mother had seen no benefit in such a pursuit.

A tureen of broth made with noodles, healthy morsels of crab, and black mushrooms was ladled into blue and white bowls with serpent motifs. Platters followed of stir-fry vegetables, turnip cakes, rice rolls, lotus leaf rice, duck with spice sauce, and braised sea bass with peppers. Shu Wei's nose dilated. "You two will not recognize—or possibly not even like— some of these dishes. They do not all originate from your province," intoned Sing How Min.

Wu Kang Ho said, "We must now discuss practical matters. Unfortunately, we were only able to retrieve a small amount of the money your father carried on his person. Someone in his ward, or possibly an intruder, removed most of his cash. This will mean that you will need to supplement the assistance those around this table will provide with your own labors." Shu Wei's stomach turned on this comment. He had strong suspicions on who this 'intruder' may have been.

"Shu Wei, I understood from your father that you have some history as a public scribe in your home town, correct?" queried Li Po Tun.

"That I do, but you must know that I had a most unfortunate encounter with the town elders." Shu Lan-lan squirmed in her seat. She wondered what the chances were that these elders might pull the truth from her brother.

"I am sorry to hear of this," said Li Po Tun. "But this is your new world, and you are working from a clean slate. This is why I discussed your skills with Fan Ching. His newspaper, *The Golden Hills' News,* is struggling and could use some new blood." Shu Wei was baffled by these Western phrases. He wondered what a 'clean slate' was. Sounded like something to do with his chalk board at school. And 'new blood?' Maybe he could have used some of that after that *jiangshi* at Immigration removed a lot of his.

Shu Wei was taken with Fan Ching's composed, almost studious bearing. Tall and reed thin, he was reminded of their scholar in Sanhou. Small explosions of dark eyebrows almost half-covered his probing eyes. He wore a newsman's uniform of suspenders over a white shirt, cuffs folded back to the elbow.

"Your talents, Shu Wei, can be quite useful to us since we publish in both Chinese and English and I am told you have a fair command of each," offered Fan Ching. "I must add, however, that many Chinese dialects are spoken in our tight little world here and a good many cannot read or speak English. That is why I am suggesting we add photographs to get our story across. I am in the process of acquiring a camera, and we'll instruct you in the operation of this device when we receive it. To get you started, I want to give you something."

Placing a muslin bag on the table, Fan Ching pulled a book out and handed it to Shu Wei. "The second edition of this book, *Through China with a Camera,* by British author John Thomson, has just been published and has an extraordinary collection of photographs, adventures, and techniques. I'd like you to take it home and read it when you have time. Mr. Thomson had a real knack for capturing the daily lives of simple people."

Shu Wei responded, "Thank you, but . . . I only fear that I will not live up to . . ."

"Let's put aside any worries for now," Fan Ching interrupted. "I am not expecting flashes of brilliance from day one. I do expect you in my shop at least two days a week in the beginning. I will pay you a satisfactory wage. I've instructed Mei Huang, our Assistant Editor, seated next to Grace here, to help get you started. I am thinking you would start in the next few weeks or so once you get your bearings and have become familiar with Thomson's book."

Eyeing Shu Lan-lan across the table, Grace Caldwell chimed in. "As for you, my princess, I have a most exciting and challenging role in mind."

Grace Caldwell was a tall woman with an authoritative presence, her voice inflected with her sturdy native New Zealand English. She wore her traditional shirtwaist with leg-of-mutton sleeves. Her hair was done up in an auburn pompadour. The only softening adornment was a circular pendant attached to a collar that extended up to her chin. Shu Wei thought he had never come across a woman with such a formidable presence. She had come to the Occidental Home ten years before and had recently been placed in the position of Head Mistress of the Home.

Grace continued, "I am in the business of rescuing domestic servants, or as you might say—little sisters—*mui tsais.* Many families are poor, illiterate, or just cruel, and choose to sell their unwanted girls. These girls are at the mercy of the unscrupulous—that is to say they are exposed to hard labor in families who take advantage of these *chattels*. But even worse fates await them as prostitutes. They are exposed to horrific abuses by cowardly men who think only of their sexual gratification."

Shu Lan-lan broke in, "I am having difficulty picturing what you are telling me. Surely there is no godly possibility I could be of help in these matters."

"I think you will find that there are many ways the Lord brings a usefulness to our lives. I will introduce you to the compassion and social justice of the Christian faith. But my methods involve more than religion. I am known to some as *Fahn Quai*, or the White Devil, to those whose victims I rescue. Some say I'm the Angry Angel of Chinatown. Still others—who have been saved from a life of abject poverty and abuse call me *Lo Mo*, or Beloved Mother."

"But how do you manage these . . . these . . . rescues as you call them?"

"We will cover those details later. For now, starting in a week or so, I will take you in to my Mission Home for three days and nights a week. You will be fed and will have comfortable accommodations. In return, and under my tutelage, you will serve as a counselor to a group of girls I will identify.

"As I understand it, your family has had connections to the silk trade. I'd like you to develop your skills in the sewing and weaving crafts so that you can bring these skills to our struggling waifs. I find that we are able to improve their morale and respectability in this way."

Shu Wei had a satisfied look on his face and a number of empty plates in front of him. Two waiters quickly swooped in and cleared the remaining dishes. Just as quickly a new round of plates was presented—this time a satisfying round of desserts: water chestnut cakes, steamed and deep fried *Mantou*, and colorful fruit melanges in custard.

"Now that you have a better picture of how you will contribute and grow in our community I must issue some warnings," said Chin Mon Way. "You will encounter all manner of people here—some wise and kind but some vile and untrustworthy. You will need to learn to observe and make judgments. The fine people around this table will not be at your side most of the time. Be wary of unprincipled tricksters and gamblers that can steal whatever money you may have in the blink of an eye.

"More precisely, you will hear about the Hap Tran Tong. This secret society's members prey on the weak and vulnerable. They are a violent group and they make good on their threats. They have many inventive ways to extract money or even blood."

"How do they do this?" questioned Shu Wei. All of a sudden he was getting that familiar pinched neck sensation. He had lapsed into a comfort zone the past few days with no sightings of his nemesis, Huǒlóng. At least he now had new friends he could lean on.

"Often by demanding money from merchants for protection against other Tongs," Chin Mon Way continued. "They run legitimate businesses that cover for their side rackets in opium or gambling. Sometimes it's the so-called yellow slave trade. Just keep a wary eye out and sniff the air for trouble at all times. And make sure you come to us if you are approached by one of these types. In time, we will rid these vile forces of corruption from our midst. The Chinese community of residents and business people here is fifty-thousand and growing. These thugs are finding fewer souls willing to tolerate their insolence."

Woo Fong said, "I might add that you both are welcome to seek advice and aid from me and my colleague, doctor Li Po Tun, as you require. My pharmacy is just up the street. And speaking of medicine, there are great perils in taking the opium. It is an easy habit to fall into and an easy purchase. But you must resist at all costs. Otherwise, you will find that your senses may be taken from you. I can provide certain medicinal remedies at my shop. But there is no easy relief for addiction."

"Let us all praise Buddha for our good fortune in having these two on our soil, and let no devils cross their paths," said Wu Kang Ho. "The night is getting late. We must let our guests retire to prepare for the busy days ahead. Sing How Min has graciously suggested we meet here again in a few weeks time."

CHAPTER TWELVE

A Funeral

The spirits in Chinatown that evening were angry. Pelting rain and angry winds assaulted Shu Wei and Shu Lan-lan as they made their way through the narrow streets to the Hop Wo building on Sacramento Street. Arriving at the top floor, they were greeted by the parties who had attended the other evening's dinner, plus another fifteen men and women. This floor enshrined the gods. Suspended in boxes lining the corridor were deified warriors, heroes, and sages. Concealed springs provided an eerie animation of javelins and other warlike weapons of menacing design.

A small cluster of dark-suited men played various stringed instruments. The pitches of these devices were both mournful and piercing. Large paper curtains dyed a deep vermillion hung nearby, announcing the names of contributors and their respective donations to this association, along with the evil spirits that have been controlled through incantations and exorcisms.

Chin Mon Way then unleashed a series of pronouncements that was in a dialect foreign and unintelligible to Shu Wei and Shu Lan-lan. They heard their father's name just as a figure in a white hood carried a pair of effigies of the devil toward the balcony windows. The group shuffled forward as these figures were being thrust violently in several directions. A low mono-tonal rumbling from some members of the group crescendoed and fell; others repeated this as though attempting a choral rapture. Suddenly, the man with the devil figures stopped his wild commotion and threw them from the balcony to the street.

Shu Wei and Shu Lan-lan, spellbound, fell in behind the group as they silently made their way to the street. The rain had stopped, leaving behind crisp night air tinged with the aromas of cooking oil and burning sandalwood. The exorcist was busy writing numerous curses in red ink on yellow paper. He then burned these on a porcelain plate. The ashes were stirred into a cup of water which he then put in his mouth. He stamped around, holding aloft a trident, and spurted this holy water in all directions. For the next several minutes he beseeched the devil's departure with a throaty yelling and howling. As a final gesture, he gripped the effigies, incinerated them, placed them again on the makeshift pyre plate and then into two bronze vessels. Shu Wei and Shu Lan-lan were given these containers to scatter the ashes to the wind as a symbolic gesture.

Shu Wei dropped his head to his chest. Shu Lan-lan stared at the dying embers and the paper particles that still drifted and swirled upward into the ink-black night air. Stars blended with these bits—one became the other.

Wu Kang Ho bent low to address the two, "Come. We will end our ceremony on the roof. Join us."

The group once again ascended the stairs to the roof where a makeshift shrine had been set up, complete with a variety of fruits, joss sticks, and a cast iron pot. Lin Feng's picture was placed on an easel surrounded by garlands of chrysanthemums, hibiscuses, peonies, and lilies. More prayers burst from random points in the crowd. Anguished moans were heard. A punk was held to light large strips of paper ensuring that the deceased will have adequate money in the afterlife.

When the ceremony concluded, Chin Mon Way came to Shu Wei and Shu Lan-lan and said, "Here, place these black bands around your sleeves for the next one hundred days. This color is worn by the children of the deceased."

Shu Wei couldn't take his eyes off the band that now rode on his left sleeve. His mind raced. *I am sorry father. I am so sorry. We will honor your life for a hundred futures and bring respect to our family again.*

CHAPTER THIRTEEN

A Discovery

The next day, Shu Wei wiped moisture from beneath his eyes. He bent to assemble the fragile remnants from their father's funeral service at the Hop Wo building.

"This will be an homage to our father so that he is always with us," said Shu Lan-lan. "We will make a modest shrine in a spirit worthy of *Shang Ti*, our Supreme God."

In the tiny backyard, no more than twenty feet to the back fence, they heard the squawks of caged birds, babies protesting, and animated chatter. Laundry hung from taut clotheslines, like so many colorful lottery sheets. A man sent aloft a fiery thread of smoke from his long pipe as he perched on a sagging wooden balcony.

With a small spade given to them by Wu Kang Ho earlier, they started digging a proper foundation for their little shrine near the back fence.

"My, the ground is hard as rock," said Shu Lan-lan.

Shu Wei took the shovel and dug with conviction until the spade struck an object that caused a small spark to fly. "What have we here? Maybe I've hit an ancient city."

"More likely it is a collection of old dog bones put there by a grieving soul for his departed pet," said Shu Lan-lan.

Shu Wei's hands pulled six moss covered bricks from the fractured ground. "These look to be from some kind of building, perhaps the one Wu Kang Ho mentioned," he conjectured. "Let's use them in giving our little shrine some permanence."

Having removed the bricks, Shu Wei noticed the dull patina of a metal object. Scraping a fine layer of dirt from its top, it appeared to be a kind of box. While Shu Lan-lan was busy setting up the easel that Wu Kang Ho had donated for the shrine, Shu Wei spaded around the perimeter of this new find. He lifted a small rectangular container from the hole. Its latch had rusted through from age.

Finally, Shu Lan-lan glanced over at this mysterious find. "What is it? Let's look inside."

"Wait! urged Shu Wei. "I am remembering the legend of *Chang'e*, the goddess of the Moon, who was warned to not open the case with the pill of immortality. When she did, she swallowed it whole instead of breaking it in two. She floated all the way to the Moon."

"My crazed big brother, that is legend. We are flesh and blood. I am certain no pill exists inside this box. If it does I promise not to eat it whole."

Pausing to weigh the words of Shu Lan-lan, Shu Wei slowly opened the box, scowling as if unknown forces would assault him. Two papers enfolded two tarnished bracelets, one of which had several words inscribed in flowing script. A series of tiny jewels, their luster faded, was imbedded on the bands. Shu Wei passed the one with the writing to Shu Lan-lan.

"This is in a language unknown to me," admitted his sister. "Maybe it has to do with the previous resident here."

"These look like they could be valuable items," said Shu Wei. "Let's bring them inside to a proper hiding place until we can decide what to do." He replaced the jeweled bands and the papers in the container and stowed it deep under his bed. The two then went back outside and continued to create their shrine, creating holes for the stubby three-legged easel and placing the mossy bricks around the perimeter.

It had been two weeks since they arrived and Wu Kang Ho thought it was a good time to plant the mulberry seedling that Chun Dai had so expertly grown from a cutting back home. He had been the custodian of the delicate potted plant ever since Shu Wei handed it off upon their arrival in Hong Kong. It had been kept in a deep window sill in his apartment over the store ever since. By now it had grown to around six inches tall, but only four tiny serrated leaves graced its stalk.

Knocking on their door at the back of the store, Wu Kang Ho said, "It's the gardener. I have something that I believe would interest you."

The door inched open as Shu Lan-lan scowled as she puzzled over the nature of this visitor.

"Oh, it's you, Wu Kang Ho," Shu Wei said effusively, warming to this chance to lighten his spirits. "I was puzzling over the 'gardener' part. I wasn't aware of the need for one to care for your vast backyard plot. But do come in with our precious plant. We wondered what had become of it."

Shu Wei dug a small hole in the middle of the yard. "I see you uncovered some ancient bricks for a sturdy foundation for your shrine," remarked Wu Kang Ho.

Shu Wei said, "Yes, we . . ." He stopped. Not certain that the box discovery should be a part of this conversation, he continued, "We thought they would help give our little easel a sturdier base."

"A wise bit of engineering," said Wu Kang Ho as he gently knocked the seedling from its container. After digging a small hole he gently lowered it into its new home. Shu Lan-lan gingerly pressed some loose soil around its perimeter. Shu Wei appeared with a glass of water, and said, "This will be our mulberry's first official drink. He had also brought out four oranges, two of which he laid at the base of the seedling and two beneath the shrine. "Now, we have paid homage to the gods and given a proper blessing for the health of our little tree and our father's heavenly rest."

CHAPTER FOURTEEN

The Golden Hills' News

In the next few days, Shu Wei was determined to probe deeper into the workings of *The Golden Hills' News*. The probing was eased considerably by the amiable disposition of Mei Huang. In fact, he thought so highly of her that he sought her out at every chance. His next chance was a round table discussion in the editing room between Mei Huang and Fan Ching. As she explained the rudiments of her duties Shu Wei was simply spellbound. Entranced.

"Our paper's so small we wear many hats around here," offered Mei Huang. Shu Wei wondered how many could he wear at a time—he conjured a stack of them precariously perched on his head. She continued, "You'll be getting a good grounding in all aspects of the news business. I edit proofs, run the darkroom, advise on stories to run, and sometimes do reporting."

"As our reporter-in-training, you'll need to start with the basics," Fan Ching said as he laid a fatherly hand on Shu Wei's shoulder. "Tell you what . . . let's go into my office and I'll start you off with a little background."

Fan Ching's desk took up the better part of the small office. Jumbled stacks of paper littered the desk, partially obscuring the editor from his guest who had just settled into a spindle-backed side chair. Memorabilia, including citations and commendations vied for space on various walls. Several yellowed front pages of back issues of *The Golden Hills' News* covered the wall behind Fan Ching's desk. Two green-globed lamps on a side table gave an eerie soft glow in the room—adding to the historic character of the place.

"First, you need to know," Fan Ching began, "that *The Golden Hills' News* was the first Asian Pacific American newspaper. Methodist missionaries were credited with its founding. Why, you ask, would a bunch of itinerant preachers want to get involved with the Chinese community? As far as we can tell, their intentions were honorable, but no doubt with motivations to increase their own flocks."

Shu Wei was once again having trouble with certain words in this new land of English speakers. He couldn't imagine why the Methodists would want more sheep. But he thought it wise not to press the issue.

"At the time," Fan Ching continued, "Chinese laborers in the Gold Rush of 1849 were being mistreated and ridiculed. The white media saw fit to publish off-color parodies and caricatures of the Chinese."

Fan Ching paused and pulled a sheet of paper from his desk drawer. A color sketch showed a squinty-eyed Chinaman with an outsized head, flowing queue, and basket on his arm. Beneath the drawing was a bit of verse:

> *Sing a song o' six taels*
> *Pocket full o' rice*
> *John is off to market*
> *To get a dozen mice.*

"Believe it or not, this is from a recent nursery rhyme book," remarked Fan Ching. "I keep it around as a reminder of how mean-spirited people can be. But, getting back to *The News*, it was started with the intent to give a more balanced picture and to dignify the tainted image of our people. And it was to do it in both Chinese and English on four pages folded in half. Unfortunately, best-laid plans don't always translate into success. That paper only lasted a few months.

"Somehow, although the next version of the paper changed hands many times, it managed to limp along for years under the same format. Of course, there were name changes, production stoppages, and months when no issue hit the streets. When I bought it, around five years ago, it was truly on its last legs." Another phrasing puzzle for Shu Wei. "My first act was to restore the name of the paper. Of course, we're far from financially viable. But the other day a butterfly with dark wings flew into my apartment. I took that as a *jí zhào*, a good omen."

Hopping from his chair, Fan Ching blurted, "Enough of the history lesson. Let's move on to what we're trying to do here." The editor put his hands on his hips and leaned backward, stretching his back. Peering out a window crusted with grime, Fan Ching pivoted to face Shu Wei.

"I, or I should say we, have only three employees: Mei Huang, plus Jake who runs and maintains the presses and a writer who helps out whenever she's available. And, even then, we find it hard to meet our expenses. So, we depend a lot on what I call our eyes and ears on the street. This is where you come in." Guiding Shu Wei back into the outer room, Fan Ching nodded to Mei Huang to join them at the table.

"We want to put out a paper worthy of reading. But, beyond that, we want it to have a wide appeal and impact. That appeal and impact is only possible when we have gained our readers' confidence. Confidence in knowing our stories are unbiased and well-founded. Confidence in knowing they are informed about critical events that affect the welfare of this community.

"Shu Wei, knowing what I do about your ability to write, I would like you and Mei Huang to collaborate as much as possible on stories. We have elements in Chinatown that are festering, poisoning influences. The Tongs are largely a menace. Some are killing innocent citizens, threatening and bribing merchants, and creating insecurity and unease. We need to print stories that put pressure on these thugs. Then, maybe our law enforcement people will have to act. Right now, they are hiding behind their badges. Of course, none of this is without risk. My life has been threatened in the past, but I will not let the degenerates get the upper hand. Through the power of the press, we can make a difference."

Shu Wei thought, *I am now living with threats as well. I guess we have more in common than I realized.* He said, "How will I start? I am new to these streets and these people."

"Not to worry," suggested Fan Ching. "Start by getting to know your neighbors, the merchants, the police, even the Tongs. You will find your story. As you have seen in Mr. Thomson's photography book that I gave you, he wanders the streets of Canton. He may find curiosity shops selling exotic wax-cased pills or swallows' nests for making soup; silversmiths, and silk mercers selling textile fabrics and delicate silks.

"Or he heads into a poor neighborhood where dingy hovels are crawling with fascinating craftsmen with their arts of shoemaking, blacksmithing and ivory carving—or even making implements of death like shiny steel daggers and swords."

"It has been a while since I have recorded anything," Shu Wei injected. "But I am pleased to get the opportunity." Deep down he felt his insecurities return. The disaster in his home town had dampened a good many of his creative urges and inquisitive instincts. But he told himself he had to try to get his self-confidence back. Mostly, he had to regain the courage to report on things that mattered—even if it meant taking chances.

Mei Huang casually put her hand on Shu Wei's forearm and said, "I will be here to guide you and support you. So, don't be bashful. Come see me as often as you like."

The pleasant tingling from Mei Huang's touch took a while to fade. He felt a closeness that went beyond an attraction. A kind of camaraderie. *We actually are in this together.*

"Now, as I mentioned I would do, Shu Wei," Fan Ching added, "I want you to have a camera to supplement your notes wherever possible. This small collapsible Kodak is discreet and quite portable. They've only been out a while but your friend Wu Kang Ho was able to get one from his trading partner in New York recently. No investigative reporter worth his salt should be without one.

"Mei Huang will help in the processing of the film. Our only other camera is a bit more bulky. It's a large format bellows style and needs a tripod. We use that one for portraits or special events.

"Now, I must give all my efforts to releasing our next issue of *The News*. The press doesn't run itself. Find me when you've had your first plunge into the real world and are ready to put a story together. I'm confident that you will find a story around almost any corner."

Fan Ching didn't know how prophetic his statement was.

CHAPTER FIFTEEN

Jun Min and The Tong

Two weeks later Shu Wei realized he had lived a life of caution up to that point. He had made certain that, even though it could be boring, he strayed only a few doors from Wu Kang Ho's store. But now he was itching to go out and explore the new exciting neighborhood. In his mind he tried on the term for the role that Fan Chin implied would be useful to the paper: investigative reporter, one that's worth his salt, whatever that means. *Maybe I'll be the best investigative reporter in the city, maybe the state. It's a lofty goal but heck, you have to aim high. Isn't that what my Auntie always said?*

His first serious foray took him further north down Dupont Street, several blocks from Wu Kang Ho's store. Boisterous conversation and the clacking of dice coming from a storefront drew his attention. A young Chinese man slouched against a door frame. He wore a smirk that joined up with a scar that ran across his cheekbone. Hard to tell where one started and the other stopped. A folded maroon headband held up a sprouting of black hair. His right hand rested on a not-so-discreetly sheathed knife that was tucked into a black sash.

"Well, aren't you the waif who has lost his way? What's your name? Where you from?" the sinister-looking man asked.

Shu Wei replied, "I'm not lost, and I live nearby. My name is Shu Wei."

"No, no, I mean where are you *really* from. You're not one of those Manchu types are you?"

"I'm from the Pearl River Delta."

"Should've known, almost everyone in Chinatown is from the Delta. Your daddy or mummy know you're here?"

"My father died on the ship, the *City of Peking*. My *niáng qīn* has been gone for some time."

"Most unfortunate. Say, come on in for some tea and games. You need to put some people into your address book."

"I really need to get home. My sister is waiting for me," said Shu Wei."

"Have a sis' huh? How old?"

"She just turned sixteen."

"Ah, almost ripe. Easily bruised."

"She works at the Occidental Home for Girls," said Shu Wei proudly. The minute he said this he knew he was being overly casual with information to this stranger. "I really do need to get going," protested Shu Wei.

"Name's Jun Min. Means clever ruler," he said as he firmly grabbed Shu Wei's elbow and guided him down a set of stairs that led to the entrance of the gambling parlor. "Gamble much, Mr. Shu Wei?"

"My parents wouldn't allow it. They said it poisons the soul and empties the pocketbook."

A heavy oak door with studded bolts swung open with a creaky complaint. Inside, on a wall next to the door was a large bar that was positioned to slide across into a metal housing on the other side of the door. Jun Min yanked the bar into place with a metallic thud. "This keeps out the curious, most especially our friends in blue."

Next to the door was a little room with a tiny window. The lookout sat in an old office chair. His bulky frame became rigid as he acknowledged Jun Min.

"This is our man, Choo Yee Kan. As you know, comes from our Chinese *zhu yi kan* meaning 'watch carefully.' He tells us his eyes burn when a bad spirit is attempting entry.

"On our left here, we call this our lounge. These old folks here are playing *Mahjong*—makes a nice comfy scene when our boys in blue come streaming in. Some say Confucius made the game up 'cause he liked birds and *Mahjong* is from *maque* or sparrow. I don't buy that." Numbered paper cards in precise lines lay in front of a cluster of men who occasionally erupted in vigorous dissent over another's move.

Jun Min kept a grip on Shu Wei's arm as he worked his way down a narrow hallway with squeaky boards, passing through several doors. He finally paused before a door with a red enameled finish.

"By the time the *jingcha*—the blue coats—get through all these locked doors we look like a social hall. By then, our dear customers are herded safely out the back door." Shu Wei felt his neck and back muscles tighten as a dull ache grew in his head. He followed his guide into a large room charged with agitated chatter and the staccato of game pieces.

"Show you around. Over here we got some *Tien Gow* going on. Some call it *Heaven and Nines*." Four men were huddled around a table with intricate combinations of black tiles with red and white pips. "Very complicated. Never learned it."

"What happens over there?" asked Shu Wei, his curiosity rising.

"Ah, now this one's for you," said Jun Min. "Step in and give 'em a try. These are *white pigeon tickets*. They're based on the first eighty characters of the *Thousand Character Classic*." Shu Wei remembered this famous poem from his studies in Sanhou when he was learning the Chinese characters.

"Go ahead," urged Jun Min. "Punch your winners on the sheets. We got boys who'll run these twice a day. Could be your day."

"I don't have that kind of money to spend. I save what little was left of my father's," said Shu Wei.

"Luck is already your middle name then. I'll spot you a few bills—a nice guy needs a break now and then, doesn't he?"

"I'd rather not. I may get in trouble."

"Trouble? Your *baba* and *mama* are gone. No one to hold you back. Live a little. No evil ghosts are gonna haunt you—punch a card, go on. I'll loan you some money," said Jun Min as he forced open Shu Wei's clenched fist and placed four dollar bills in it.

Shu Wei's hands turned icy. He was not at all comfortable with taking a stranger's money. "How soon do you need this back?" Things were happening way too fast for him. He remembered the warnings the elders gave him that night of the dinner at the Silver Dragon. His instincts told him that one of them no doubt applied in this case.

"Hey, not to worry. You're my new pal. Don't you raise a frown about that."

Shu Wei nudged his way into a small group of men and laid enough down for one sheet. With some guidance from Jun Min he punched his character selections and, with a trembling hand, deposited the document into a slit on a bright red box with a brass latch.

Taking a stronger hold on Shu Wei's arm, Jun Min said, "You're not leaving just yet! I have another special treat for you."

Sensing the potential peril of resisting, Shu Wei allowed Jun Min to lead him back into the corridor to a stairway that led to the lower level. The well-worn wooden steps gave beneath his feet. The hallway on this level narrowed, funneling toward the end. Or was this his imagination? He was prone to occasional spells of claustrophobia. Then, more mystifying closed doors. Some unfamiliar smells added to his unease. He glanced backward, assessing his chances of escape. Not good.

Shu Wei was escorted into an airless low-ceilinged room that was clearly designed to be concealed from public view and access. When he focused, he was both revolted and fascinated by this smoggy underworld.

"Here, my new friend, is where you can take the pipe and enter a world where your worries go up in smoke." Jun Min let out a little whimper of a laugh, pleased by his cleverness.

Shu Wei scanned the murky room where bodies, clothing, and various exotic devices lay scattered haphazardly. Two men lounged on padded benches, each with pipes in their mouths and legs akimbo. Others kneeled cross-legged on a large cabinet. All occupants were in a daze, oblivious to their visitors.

Jun Min said, "I happen to have a pipe that should suit you very nicely. It's my favor . . ."

"Oh no, I don't do that sort of thing. I have stayed my distance from tobacco."

"You will receive the fragrant fumes of the immortals at the very first breath. Here, let me show you."

Jun Min lifted a long-stemmed bamboo tube attached to a ceramic pipe-bowl. "Simple. You put a small pellet of opium in the bowl and hold it over an oil lamp. That gives off the good vapors that will send you into the calmest of heavens. We call it the *yen chiang*—the smoking gun. And, you should know that it goes back to the Yellow Emperor, the very founder of the Chinese civilization. A red-faced god with six arms appeared before the Emperor one day and blew a mighty breath across the earth, producing a bamboo pipe; another breath the poppy; and a third huff made a flame."

Shu Wei tentatively drew on the pipe and immediately belched a cloud of dense oily smoke that reminded him of the bonfires lit from the waste of harvested crops in his town of

Sanhou. A more painful image came to him: the smoky mass that accompanied the fire at his father's shop when Huǒlóng worked his revenge. The second draw from the pipe seemed easier. His body grew relaxed, and he experienced a calming euphoria. Maybe this is just what he needed. He'd been too wound up. *But wait! What am I doing? I need to get out of here!* he thought, his panic rising.

Jun Min reached into a cabinet adorned with animal shapes in metal relief. "For me, you need personality in your pipes. This one has an ivory stem with a ram's head bowl made of white porcelain; gives me a nice warm rush—not too sharp, nicely balanced."

Leaning on one elbow, Jun Min held his pipe over an oil lamp, drew a long breath, and exhaled a helix of blue-gray haze.

"So, it is now time to inform you of the terms by which you must abide. Since I have loaned you a goodly sum for the gambling and allowed you to partake of my opium pellets, your total cost is a mere five dollars. I will need to receive this in three weeks' time or your life will quickly be a troubled one. I am sure you and I will be fast friends after your willing compliance. Oh, and one more thing. You will shortly be meeting my partner. I believe you may have encountered him already." Shu Wei wondered about this "partner." The burning in the back of Shu Wei's neck returned, complete with stabbing spasms across his shoulders. Now mystery was added to his anguish over his debt to Jun Min and his taking the pipe.

"But that is a sum I will have a lot of trouble coming up with," Shu Wei said, all too aware of his voice breaking. "I told you my father died, and he had very little money left."

Jun Min's face drew taut and seemed to be heated from within. "I will not hear of your woes. I have already given far more favorable terms to you than our other customers. Besides, I find that all people are creative when it comes to finding money. Now go."

Clutching Shu Wei's shoulders with both hands, Jun Min pressed on Shu Wei's upper spine, escorting him out with a convincing force that left no room for argument.

CHAPTER SIXTEEN

Yong Qiang

Shu Wei staggered back south up Dupont, still mildly tipsy from the effects of the opium. He had no idea what he would do now. *I've gone and done it again,* he thought. He was turning the corner onto Clay Street toward Wu Kang Ho's store, when he ran headlong into Huǒlóng.

It seemed Huǒlóng had transformed himself into an urban street hooligan. No longer wearing the flamboyant cape with the figure of the Fiery Dragon, he had on a plain black suit and bowler hat tipped rakishly over one eye, a brown feather implanted in its band. His nails were long and pointed with studded shields on the little fingers. An oily balm had been lathered on a scar on his left hand. The ring on his right hand, which Shu Wei had seen at the time of the fire at his father's store, bore an embossed image of two serpents in combat.

"So good to see you again. We now have a chance to become closer friends," said Shu Wei's nemesis as he looped his arm around Shu Wei's.

"How did you know where I . . . I have to . . . I mean . . ." stuttered Shu Wei.

"That's okay. Lots of people are speechless around me. Some even end up that way permanently—if you know what I mean." Huǒlóng grabbed the sleeve of Shu Wei's blouse and dragged him into a grimy side alley.

"Why are you following me? Haven't you made our lives miserable enough?" hissed Shu Wei.

"Whoa, my feisty one! I have big things in mind for you. You tried to get too close to our operations in Sanhou. Luckily, our Town Constable was attentive and smelled the proverbial rat. Now I see you have met my partner, Jun Min. We run the Hap Tran Tong, the biggest there is."

"Who are you? What do you want from me?" demanded Shu Wei.

"You can call me Yong Qiang, brave and strong."

Shu Wei thought he was going to gag. Surely a name suggesting a coward would be a better fit after the despicable acts the man had committed against his family.

Yong Qiang continued, "You and I are going to share a dirty little secret. Maybe more than one. Before I say more about that, let me mention some ground rules. For starters, you will not mention the little collaboration we are about to engage in to my partner, Jun Min. If I discover a word—a single word—of this has gotten out, your life will be over. Along with your sister's.

"Our Tong is very prosperous, markets are many; our Hong Kong contacts bring us a healthy trade in silk and tea. We deal in opium, of course, but have to rely on our quiet dealers who find discrete places in the ship holds. The prostitution and girl slave markets are booming. We're proud of our accomplishments.

"Now, A few words about our Tong and our secret mission. We have some eight highbinders—the *gweilos'* name for hatchet men. These *boo how doy* are highly trained and fearless. They close out their missions in an expeditious manner. I control all but two of them. But soon I will control them all. You will get to know our lingo. If you hear one of them saying,

'We'll need to wash his body' this, simply put, is a kill order. A rifle's called a 'dog'; a pistol a 'puppy.' Bullets and ammo are called 'dog feed.' And when you hear the expression, 'Let the dogs bark,' you will know that's when the order to fire has been given.

"I will introduce you to my highbinder friends, my *boo how doy*. I will instruct them to leave you alone. Like I said earlier, you will be of more value to me alive than dead. Now, *What value?* you ask. I have suspicions that my partner, Jun Min, has been skimming the earnings off our companies. I am pretty certain that he has been handing money to others outside our Tong to avoid taxes and to fund his own activities. This has to stop!"

Yong Qiang's rage caused spittle to leak from the side of his mouth and his body to tremble. Shu Wei drew back and put his hands up in mock defense.

Pausing to collect himself, Yong Qiang continued. "This is where you come in. I need someone on the inside—someone that he won't suspect—to help get information. The best way would be to take notes or use one of those new-fangled western cameras. I know you're at least good at taking notes." His mouth formed a smirk of derision. "You don't have a camera by any chance, do you?"

Shu Wei felt a surge of acid building in the back of his throat. *This is uncanny,* he thought. *I must be dreaming this. How can he know this?* He heard himself blurt out, "My friend, Wu Kang Ho, gave me one when I got here for something to do. I could use that . . . as soon as I learn to use it, that is." He didn't believe he was actually confessing but, at this point, he thought the camera could become useful.

"Excellent. Knowing your cagey little ways in Sanhou, I knew I could count on you."

If it's possible to choke on one's thoughts Shu Wei would have been writhing on the ground. *My 'cagey ways?'* This monster was asking him to look into fraudulent activities when he'd punished him for doing that very thing in his hometown.

"Our dealings will need to be foolproof, otherwise both our lives are in danger. I'd hate to sacrifice a useful tool, but better you than me," said Yong Qiang.

"How will I manage to get the information you need? I already owe Jun Min money. I will have to clear my debt before this assignment will work."

"Ah, ever the nimble thinker. I will give you a fair stipend once I feel you have satisfied my demands. But if you don't deliver, not only will you not get paid, I will see to it that your queue is wrapped around your neck until all life is drained away. Now, we will need to meet to discuss the specifics of this plan. We will meet in two weeks time in the basement of Hong Lu's Fish Emporium. That's at the corner of Fish Alley—Washington Place to you—and Jackson Street. Two o'clock. If you're not there I know where to find you. Or, let's say, my men will know how to access you."

"How do you know . . .?" Shu Wei thought better of finishing his question.

"Let's just say my eyes and ears are in many parts of Chinatown. Now get on."

Shu Wei trudged back to Wu Kang Ho's store. His sister was folding a skirt on her bed when he walked in. "Why the long face? And what is that vile odor I smell? You reek of smoke and mold. What have you been up to?"

Shu Wei threw himself on his bed and drew his curtain closed without responding. He sat, arms wrapping his legs, trying to become small. He felt alone and vulnerable. His sister would never understand. Besides, he didn't want to get her involved.

"Shu Wei, please speak to me," Shu Lan-lan said. "There is no reason to retreat inside yourself." She pulled at his privacy curtain, but Shu Wei yanked it back, almost pulling the entire rod down.

An angry stream of pent-up emotions coursed through Shu Wei's body. His sister left him alone, and he finally drifted into a disordered state of sleep. In his dream he was fulfilling his duties as Town Scribe when he tipped over his *yàn*, his inkstone mortar, while he was grinding his ink stick. He watched as the liquid spilled out, casting a black, impenetrable stain all over his work.

CHAPTER SEVENTEEN

The Fish Emporium

Two weeks later, Shu Wei arrived at Hong Lu's Fish Emporium in the early morning. The door was locked. He knocked tentatively. Someone inside slid back a small panel covering an opening in the heavy wooden door. The door opened a crack, and Yong Qiang fingered a signal for Shu Wei to enter. Empty bins gave off a rancid fishy smell and the oily rubber aprons still hung on pegs, but apparently, fish had not been sold there in some time. A single light bulb hung over a counter in the back, providing more shadow than light, and giant hooks with pointed ends hung along the far wall. Even in the half-light Shu Wei could see the dark smears of dried fish blood staining a giant chopping block. Cleavers and gutting knives lay on another table. A chill traveled down Shu Wei's spine.

"Get your scrawny self inside before the whole street wants in," Yong Qiang commanded. "Welcome to our private clubhouse," he quipped once Shu Wei was inside. "My friend Hong Lu, the fish merchant, is a wise businessman. He decided he was better off pursuing other ventures. Okay, I helped him make that decision, but he hasn't regretted it. The appearance of legitimacy is striking, don't you think? The sign and all?"

Shu Wei wasn't sure where it was all going. He hadn't had much sleep lately, and things were moving way too fast. His mind felt like it was filled with the dense San Francisco fog that swirled outside.

Yong Qiang motioned to Shu Wei to join him on a cob-web-draped couch behind the back counter where the light bulb now flickered. When he sat, a protruding spring launched him upward in a fright.

"You seem jumpy today, my friend. Once we get to know one another better, you'll be more comfortable. Now, let's go over some basics. First, you are going to need to get to know Jun Min better so he will treat you as a member of our tribe. I will play along. Second, you will do whatever is asked of you. If I can be candid, I will personally rip your heart out of your body if you go against me. Understood?"

Shu Wei stuttered, "Y-yes. I under . . . under-stand."

"What was that? Convince me. Do you understand?"

"*Yes, I understand!*" Shu Wei tried on a louder voice.

"Better. Now this is my plan. We keep ledgers for our main enterprises, mainly our export and import companies. Of course, as partners, Jun Min and I keep track of our other busi-nesses—special accounts I call them—so we each get our share. We both check them over with each other monthly. But one day another of my colleagues made a big discovery. He found a loose floorboard beneath a rug just near the locked cabinet where we keep the special records. When he lifted it, he found a second set of ledgers. My partner, Jun Min, the nervy little dev-il, has been keeping two sets of books behind my back.

"Turns out, the second set under the floorboards is the ac-tual record for our side deals . . . I mean, the special accounts. So, this is where you come in. I want you to take photographs of these books and anything else that I find suspicious. I will cook up a scheme that will get him and his boys away from the headquarters every so often. I know nothing about using that camera-thing, but I will find a way to get the pictures developed and use them as evidence.

"When I first found out about this I was going to take out my favorite dagger and do that cheat in. But then I thought that wouldn't get me my money back. Of course, the knife's still an option. But, there's always the chance I could wind up in jail with all those other crusty unsavories, including my rotten-to-the-core partner. So I am looking into hiring me a big New York-type lawyer.

"What are the next steps you ask. We will meet again in this special place, this *maison de poissons*. Hah!! Didn't know I speak *Français*, didja? Doing some business with a little succulent sweetie in gay Paris. Booming commerce in exotic fruits.

"So, one month—no, I will grant you five weeks from today. Same time. *Comprenez vous?* I want you to take a crack at our friend, Jun Min. Get to know him—everything about him. Oh, there's one more thing. I'll need your company in two weeks for a little errand. You'll be meeting me in the alley behind our headquarters."

Shu Wei realized that his mouth was still wide open. Breathing through his mouth instead of his nose had mostly avoided inhaling the stench, but needing to reply to Yong Qiang, he inhaled and almost gagged. "Yes, two weeks at your headquarters and five weeks back here." *A lawyer? He would get a lawyer?* Shu Wei thought. *How can a criminal sue another criminal? What could possibly come of that?* But, he knew the evidence he collected would come in handy for his own purposes. It's just that the collecting part was not going to be easy.

"My scuzzy little scribe, I think you will work out fine. Just remember, if you mess up, it's lights out. And don't forget your camera for our next session. Now, get out of here. From now on we use the back door."

Yong Qiang unlatched the long cast iron locking bar and opened the back door. Shu Wei stepped into the pitch-black alley. As he did so, two emaciated cats leaped from partially open trash bins, yowling.

CHAPTER EIGHTEEN

A French Connection

Shu Wei pulled the crusted metal box from under his bed. Carefully, he took one of the bracelets from the box and placed it in the pouch he had brought with him from Sanhou. As he closed the box and replaced it beneath the bed, he glanced around like an anxious burglar. Shu Lan-lan would be home at any minute; nothing must interfere with his secret mission.

In his recent wanderings a pawn shop on Bartlett Alley near Pacific had caught his eye. Immediately he knew what he had to do. He could not count on getting paid from Yong Qi-ang and he guessed it would be some time before he earned a real salary from *The News*. Therefore, his indebtedness to Jun Min required some bold thinking. Jun Min was not one to, what was that fishing expression he had learned the other day, 'let one off the hook.'

Shu Wei's strides grew more vigorous as he headed north down Dupont Street. He found that his mood lightened when he walked purposefully. And, it was Sunday, a day when more families were out. The women wore brightly colored jackets and wide silk pants patterned with colorful banding. A few of the people stopped to purchase lilies from the flower vendor or fish for their Sunday meal. Others were headed to the Plaza— Portsmouth Square—to spend time catching up on the affairs of friends and family or to simply retreat from the hustle and bustle of Chinatown.

A bell tinkled brightly over the front door, announcing Shu Wei's entrance to Quincy Baron's Pawn Shop. A small forest of goods with little white tags sat on several tables: ivory-tusked jade elephants, pagodas of metal and lacquered wood, squatty bronze Buddhas, elaborate watches and clocks, urns, and candlesticks. Seeing no one, Shu Wei busied himself by scanning the collection of leather- and cloth-bound books that overflowed shelving on a far wall.

"Why, hello son," barked Quincy as he emerged from a curtained doorway. "Didn't hear you come in. Guess I'll have to get a louder bell. Sometimes I lose myself in something in the back."

Quincy was one of the many white merchants in Chinatown who thrived on a lively commerce and engaging repartee with his Asian customers. A rotund man in his sixties, his jowly face had a frosting of tightly-trimmed white hair that stretched from ear-to-ear with a tufted clump at the chin. His receding hairline was edged by a sea of tiny freckles. Two brass buttons strained to hold his striped vest in place. A gold chain dripped from his vest pocket and disappeared into double-pleated pants.

"So, what might I do for you on this fine day?" Quincy asked as he closed a sliding cabinet door. "I see you're eyeing the books. I've got some good ones—bestsellers. How about *The Red Badge of Courage,* by Stephen Crane? Just got that one in. It's about a young man fighting in our civil war. Or maybe *Treasure Island,* by Robert Louis Stevenson. Now that's a real pirate adventure story. Ah, but this one I know you'll like: *Water Margin.* I'm sure you know this Chinese classic set in the Song Dynasty about a group of outlaws who . . ."

Changing topics mid-sentence, Quincy moved quickly on to a glassed-in case. "Boy your age should have a set of the *Encyclopaedia Brittanica* here, or maybe this *Penny Cyclopaedia.*

Now that's a fun one—for just a penny you get a little newspaper-like issue each week, full of the latest information. Ah, but wait. I'm nattering on like a magpie. What's on your mind, son?"

Shu Wei was spellbound with the wealth of interesting items. It took him a minute to re-focus on the purpose of his visit. "I-I've come to pawn this piece of jewelry and would like to know how much I can get for it," he said.

"Well, son, let's have a look. This is a very pretty bracelet. Your family's?"

"It must belong to some family but not ours," replied Shu Wei. "You see, my sister and I just settled in Chinatown and we're staying at Wu Kang Ho's store for the time being and we found some items in a box in his backyard and our father died on the way from China and we're out of money and wonder if . . ."

"Whoa, whoa, my friend," Quincy pleaded. "We'll get to your life history, but first, let's have a look at what you have."

Quincy pulled his loupe from a drawer and planted it in his left eye. Peering at the piece, his head bobbed back and forth to get a proper reading.

"This seems to have some lettering on the back. Ah . . . French at that. It seems to have a good pedigree. No plating—seems to be solid gold or an alloy anyway. The stone sets are still solid and these are most likely sapphires and red onyx gems. These will clean up nicely.

"Hummm. Looks like it says '*A notre fille, Marie.*' That means, 'To our daughter, Marie.' Could have been a present from her parents. Interesting. I believe my mother had contact with a woman by that name that used to live where your friend's store is now. I don't recall what her last name was. A very bad thing happened to her as I recall. Have to do some research on this. I'll ask my mother, Evelyn. She has a dossier on the world.

"Ahh, this bracelet takes me back to my days in Paris when I used to work in the jewelry trade; I even met Louis Cartier, the famous jewelry designer. But, there I go again, rambling off . . ."

Shu Wei had only heard half of Quincy's discourse. And he understood far less, his mind being consumed by more consequential things—like getting money for survival.

"Tell you what," Quincy said finally. "I'm going to go ahead and take this in but I'm not sure about the price. Can you come back here in a few days after I've had a chance to be more certain about its true value?"

"Oh, but, sir, I am in need of the money at this very moment," blurted Shu Wei, all too aware of his voice rising an octave at the end. You see I am working for *The Golden Hills' News,* and I won't get paid for . . ."

"Ah, *The News,*" Quincy broke in. "Are they still around? Must've died a thousand deaths by now. Okay, I'll give you three dollars now since I'm certain it's worth at least that. When you return, we'll settle on a firm price. Of course, that still won't be its true worth. I have to hold back a little something for the business. Does that work for you? By the way, what's your name, lad?"

Barely able to stand still, Shu Wei sputtered his name. He fingered the bills in his pocket as he bolted from the shop. His sense of triumph quickly waned when he realized that now he would have to keep even more secrets from his sister. The lies were piling up. He wondered how much of this burden he'd have to bear before the gods punished him. Well, at least he had a few days before he needed to face Jun Min again. Ah, but no, Jun Min didn't seem like the patient kind. Shu Wei knew he needed to get the money to his tormentor sooner rather than later.

CHAPTER NINETEEN

The Baniers

Shu Lan-lan hated confrontations. Especially with her brother. Her birth zodiac sign was a snake. It meant she had endless sympathy in helping others, a strong will, and a hatred of failure. Nonetheless, she had usually been the one to compromise. But now she needed to muster her resolve.

She tried the door knob to their room. It turned but the door wouldn't open. "Shu Wei! Are you in there? Open the door, Shu Wei! I need to talk with you."

Shu Wei's behavior continued to affect Shu Lan-lan's typically even-tempered demeanor. She found she was even getting cross with the girls at the Home, and they certainly didn't deserve that.

She heard a scraping noise—Shu Wei moving a chair away from the door knob where he had wedged it.

"What is this all about? Why did you have a chair against the door?"

"I don't want any more people snooping around in our things," explained Shu Wei. "Someone moved the box under my bed."

"That someone was me. I noticed a cord sticking out from under your bed and thought that was strange, so I investigated. What I found next troubled me greatly. The cord belonged to a pouch and the pouch had money in it, but one of the bracelets was gone. Now, can we have a little chat about all of this?"

Shu Wei crawled into his bed, pulled his knees to his chin, and let out a furious explosion of air. "Dear sister, I can explain what I can, but some things must be left as they are. You see, I needed the money so I took one of the bracelets in the box to the pawn shop. That's where the money came from."

"You *needed money*? For what? Wu Kang Ho and the Association have given us a living allowance to sustain us until we can earn a steady living ourselves."

Shu Wei shuffled over to the tiny window beneath the stairs and stared at the pitiful stub of their mulberry tree. "It will do no good to pester me about this," he insisted. "I . . ."

"*Pester you!*" hissed Shu Lan-lan. "I am not pestering. I need to know what is going on with you and why we can't talk things over."

Shu Wei retreated to his bed, flopped face-down and yanked the curtain across, causing the rod to vibrate. Shu Lan-lan's head sagged. She felt empty inside. It seemed futile.

The next day, Shu Wei and Shu Lan-lan decided to take in the remainder of the items from the box. Shu Lan-lan felt it was a victory of sorts. At least, a path of communication had opened up with her brother. The hardest part was telling Wu Kang Ho what had transpired. After all, they had found the box on his property. After an initial burst of annoyance and a lecture on trust and honesty, Wu Kang Ho agreed to join them on their trip to the pawn shop.

When they arrived at the pawn shop, the familiar tinkling of the entry bell alerted Quincy Baron to his visitors. He was rearranging a series of pocket watches on a shelf at the back counter. Two handsome Elgin watches, with their casings open, lay next to a Waltham gold-filled hunting case. With his back to the door, Quincy ran a dust cloth over another prized watch, a Hamilton 940 railroad model, and said, "Come in, come in. Right with you."

Turning around, Quincy exclaimed, "Aha! I see you've brought your family. I'm glad you came back. I . . ."

"You could say we're almost family but that would take a while to explain," Shu Wei broke in. "I am Shu Wei, and this is my sister Shu Lan-lan. Our dear friend, Wu Kang Ho here, has nicely put us up in the back of his store. I think I already mentioned that my sister and I are new to Chinatown."

"Well, almost-family, I have some interesting news for you. My mother and I have researched the writing on the bracelet. There is a good bit of history here. And, now, it looks like you've brought more treasure. Shu Wei handed the other bracelet and the two rolled-up paper documents to Quincy.

"My, my, this only adds to the intrigue," said Quincy. "Before we look at these additional items in more detail, I want to introduce you to my mother, Evelyn Parkford. Mother! We have visitors."

Evelyn still bore the trappings of a once-prosperous life. Her wavy ice-gray hair was anchored at one side with an elegant clip. Evelyn's shallow-set, azure eyes sparkled as they scanned the faces of the visitors. Her warm smile spoke of assurance and grace, and her buttermilk-pale skin and finely sculpted face, neck, and hands were lightly marbled with fine wrinkles. A colorful necklace of mollusk shells hung atop her loose-hanging silk day gown with aquamarine accents.

"Evelyn, these nice people came to hear about what we, or I should say, *you,* found out about the bracelet."

"Well, aren't you a fine-looking group," exclaimed Evelyn. "And I should say you've come across a very interesting bit of history with your digging."

"I knew mother would be useful," offered Quincy. "Nothing much escapes her in this town. Some say she has the smarts of a crow and the ears of an owl."

With an attentive audience, Evelyn needed no prompting to continue. "Quincy is right. I've seen all sides of a long life. My son and I knew the good side of that life once. My husband, Claude Parkford, was a supplier to the builders of the Transcontinental Railroad. We lived very comfortably on the lower slopes of Pacific Heights—that is, until he decided he would cavort with a stable full of loose women. So much for the family's fortune.

"Thankfully, we had had the foresight to set up a trust fund for Quincy's care and education. He graduated from the College of Santa Clara with honors and couldn't wait to take on the European continent, where he spent two years at *L'Université de Paris.*

"Quincy fell in love with Paris. But he felt he needed a practical career if he were to survive *les défis de la vie*—life's many challenges, especially in a foreign country. He returned to San Francisco in 1889 and started a company on Sutter Street dealing in jewelry and gems.

"When he began dealing less with the French and Europeans and more with the Chinese, he relocated to Chinatown. Then, when trading got more regulated and messy, he went into the pawn business."

"Evelyn hung around San Francisco while I was gallivanting in Paris," Quincy broke in. "Since my father, Claude, spent most of his money on his hussies, she was left with little to work with. After I got into the jewelry business in Paris, I began working with Levison Brothers here in San Francisco on Washington Street. I introduced Mother to Louis, one of the founding partners, and that was the beginning of a long friendship. She managed their books and even worked in sales for a while. Then Mother set up her own shop on the edge of Chinatown. She sold some of Levison's more exotic goods like gold quartz, moss agate, watches, and other items. So, many specimens of society passed through her front door at the time. One of the more eccentric was this Marie woman."

"Oh yes," Evelyn broke in. "Marie Banier was a many-sided woman. She . . ."

At the mention of the name 'Banier,' Shu Wei gasped abruptly.

"My, Shu Wei," said Quincy, "are you okay?"

"I—I'm fine," Shu Wei assured. "It's just that Perrier Banier is named, along with Marie, on these documents."

Evelyn continued, "That would make perfect sense. That's why we went ahead and did further research. Even though Marie's son was born out of wedlock and no record of any father exists, we found a birth certificate. Perrier today, we discovered, is in his thirties and is employed at the *Alliance Française de San Francisco* at 414 Mason Street. He teaches French there.

"Anyway, back to Marie. She would pop into my antique shop now and again. This was thirty years ago or so. She'd had a rough life by then.

"She would regale me with her tales of growing up in aristocracy in the small burg of Bussy St-George, just outside of Paris. Her father was an elite colonel in the French Army—he was killed when Marie was only fourteen, in the final battle of the French conquest of Algeria. Her mother, Anne-Pierre Laiseaux, sold the family's extensive land holdings and moved into a flat over a chocolatier on the *Avenue des Champs Elysees*. Her mother took the proceeds from the estate sale and a military benefit from the French Army, and invested in three properties in the Montmartre District of Paris.

"By the age of twenty-six, Marie was developing into an up-and-coming artist and began frequenting coffee houses. Her several dalliances with various *au courant* artists were uniformly calamitous affairs."

Evelyn drew in a deep breath and with a palsied movement, smoothed her silvery hair. "But the ultimate blow came when her mother committed suicide. With both her parents gone, Marie decided she needed to get away. She came across an article about San Francisco in the daily, *Le Petit Journal*, prompting her to make the trip across the ocean.

"Apparently, upon landing on those shores," continued Evelyn, "her bloodline, charm, and wit brought her access to the best of society in that day. Through her clever ways, she slowly amassed a small fortune. But this only led to her downfall. Her associations were increasingly with malcontents—a throwback to her Paris days.

"Eventually she met up with fates beyond her control. Newspaper accounts at the time noted that she was found dead in the ransacked boudoir of her dwelling with severe wounds. Whoever committed the crime either had a momentary bout of mercy or was unaware that a one-year-old boy, her son, was in an adjoining room. This all happened on the site where your friend here, Wu Kang Ho, now has his store. She, no doubt, had become concerned about her safety and decided to bury these valuables in a box in the backyard of that earlier house.

"To finish the story, a male suspect was detained at the time, but was judged not guilty and the matter was forgotten . . . until, that is, you found the box."

"Here, let's have a look at those documents," suggested Quincy.

Shu Wei unrolled the three furled certificates which carried a thin crust of gray-green mold and grime. He spread them out and held them down with two brass lamps on the counter. Quincy smoothed the creased parchments under his palms, his squinting eyes poring over the documents.

"Well, well," Quincy began, "these are most interesting. Two of these with the heading, *Acte de Propriété*, are deeds to property in Paris that are made out to Perrier. The other is a certificate of deposit for a sizable sum of money at the *Crédit Lyonnais* bank in Paris, also naming Perrier."

Addressing Wu Kang Ho, Quincy continued, "I would suggest you contact Perrier so that there can be a full disclosure of this situation. I'm afraid the bracelet we have in our possession, as well as the one you have here, will legally belong to Mr. Banier's estate. If Monsieur Banier has a sense of fairness, I should think he would offer some kind of gesture in kind to you all—if you get my meaning. These will be of significant value to him for sure . . . providing, of course, they are authenticated properly."

"I take this to mean that we owe back the money for the first bracelet then," Shu Wei said, his voice fading to a near-whisper.

"Let's see how things develop," Quincy proposed. "Of course, the bracelet rightfully belongs to Perrier. Even if there's no will, ownership by Perrier is implied since he was the only known surviving kin. We'll worry about the money in due time."

"You've been most kind, Mr. Baron, to share this information," Wu Kang Ho said. "Now we'll take the next steps and get in touch with Mr. Banier."

Shu Lan-lan's hand was on the doorknob of the shop, preparing to leave, when Evelyn charged after the three visitors.

"I almost forgot a critical point." Evelyn held the shop door open as she spoke. "My son says you're with the newspaper, Shu Wei. Is that correct?"

"Yes. Why?"

"Well," Evelyn continued, "There may be a news story there somewhere."

"Story? Where?"

"The whole Marie thing. You see, I have good information that her killer may reside at the Globe Hotel. The blokes at the local precinct have had their eyes on a few residents there for some time but haven't had enough evidence to bring anyone in. You might want to dig into it a bit."

Shu Wei thanked Evelyn for her advice but thought to himself, *Globe Hotel. I've heard that is the notorious place where the burned-out and crazy people live. My fù hé, my burden, is already bigger than a field ox could bear.*

The tightening sensation at the back of his neck returned with a vengeance.

CHAPTER TWENTY

Smugglers

It was time for Shu Wei to meet up with Yong Qiang again. Dawn was just spreading its first rays in an alley just behind the Hap Tran Tong's headquarters on DuPont Street.

"Well, it's my new accomplice!" sneered Yong Qiang. "Delighted to see you so bright and early." Shu Wei didn't like the implication of the word 'accomplice.' That was the absolute last label he wanted to inherit. *I am the furthest thing from being an accessory to your wicked deeds,* he thought. Or was he? The irony was that he would need to think more like a criminal if he wanted to fully understand the operations of this group. And he couldn't afford to give the slightest hint that he had actually become a double agent, a term that he had learned from reading James Fenimore Cooper's *The Spy* as part of his English studies in Sanhou.

Yong Qiang motioned toward a polished ebony carriage. A striking chestnut-colored horse waited calmly for the direction of its Native American driver, a man Yong Qiang referred to as Gray Wolf.

The two climbed aboard for their trip across town. They drove south through an area that was once home to stately mansions, but had fallen into disrepair. Now a workingman's neighborhood, the modest wood frame structures were clad in weathered clapboard siding. Five minutes later they arrived at a small inlet along San Francisco Bay with a sandy beach.

Yong Qiang and Shu Wei climbed from the carriage and set off toward the shoreline where they were going to meet Johnny Two-Fingers at a rusty tin fishing shed.

"Do not say anything to Johnny about his hand," advised Yong Qiang. "Most of his fingers were hacked off in a Tong battle a while back."

They found Johnny supervising a crew that caught bay shrimp and squid to be sold locally or shipped to China, Japan, and Hawaii. Johnny motioned to two men that were tending their woven baskets laden with part of the day's haul. They wore broad sedge hats and were covered in slime from their rubber boots to their heavy jackets. It was time for them to work their magic in placing opium in their loads headed for Los Angeles.

"For this transport, we must have watertight false bottoms built into the shipping containers for the fish," Yong Qiang said in a lowered voice. "Of course, I ensure that the handlers and customs officials up and down the coast are properly compensated for their efforts. If a shipment's weight is ever questioned, our crews simply point out that more ice is necessary due to engine overheating.

"Today marks our largest shipment to date—five hundred pounds of opium." The sparkle in Yong Qiang's eye was impossible to ignore. "Out of the fleet of twenty-five small boats, our fishermen operate four. These will transfer the valued cargo to two steam packets. Our trusted shipping handlers relay payments back from clients in the very same false-bottomed tanks."

Once in Johnny Two-Fingers' shed, the three men shared a steaming pot of tea and stale biscuits before pulling out the ledger that tracked the contraband. Marks were made. Johnny snorted and slapped Yong Qiang's shoulder before they parted.

"Hey, Scribe!" said Yong Qiang as the two walked back to the carriage. For a minute Shu Wei didn't register. *Scribe? Oh, my eternal god.* It was a title that he really didn't care for anymore. "See this ledger? I'm returning it to our locked bin at headquarters. I'll bet my slippery partner will create his own version. And that's for you to find out. Could be more in it for you, if you come through. *Comprenez vous bó zi?*"

Shu Wei could only nod.

As they were about to climb back into the carriage Shu Wei's arms were suddenly brought together behind his back. His nose was shoved against the side of the carriage, his nostrils expanding at the smell of the recent coat of glassy varnish. He could feel cold steel being pressed into the taught tendons of his neck.

Johnny Two-Fingers whispered into Shu Wei's ear, "You see nothing here, nothing. Only beach and boats. Good views. Town have big ears. You let out secret, you end up like little fishies at market, split down middle. Hah!"

"I understand completely," stuttered Shu Wei, "I-I saw nothing."

"Ho-o-a-a-h, ha!" bellowed Yong Qiang. "Johnny here's serious about his livelihood. Too much at stake. Big money. Likes to double-lock his door, get it? Now, climb on up."

Shu Wei's legs almost caved beneath him as he lunged for the grab bar on the side of the carriage. Pulling himself up to the seat, his pulse throbbed frantically. He rubbed his neck where the pistol had been held, his body rigid in the cushioned seat, and fixed his gaze on the swarm of flies fluttering about the horse's auburn mane.

CHAPTER TWENTY ONE

Alliance Française

Two days later, Wu Kang Ho, Shu Wei, and Shu Lan-lan trudged up the Clay Street hill from Wu Kang Ho's store on Waverly Place. A diaphanous cloud of mist still clung to the higher reaches of buildings, the remains of a persistent blanket of fog. Moisture from overhanging eaves and balconies fell to the glistening cobbles and sidewalks below. The dampness seemed to intensify the array of aromas in the heavy air from the fish houses, lumberyards, cigar factories, and horse stables.

"Hurry along now," ordered Wu Kang Ho. "Mr. Banier has been nice enough to invite us to his office. We mustn't keep him waiting. By the way, he was quite excited over the phone when I told him the news about the box you found."

"We have yet to take a cable car since we've been here. Can we ride one today?" suggested Shu Wei.

"Yes, since we won't be taking a horsecar. There aren't many left anymore," said Wu Kang Ho. "They give a nice smooth ride with the horse pulling the car on the rails, but unfortunately, they give off a smell with their blend of smoky coal-oil lamps, sweating horses, and a stink coming up from tobacco juice in the straw on the floor. I make sure to take the cable car now."

"Why do they call it a cable car?" asked Shu Lan-lan.

"Well, said Wu Kang Ho, "about twenty-five years ago, a clever man named Andrew Hallidie buried a cable—a wire rope—beneath the street. If you look down, you'll see a slot running between the two rails that the car runs on. The cable car mechanism grabs on to that cable to make it go forward. A special brake keeps it from going too fast downhill. So, all those poor horses who used to slip and slide, pulling cars on the cobbled hills . . . well, hopefully they're enjoying some grassy pastures now. Let's get on here at Powell Street," he suggested. "If we're lucky, they won't kick us off."

A cable car painted a deep forest green and ivory slowly screeched to a stop, the sound of metal-grating-on-metal. Shu Wei and Shu Lan-lan latched onto poles and stood near the front on a narrow running board close to street level. A large man handled the grip—a vice-like lever used to control pressure on the underground cable that powered the car. Wu Kang Ho sat on a slatted wooden bench. A couple of women sporting parasols and broad-brimmed flowered hats promptly got up and moved, mumbling something about "these Johns." Some older white boys pulled on Shu Wei's *bing,* the queue that hung invitingly down his back. The two tried to act nonchalant and, in fact, were too preoccupied with the passing scene to give the boys much heed.

The grip man exerted his will on the lever again, making the car lurch forward after each stop. When they stopped at California and Powell at the top of the hill, their mouths fell open at the sight of the Leland Stanford house. It stood as a prominent monument to Stanford's stature as one of the Big Four who owned the Central Pacific Railroad. Wu Kang Ho said that the *San Francisco Newsletter* once named it "the most elegant home in America." Behind it, at Mason Street, rose the towers of the impressive Hopkins home which housed the Hopkins Art Institute.

Shu Lan-lan let out a squeal as the cable car plunged down Powell from California Street. With her blouse flapping in the wind she said, "I truly hope our lives don't end here. I don't know what keeps our little train on the tracks down this steep hill."

The vista opened up as they approached Union Square with its collection of churches, residences, and shops. The square itself was a formal arrangement of gravel paths, running diagonally from corner to corner with others at block mid-points, all of which met at a small circular paved area in the center. Informal plantings set in the grassy areas defined by the pathways included exotic species: Norfolk Island pines stood next to Dracaena palms and New Zealand flax. Carriages stood along the curb at Tiffany's, with their drivers awaiting their passengers while they enjoyed a smoke-filled chat with one another.

The building at 414 Mason was a handsome eight-story building, in the style of an Italian Renaissance palazzo. A sign carved into the limestone announced the primary tenant: The *Alliance Française de San Francisco.* The three entered and crossed the marble-tiled floor to an impressive oak desk with a green vase brimming with sunflowers. "We have an appointment with Mr. Perrier Banier," announced Wu Kang Ho.

The woman at the reception desk wore a maroon and powder blue bodice with lacy trim, cinched tightly at the waist. Her auburn hair was captured in a bun on top of her head that completed the severity of her facial expression.

"I am sorry but your likes will not be permitted to see Monsieur Banier. He will not . . ."

At that moment, a man sporting a gray tweed sport coat and dark blue pants appeared from a door off to one side. Smoke from a glowing cigarette dangling precariously from a corner of his mouth, hovered above a head of tousled hazel hair.

Cigarette bobbing up and down, Perrier Banier snapped, "Ah, Sylvie, that is quite enough. These are friends with important news. Come, come. This way. You must forgive my secretary. She has only recently come from a small town in France and is still wary of so-called foreigners. I remind her often that she herself hails from foreign soil."

Once inside the office on the top floor, the trio marveled at its coffered ceiling and hand-painted panels of the French countryside. Perrier suggested, "Please sit. I will have my aide bring us all some tea which, by the way, is from one of your fine shops in Chinatown."

Wu Kang Ho spread the two documents on a large oval table and laid the bracelet on the table. "As I mentioned in our conversation the other day Mr. Banier, Shu Wei and Shu Lanlan here have uncovered some items that I believe you will find of considerable interest."

Perrier ground his smoldering cigarette in an ashtray. His eyes darted across the pages as he laid the papers beside each other. Reinserting the now-lifeless cigarette in his mouth his chiseled face grew taut. Ashes fell to the carpet as he drew one and then the other document closer for inspection. He exhaled a heavy breath of nicotine-laced air, then dropped heavily into a couch upholstered with blue and gold fleurs-de-lis.

Perrier's eyes drew cloudy as he turned his face to his visitors and said, "*Sacré bleu!* These are indeed from my *maman.* As you might know, I do not know who my father is. Whoever this man is, we think he was accused of killing my mother when I was only a year old. But there is no evidence. After my mother's death I was sent to a Catholic orphanage.

"Over the years though, the church helped me research the history of my mother's family. By that time there were no living relatives. But, my grandmother—Marie's mother—Anne-Pierre Laiseaux, had kept a rather complete diary and, I learned, stored it in the family crypt in the Père Lachaise Cemetery in Paris where her husband had been given a military burial.

"When I reached the age of sixteen I was told that I must leave the orphanage. I was terrified. After a couple of years of living on my own, I decided to sail to France. I ended up in Paris hoping to trace my mother's footsteps as best I could. I had to go to the French authorities to get a release of my grandmother's diary.

"My explorations were fruitful, maybe too fruitful, because the diary not only exposed the vulnerable nature of both my mother and my grand—" Perrier stopped, falling silent, as his shoulders sagged, and he pulled in a restorative breath.

"Shall we take a little break?" suggested Wu Kang Ho. "Perhaps a tea break would be nice."

Perrier signaled to his aide for more tea. The group around the table stretched back into their chairs.

"In the end, my stay in Paris was rewarding," Perrier continued. "I learned to speak French and ended up working for a newspaper for a few years. At the age of twenty-two, I decided to return to San Francisco. I had a colleague at the newspaper that became Assistant Director of the *Alliance* and was looking for an editor for their journal. And that's how I ended up in this building.

"But, back to our story at hand. I truly hope that my mother's killer will be found and brought to justice. In the meantime, I am incredibly grateful to you three for being honest enough to bring these documents to me. While they won't bring my mother back, they represent considerable monetary value and are of infinite sentimental value, as you can imagine."

Shu Wei picked up on Perrier's thoughts about his mother's killer. And, Evelyn Parkford mentioned something about the possibility of suspects at the Globe Hotel. *May be a story with promise after all*, he thought, his mind churning. And what about Perrier's newspaper experience. Maybe he'd be interested in *The News*.

Monsieur Banier stood, approached Shu Wei and Shu Lan-lan and put one hand on each of their shoulders. "I wish to reward you for your kindness. When I am able to convert these certificates of deposit into cash at the bank in Paris, I will convey a good sum to you both. It is the least I can do. Of course, under the circumstances, the verification of the legitimacy of the documents and my claim to them will take a bit of time. But, rest assured, you will get your money."

Shu Wei and Shu Lan-lan stood, words failing them. Shu Wei's chin began to tremble as he confessed, "We are most thankful. I must also tell you about another bracelet that belonged to your mother. Before we discovered the story behind it, we pawned it at a shop in Chinatown. It was given to your mother by her parents for her 'coming together' or something like that."

Shu Lan-lan gave a gentle nudge to her brother's ribs and said, "He means a present for her 'coming of age.'"

"Yes, I think I had guessed his meaning," said Perrier with a smile that elevated his cheekbones. "Tell you what. If you lead me to this pawn shop, I will buy it back and keep it as another keepsake of hers. I can certainly afford to do that now—thanks to you both."

Wu Kang Ho extended his hand and said, "My store is now on the former grounds of your mother's house. We are permanently bonded to your family and this will stand as a reunion of sorts with your mother. In China we would call this *ku tian* or 'bittersweet,' in this country. He handed Perrier a gift box of dried candy ginger. "We would be pleased if you could join us some evening soon for a small banquet."

"I would be most honored," replied Perrier. "I would think it also appropriate that you attend a dinner at the *Alliance*. We have a most capable chef and will serve food in the French style."

On their way out the three passed by the reception desk once more. Wu Kang Ho offered a '*bon jour*' in the Chinese style: *zai jian!* The receptionist only glowered and repositioned a flowered metal hairpin in her unruly bun. She swiveled her squeaky chair so that she faced away from the departing visitors. In doing so, her bun came flying apart and the pin skidded across the marble floor, drawing a smile from Shu Wei.

CHAPTER TWENTY TWO

The Hong Kong Garden

A week later, before the dinner with Perrier Banier at the Hong Kong Garden restaurant, Mei Huang met Shu Wei at six in the evening at *The News* offices. Twice a month Shu Wei joined her to explore techniques in photographic imaging and developing. She even had him experiment with three-by-four and four-by-five glass negatives. These sessions were instructive but also came with a bonus: the chance to spend time with Mei Huang. Her easy demeanor and patience was a balm for his troubled spirits, at least temporarily. Beyond that, on a deeper level, Shu Wei felt the onset of a collaboration, a kind of alliance of kindred souls and instincts. Plus, he had to admit, he simply found her very attractive.

"Photo journalism is a blend of technical skill with the camera and an eye for the unconventional," Mei Huang suggested. "I don't mean bizarre necessarily, but what you feel a reader would be attracted to. When you combine a captivating photo with a story of interest, you draw people in with the texture and flavor of everyday life. This means, of course, that you will have to work up the nerve to not only photograph people but get their story as well. Or try other sources if they aren't willing to talk.

"I must remind you, though, that there are hazards. Not everyone wants to be photographed or imposed upon. I've had situations where my camera has been broken and I've gotten a bloody nose just because I thought I was invincible. So, just use caution and common sense."

Following their session, Mei Huang and Shu Wei made their way down Dupont Street toward the restaurant. Shu Wei paused to photograph a small cluster of men gathered around a horse-drawn cart piloted by a man in a floppy hat. Mei Huang said the man's father worked in a slaughterhouse at Hunter's Point. The son did a good business from selling items salvaged by his father: pig intestines, cow stomachs, duck and chicken feet, and other discarded organs. Shu Wei turned his eyes away, quivering, thinking of the fish emporium where he met with Yong Qiang.

Turning west up Jackson Street, they passed St. Louis Alley where a woman was burning prayer papers in a square incinerator can—a Buddhist ritual he had discovered that was practiced twice a month, at half-moon and full-moon. She doused them in a street puddle to extinguish them. Wooden balconies on decaying house fronts sported scraps of colored fabric and gilt paper. Trails of thin blue smoke from joss sticks mingled with the aroma of sandalwood, meant to repel the devil and his emissaries. Further along Jackson Street, hooks held ducks split down the middle and flattened out like sheets of wrapping paper. Cubes of roast pork sat next to dried herbs and platters of cheeses. Shu Wei wanted to photograph all of it, but he held back.

Two young boys were playing in front of a basement stairway at the Hong Kong Garden, a four-story building with a bright green awning. The front was painted with light colors, veined to simulate marble. The words "beef porridge, fish, and wonton" had been painted on a short wall to one side of the stairwell. "I have eaten downstairs a few times," said Mei

Huang. It's for the workers or unemployed. It's always good to keep friends with this group. I keep my ears tuned; they're often open in their conversations. The top floor, where we're going, is reserved for the Chinatown elite and their guests. Folks on that level usually keep to themselves in their private corners."

As they climbed the stairs they passed waiters carrying trays on their shoulders and speaking in urgent voices. The rattling of pots and dishes in the kitchen on one floor faded as they approached the top-floor entry to the restaurant. Shu Wei had never seen a more luxurious layout. Banquettes, upholstered in tufted black velvet with puffy silk pillows in different colors, framed the sides of an entry vestibule.

Off to one side a quartet played softly. They blended an *erhu*—a two stringed fiddle—and a pear-shaped fretted lute, a *pipa*, with two *dangus*—small flat drums with handles.

Several giant lanterns with intricately etched glass globes hung overhead. An adjacent wall of vertically banded wood and glass let in bars of subdued light that skidded across a dark polished wood floor. Ahead, a high screen of fretwork held up by gilded columns let in shafts of brighter light from a skylight in the main dining room. More elaborately tasseled globes hung as accents over each table. Beyond, an outdoor terrace beckoned with a lushly planted garden.

Shu Wei, Shu Lan-lan, Wu Kang Ho, the doctor Li Po Tun, Grace Caldwell, Fan Ching, Mei Huang, and Chin Mon Way of the Hop Wo Company began claiming the open-backed enameled chairs that flanked a long rosewood table. Two giant ceramic vases with sprays of camellia, osmanthus, narcissus, and plum blossom rested on a vibrant blue-and-emerald-green runner. Decanters of red wine were placed at intervals between tureens and flower displays. The wine was the gift of Perrier Banier who occupied one end of the table. The restaurant owner, Wu Fang Lee, sat at the other end. Two young women, in patterned flowing trousers and contrasting jackets, noiselessly placed menus on each guest's plate and offered cigars from a platinum tray. A phalanx of six waiters in stiff white jackets stood poised behind them.

Chin Mon Way rose and said, "It is indeed a great privilege to begin with a toast to Mr. Perrier Banier who has graciously endowed the event this evening. At his request, I invite him to say a few words."

Chairs scraped and glasses clinked as the attendees rose and saluted their host with muffled clapping. Perrier began, "A good many of you may know, by now, the amazing discovery of some papers and jewelry on the property of Wu Kang Ho's store. For those who haven't heard the story, I will not burden you with the long version. Briefly, my new friends here, Shu Wei and his sister Shu Lan-lan, uncovered a box in the backyard of Wu Kang Ho's store. In that box were highly valuable documents to me—both monetarily and personally. These date to the time when my mother occupied a building on that same site. She must have had an intuition for she buried them some time before she met her death at the hands of a cowardly assassin. Whoever this man is, he may also be my birth father. I have long fretted over the fact that he has not been brought to justice, which has only deepened my grief over losing my *maman*."

Tugging at his collar and playing with his shirt cuffs Perrier continued, "However, because of the papers she left behind for me, I have acquired a wealth I never dreamed of having. And, I must say, the fact that Shu Wei and Shu Lan-lan, along with Wu Kang Ho, brought these to my attention is an act of true kindness and honesty. For this reason, I would like to honor these two young people with a gift that will serve as an endowment for their future livelihood. I will also be setting aside a stipend for Wu Kang Ho for his part in this."

Before Perrier could continue, the group burst into hearty applause. "Wait . . . I have not finished. I asked Shu Wei to tell me who he would suggest might be a candidate for an additional gift that would benefit the community. Without hesitation, he replied '*The Golden Hills' News*.' So, when I receive the funds, I will deposit a sum in Wu Kang Ho's bank sufficient for Fan Ching to continue to operate his newspaper for the next few months. This should keep the creditors at bay and give the paper a better chance to focus on important stories and grow their advertising and circulation."

Fan Ching rose from his chair and, with a nod, humbly offered his hand to Perrier in a gesture of *guanxi*, a symbol of a new relationship. Mei Huang followed closely behind, dipped her head briefly and said, "*Xièxiè*," thank you.

Fan Ching flicked a spoon in a staccato against a drinking glass. The murmur of conversation slowly ebbed. The group stood in clusters with looks of anticipation.

"I also have an announcement," said Fan Ching. "Over the past little while, I have gotten to know Monsieur Banier and, in the process, discovered his background in the newspaper business. It is my great pleasure to inform you that, by mutual agreement, Perrier will be *The Golden Hills'* new Executive Editor. In the beginning at least, he will retain his position at the *Alliance*. We are honored and privileged to have Perrier as a part of our team. We look forward to a long and fruitful partnership." As the group applauded, they realized the entire dining room was clapping along.

"We would sing your national anthem, your 'Marseillaise,' Fan Ching broke in, "but I'm afraid we are not in good enough form for that. One thing we are not lacking however, is a sense of gratitude that will remain with us forever. And, rest assured, we will learn your anthem and try our best to sing it at our next gathering."

Perrier responded, "I will certainly not expect you to tackle our anthem . . . as long as you hold no hopes of me diving into the tune of *Li Zhongtang*, the lovely song you use for diplomatic missions to our land."

Later that evening, Shu Wei and Shu Lan-lan, still sated with the food and conviviality of the banquet, kneeled before the mulberry plant in their backyard. Its yellow-brown branches were beginning to spread, its modest shafts now populated with infant buds. A small bird settled deftly on the wooden fence nearby, sending throaty squawks into the evening air.

The semicircle of rocks at the tree's base was growing. Shu Wei placed another "prayer stone," this one to commemorate the spirits' granting of good fortune: the chance encounter with Perrier and *The News*.

CHAPTER TWENTY THREE

Shu Lan-lan

While Shu Wei was getting himself more tangled in the web of the underworld, Shu Lan-lan was undergoing her initiation into life at the Occidental Home. Mother Grace felt Shu Lan-lan ought to be immersed in all matters of the Home if she were to play an integral part there. This meant spending time in the laundry, the kitchen, and at waiting tables and sewing. Although Shu Lan-lan had helped her mother with many household chores, helping with the care and feeding of almost seventy young girls was quite another matter.

She discovered early on that the place she least liked to be a part of was the laundry room. The damp heat combined with the incessant noise of the machines often gave her a headache that lasted well into the evening. But it was the sorting that was the worst. Stale and often malodorous heaps of linens, towels, clothing, and tablecloths had to be separately staged in front of three large washing machines. Once the bulky items had been wrung of most of their moisture, Shu Lan-lan stood on a wooden box and fed them through a hand-cranked mangle. She had to discipline herself to take breaks to avoid cramping in her arms.

Work in the kitchen was less arduous, but required tolerating the three matronly cooks who ran the operations with military discipline. On one occasion, Shu Lan-lan's lateness caused the sizable German woman to unleash a caustic dressing-down. Shu Lan-lan had to use her apron to manage the cascade of tears.

At least Shu Lan-lan wasn't the victim of burns that befell many of the younger girls. Kitchen work was dangerous. Shu Lan-lan learned to administer quick treatments of sterilizing ointments and gauze padding. Her own mishaps came more from chopping, dicing, or peeling. On one occasion, she forgot to fold under the tips of her fingers as she worked on chopping onions. A minor wound drew blood causing her to panic and dump the entire tray of twenty diced onions on the floor.

Shu Lan-lan found the best opportunities to get to know many of the girls were during her stints in the game room. Her job was to keep the pieces in their proper boxes and to monitor the six tables where games were played. She quickly learned that innocent-sounding games like Tiddlywinks, Spoof, Man in the Moon, and The Rival Policemen could easily spark aggressive behavior and all-too-lively competition. This led her to invoke "Shu Lan-lan's Rule": play peaceably or not at all.

Mastering the art of forceful dispute resolution gained her the respect of most in the room—all except the notorious eleven-year-old Fan Foo Lin, who accused Shu Lan-lan of picking favorites. She brought a hemp doll to the game room that she would blatantly stab with a hat pin as Shu Lan-lan neared her table. Shu Lan-lan briefly considered bringing this to the attention of Grace Caldwell. Instead, she found a doll from the "secret" storage bins in the closet beneath the stairwell, complete with a wig and several changes of clothing, and gave it to Fan Foo Lin. After that, Fan Foo Lin sought out Shu Lan-lan whenever the doll underwent a wardrobe change, which seemed alarmingly often.

Shu Lan-lan's work in the dining room was uneventful for the most part. It involved setting the tables for lunch, clearing the dishes, and putting out the weekly flowers for each table. Mrs. Blakewell, the overseer of the dining room, was a stickler for detail, including the correct placement of napkins and silverware. Chopsticks were to be placed at the head of each plate. The girls who arrived early often accumulated several pairs and built elaborate structures from them, inviting the wrath of Mrs. Blakewell. She drew up an edict for those tables guilty of such infractions that eliminated dessert or required them to stand for the entire meal, sometimes both. This could result in retaliation by the others as they clacked their chopsticks together in protest. Shu Lan-lan was charged with helping to quell these disturbances.

One evening, working with the evening crew, Shu Lan-lan entered the dining room and found every girl with her head down on the tables. The room was eerily quiet. As Shu Lan-lan tentatively eased her way into the room they all rose at once and belted out a spirited Happy Birthday song, first in Chinese, then in English. Shu Lan-lan had forgotten her own birthday! As tears flowed down her cheeks, she joined the line as it snaked its way through the dining room and even through the kitchen—much to the amazement and delight of the cooks. When she sat down for her special meal that evening each girl came by and presented gifts: *zhézhǐ* boats and hats that they had made in their Chinese paper-folding class.

But, of all the roles and experiences at the Home, the sewing room was Shu Lan-lan's favorite. She spent many hours with Grace learning the mechanics of the sewing machines—more hours spent trying out the various stitches, loading the thread, "walking the foot" of the machine, and properly oiling and caring for the parts. Rumor had it that these foot-operated, treadle-powered machines would soon be replaced by electric models.

In fact, to her great satisfaction, Shu Lan-lan learned that in another two-to-three weeks she would be transitioning away from the laundry and kitchen operations and over to the sewing program. It was Grace's intention to groom her for the full-time position she herself once filled when she first arrived at the Home. Shu Lan-lan felt honored that she had been singled out to train for this responsibility.

Shu Lan-lan's second favorite activity was reading folk tales to the girls—particularly those stories that she felt could inspire them. She also found her own muse in many of them. One of her favorites was the one about Hua Mulan.

"This story concerns a family that lived in the hills of the Wei River Valley, the birthplace of Chinese Civilization," Shu Lan-lan began. "The Emperor's Army was building great snaking dragons of stone: walls to keep out invaders. Hua Mulan took action when she found out that her father was being recruited for the project. She knew that he had already served and was too old for duty. Her younger brother was likewise ill-suited, given his young age.

"Hua Mulan disguised herself as a man so that she could, unbeknownst to her father, serve in his place. Cleverly dressed in her father's re-tailored military uniform, she was accepted into the Army. After years of courageous fighting, she returned to her family, a true hero. When the Emperor wanted to reward her with an appointment to a high office she declined, accepting a fine horse instead.

"So you see, girls can be courageous and accomplish great things," advised Shu Lan-lan. "You can become your own version of Hua Mulan. You will build new skills and self-respect here in the Occidental Home so that you can create your own future. I too, have had upsetting experiences where I lived in China. But here, in Chinatown, I feel I can grow stronger and learn to trust people again. Now, let's write down our wishes and dreams and put them in this big basket. Tomorrow we'll talk more about these and how each of us will make them come true."

146

Several evenings later, Shu Lan-lan wrestled two large trash cans from the closet inside the back door. She hated this duty the most. The stench overtook her even as she held her breath. As she dragged the cans down the back steps toward the alley, she sensed things were not right. As fog pirouetted around the only gas light in the alley, an eerie blanket of yellow-gray light was cast over the yard. Normally, the Home's guard dog, Bruiser, would run up and plead for some scraps from the cans. A slight breeze pierced the leaden air and ruffled Shu Lan-lan's work apron.

The blow to her stomach came out of nowhere. The air was knocked from her lungs. A log rolled away from her toward the bushes. She collapsed backward, her head striking a square of brick paving stones. Nauseating pain rippled through her. She sensed a warm liquid oozing from the back of her head. The dog's angrily snapping jaw threatened her. Viscous strings of the dog's saliva landed on Shu Lan-lan's chest. Jun Min pulled back on the animal's neck chain, causing it to cough a raspy growl.

"I know who you are, you *hú li*, you scummy little vixen," Jun Min boasted. "You're workin' for that White Devil . . . the very one that's takin' my girls from my clients. This is just a warning to you folks. We're gonna storm the place here. Just you wait. Take all my girls back."

"How do you . . . know who . . . who I am?" Shu Lan-lan asked in a quavering voice, still struggling to regain her breath.

"Let's just say I have my sources," retorted Jun Min. As he fled out the back gate, he pivoted and shouted, "One last thought. You might have your little angels stop feeding your guard dog contaminated food. It's hard on the poor thing's health."

Shu Lan-lan's blurred eyesight only allowed her a shadowy glimpse of Bruiser's limp form sprawled nearby. The back door burst open just as Jun Min disappeared down the alley.

"I heard Bruiser barking so I thought I should . . . my heavens child!" cried Mrs. Blakewell. "What in the world . . . why are you sitting on the ground? And why is Bruiser lying there twitching?"

"That wasn't Bruiser barking," said Shu Lan-lan. "that was some horrible man's dog. The man who attacked me. I think I hurt my head. Please check on Bruiser—the man said something about contaminated meat."

Mrs. Blakewell whimpered a "Oh, my Lord!" when she saw the blood now oozing from Shu Lan-lan's head. "We'll need to get you to doctor Li Po Tun right away."

Others, upon hearing the commotion outside, came pouring from the kitchen door. Grace fell to her knees beside Shu Lan-lan, wiping the young girl's brow and trying to calm her. Mrs. Blakewell raced over to Bruiser, now lifeless, with foamy saliva slathered over his muzzle. A piece of meat, partially eaten, lay beside him. Grace discovered later that the meat was laced with *gu* poisoning.

Grace's instincts told her that these barbaric acts had to be Tong-related. She trembled upon hearing Shu Lan-lan's report of the man's threat to storm the Home and kidnap her girls.

"I'm afraid we'll have to increase the security immediately," Grace said as she rubbed her forehead. "We'll need more doorkeepers at the front and back doors on a permanent basis. One of the doorkeepers will accompany you, Shu Lan-lan, during your travels to and from the Home." It was necessary. Grace knew that the threats the Tong made were never idle ones.

CHAPTER TWENTY FOUR

A Raid

Shu Wei was furious, confused, and scared when he learned of his sister's incident at the Occidental Home. "Who would want to do such a thing?" he probed. "How did they know it was you and how did they know you take the trash out at that time?"

"If only I could answer just one of your questions, but I can't. My thoughts ran to the man on the ship. Do you think there is any connection? Although, as I think about it, this man did not match that man's appearance."

"Tell me, did you get a good look at the man? Can you describe him?"

"Well, the light was behind him and I was in a state of shock during the whole thing, so I'm not sure my version would be accurate. But I'll try. My headaches sometimes get in the way of clear thinking."

Shu Lan-lan's description confirmed Shu Wei's biggest fears. It had to be Jun Min. He turned ashen, then spun from her.

"Are you okay? You seem unsettled. Do you know this man?"

"N-no, no!" Shu Wei rasped all too quickly. "It's just terribly upsetting that you had to be drawn into this . . . this . . ."

"This what? What am I drawn into?"

"The awful thing that happened to you in the backyard. My thoughts are now even more dark. What if there is someone at the Home that is a friend of the Tongs? What if that person knows everything that goes on there? I think we need to discuss this possibility with Grace. Or maybe I'm just over thinking the whole thing."

"Now you've got me even more scared. I will be forever looking over my shoulder. Maybe I should just work for Wu Kang Ho at his store."

"No, don't give up what you enjoy. The girls would be heartbroken. This person . . ."

"You say 'this person', but what if there is more than one?"

"A-a-yah," blurted Shu Wei. "I am worrying us both sick. I need to stop. As our Auntie Chun Dai used to say, 'Quiet thoughts mend the body.' Let's get some sleep."

Several days later Shu Wei quickened his pace on the way to the Occidental Home. Shu Lan-lan begged him to slow down. Intense pinching sensations came and went in her head sporadically. The effects of her beating made even the act of walking laborious. She conjured images of Fan Foo Lin jabbing her doll with pins. Dr. Li Po Tun said that this pain would lessen over time, but she was now more concerned with her paranoiac feelings—especially since she considered herself a high-spirited young woman. And she had still failed to reach her brother. It was like playing the classic game of tangram. So many pieces with so many possible combinations.

A crimson sky dusted with cottony clouds lidded China-town. Merchants were busily readying their shops for the day. Shu Wei loved the sweet aroma of wood sap at the wood carver and the clanging of hammer on metal next door at the tin shop. Further along, a tailor was hunched over his work with a visor askew, his fingers nimbly feeding a needle into a brown tweed suit coat.

Shu Lan-lan finally decided to speak openly to her brother of her growing malaise: "I must say that I am more than a little jittery after my encounter in the backyard of the Home," Shu Lan-lan confessed. "I am beginning to have suspicions about everyone and anyone, even the green grocer. As you know, I enjoy all kinds of company. I don't want to show my *kǒng pà*, my fear, to the girls."

"Of all the years that we have been brother and sister, I have not known you to be sullen. I am afraid that I am the one that has soured your thoughts and driven you to question *me*. For that I am sorry."

"Come, we have missed the morning breakfast, but I'm sure my friends in the kitchen will take pity on us," Shu Lan-lan advised.

As the two reached the front steps of the rusticated brick building of the Occidental Home, three animated girls of various ages rushed from the front door of the Home past the two burly doorkeepers to greet the visitors. "Auntie Shu," they exclaimed, in an almost perfect chorus. They smothered Shu Lan-lan with vigorous hugs.

"So, you have made good friends here I see," said Shu Wei as he nearly tumbled off the shallow landing to avoid them.

"Come children, you should finish your morning chores," admonished Grace Caldwell, patting two of the girls on their heads. "Why, hello, Shu Wei. A pleasure to see you again. Now, come in. Come in. We're all a little edgy here as you can imagine after our little incident a few days ago. Your sister is a real trooper. Unfortunately we lost our dear friend, Bruiser. We're currently in the process of tightening our security around the Home. But on to more pleasant things.

"I don't know if I told you, but my first real responsibility at the Home was as the primary sewing teacher—a role that I hope to have your sister fill. "In fact, I understand your sister wants to show you her sewing group first," said Grace. "Then we'll all assemble in the chapel room."

Shu Lan-lan looped her hand through her brother's arm and ushered him into a small room alive with activity. Two children in thin white smocks, heads down, were busily hand stitching a pocket on an apron. Three others were huddled over a quilt composed of colorful squares cut from old clothing. They took turns experimenting with the iron treadle that drove the New Home sewing machine mounted on an oak console.

"I am glad our mother and Auntie shared their sewing knowledge," said Shu Lan-lan. "I'm building on that—always thinking of new projects. Mother Grace knows a lady who may donate a loom to the home. But for now, we're sticking to the basics. The girls are just happy to be doing work that's not forced on them."

"Where do these girls come from?" asked Shu Wei. "They all seem so thin and most have sad eyes."

"They have been rescued from a life of prostitution or enforced hard labor," replied Grace. "Some were even sold by their parents and shipped over from Hong Kong. One fifteen-year-old, Ah Chung, was taken from her mother by Tong members. She would have had to come up with two-thousand dollars for her freedom. I'm told it was the Hap Tran Tong that held her captive in a brothel." Shu Wei let fly a half-choked gasp.

"Are you okay?" asked Mother Grace. "Was it something I said?"

"I'm fine. I was shocked that someone could do something like that."

"Let's go see what our little performers have in store for us," suggested Grace. "Every month our house manager, Margaret Culbertson, works with the residents to put on a skit or a musical concert. Then there will be a prayer period followed by lunch, classes, and more chores. The older girls get to stay up later after dinner to read or do special projects."

"What kind of prayer do they have here?"

"It's based on the Presbyterian faith. It's Christian. They speak of a god and something called the Scriptures. Our prayer leaders speak in Chinese, but we have an interpreter at other times since not many of the girls speak English."

"We have just freshened our chapel," said Grace. "Our girls have been scouring, sweeping, and dusting. A friend of the Home provided the beautiful fish net draped over our heads, in honor of Fon Lai, who was rescued recently. The flowing curtains gracing our windows are the work of the sewing group. Our chorus is in final preparation for our annual meeting event where important donors gather with us. So, they will need to be in fine voice."

Thirty girls sat primly in chairs facing an assemblage of staff and guests. Mrs. Culbertson, who also served as the music director, raised her hands to ready the group. Following an uneven beginning, rows of heads bobbed along in time with the piano, blurting out Chinese renditions of "When You Were Sweet Sixteen." A brave but more tentative version in English followed. When the singers plunged into "Kiss Me Honey Do," a crescendo of giggles nearly drowned out the plucky piano and obscured many of the lyrics. Mrs. Culbertson then fearlessly tackled the new Scott Joplin piece for piano, "Swipsy Cakewalk."

The meager audience was spellbound by the performance. Vigorous clapping prompted several stiff bows on the part of the singers and Mrs. Culbertson. Grace rose, letting out a high-pitched whistle, surprising even herself.

"We are blessed to have such a divine and spirited group of girls," Grace began. "And now, I have the pleasure of announcing something joyous indeed. I have gotten us an invitation to sing at the Old Saint Mary's Cathedral in a few weeks. It will take a lot of hard work, but I am convinced that it will be a splendid affair."

After lunch, Shu Lan-lan and Shu Wei passed by Mother Grace's office where she was conferring with three men, all wearing badges.

Grace beckoned to Shu Wei and his sister, "You two are invited to join us on this next raid, but you'll need to stay out of the way. Meet Frank Growman, the Sergeant of the China-town Squad, who will lead the mission."

Growman stood, arms stiffly at his side. The insignia of the San Francisco Police Department stood in relief on a narrow-brimmed bowler. His ruddy face with its prominent chiseled jaw seemed inhumanly square. A pair of steel blue eyes was hooded by wiry eyebrows, flared like magnetized iron filings. A drooping brown mustache sprouted just below his nose. Sparks of light bounced from a seven-pointed-star badge affixed to a pocket of a crisp six-button double-breasted coat.

Grace continued, "Charlie Rumford and Sam Ponderson here are coming along as back-ups. Their sources have obtained details on the building we are about to visit. The building fronts on Pacific Street, near Stockton Street, with a vacant lot on one side. Access to the captors' apartment—we call it our "target"—is by way of a window at the rear of the lot. We already know the exact layout of the target, including the location of the closet where the girl is kept. Her captors have a regular routine. We have spotters at the building to know when they leave. We'll wait until they give us the ready signal."

Addressing Shu Wei and Shu Lan-lan, Mother Grace said, "Remember what I said, keep your distance. We can always have trouble. The neighbors get curious if they smell some-thing."

"We will be careful," agreed Shu Wei, wondering what they could possibly smell.

154

The signal came later that afternoon. Shu Wei could see the spiraling motions of the spotters' hands. Ready. Shu Wei watched as the spotters placed a ladder just below the window after the captors had left. The rescue team swung into action.

Huddling briefly with his two back-ups Sergeant Growman pointed to a fenced area across the vacant lot where the two backups were to be positioned. He had demonstrated earlier the coded set of hand signals the three would use during the rescues. This allowed him to work alone to minimize the commotion. Mother Grace planted herself, hatchet concealed in the folds of her skirt, alongside Shu Lan-lan and Shu Wei who stood in anticipation across the street.

Sergeant Growman ran into his first setback. The window was locked. Taking a small crowbar from his jacket's inner pocket, he jammed it between the upper and lower window unit. His only recourse was to smash the window. So much for stealth.

Across the lot, Sam signaled an alert. Growman had apparently already seen the window of the neighbor's unit being raised on the floor above. While Growman dispensed with remnants of broken glass from the window's frame, the neighbor above launched himself half way out his window and spit out: "What's going on down there? You guys crooks? I'm gonna call the cops."

"No need," responded Growman, "we are the cops. Now go back inside."

Again, from upstairs, "Y'aint no cops! When the hell do cops break into a place. I'm gonna call."

From Growman, "Go ahead, call!"

Finally, Growman shinnied his bulk through the window frame. He had performed these rescues many times but they were never routine. Later, at the station-house, he recorded the events and his account of what he'd seen. The disorder inside the apartment had been appalling. Dishes, layered with films of petrified food, were stacked in crazy piles on the counters; some lay in shards on the floor like ceramic puzzle pieces. A cat box was heaped with feces, some appearing to be of human origin. A rodent with gray spiky fur skittered from a hole in the sink cabinet. Gouges in the wall were rimmed with bloody smears. Roaches feasted on opened cans of food defiantly ignoring Growman's stomping feet.

Then came the moaning, whimpering sound. It came from the closet. The door was locked. The shuffling sounds inside the closet grew softer and stopped, became mere murmurs.

When he bashed the door knob with the steel bar, the voice inside released a blood-curdling shriek. In that closet, Growman found a girl no more than fifteen years old, with lumps, bruises, blisters, and wounds covering her skin. Limbs folded in protection mode, the girl pressed backward into the dirty mops and buckets and lowered herself into the rags that formed a makeshift bed.

Growman reached out for the girl just as he heard a loud banging coming from the front door. It was the upstairs neighbor.

Temporarily leaving the girl, he raced to the window and gave a signal to the back-ups. When he returned, the girl had pulled the door of the closet closed. When Growman yanked the door knob toward him, the door's hinges gave out. He fell backward onto the floor, beneath the door, the girl beating on it from above.

At that point, Sam had reached the building and heaved himself through the window, careened across the room, and finally restrained the girl who lay confused, uncomprehending. Her raggedy pajamas bore the stains and blood of an abusive existence. Slowly, Sam's reassuring words began to settle the trembling girl.

Charlie, with his ballooning girth, came tumbling, almost rolling, over the window sill and yanked the door off his struggling boss. "Glad you could join the party, Charles," Growman muttered, rubbing his sore stomach.

Charlie loaded the girl over his shoulders and headed for the front door of the apartment. As he approached the stairwell, he was confronted with an ox of a man in a flannel robe, wielding a metal bar. "Whatcha doin' you louts?" the man said in a thick New York accent. "I knew you wasn't cops. You're stealin' my friend's housemaid."

"Back off buster," came a voice from below. Grace, eyes aflame, raised her hatchet. "One more step and I'll part your skull with this," she threatened.

The hulk retreated. Baffled by the wild-eyed woman, he stumbled back up the stairs. A phalanx of Charlie, Sam, and Growman led the girl down the stairs and out the front door. A small crowd of onlookers hooted their approval as the girl was laid upon the ground, unconscious. Growman snapped open a tube of smelling salts and waved it under her nose, reviving her. On schedule, a police wagon arrived and gathered up the exhausted group for transport back to the Home. Once in the carriage, the girl immediately collapsed into Grace's arms.

Shu Wei was still snapping photographs of the crowd from his position in the police carriage. Shu Lan-lan sat beside him, terror-stricken, prompting Mother Grace to explain: "Okay, I should be introducing our new resident. Her name is Bo Cai; she is seventeen. She came over from China two years ago with an uncle who sold her to support his addiction to the bottle and the *fantan*. He placed an ad in a local underground newspaper. The highest bidders were a couple whose own daughter had died mysteriously at the age of six.

"We know through sources that Bo Cai is lucky to see this day. The conditions were some of the worst we have encountered. But it took a lot of careful planning since the captors wouldn't leave the apartment for days at a time.

"Did you manage to get some pictures?" she asked Shu Wei.

"I did indeed—even got one of you with your ax raised on the stairway."

"That always gets people's attention—especially since it's a woman doing it," Mother Grace said. "The rather colorful rumor has it that I am in the habit of draining the blood from the arteries of newly captured girls and drinking it to keep up my vitality. You can be assured that this is not the case. My resolute nature is inherited. My father was a prize fighter in New Zealand."

"It was most impressive," Shu Wei said. "I have plenty of pictures to go with my story—that is, when I get around to writing it. And, of course, I will need your permission to interview Bo Cai."

"We will need to give our Bo Cai a few days at least. The first week, our girls are the most fragile. Some even want to return to their captor's place. For now, we'll need to get some hot tea and food in her. She's been through enough for several lifetimes already."

CHAPTER TWENTY FIVE

Two Different Worlds

The first rays of daybreak had begun their dance on the floor next to Shu Wei's bed. His trepidation about visiting Jun Min had started early—very early. He had spent the night tossing and turning. Thoughts were his enemy these days. They tumbled in his brain until they became a festering muddle of night terrors. But this morning he also felt the push of obligation— obligation to satisfy Yong Qiang but also the more important obligation to press on for the sake of family.

He got dressed and downed a hasty breakfast of black sesame porridge and a salty pancake that Shu Lan-lan had made the night before. Once outside, the cool morning air freshened his senses just in time. He had forgotten his notebook and the money for Jun Min.

As Shu Wei descended the steps of the Hap Tran Tong building he saw Choo Yee Kan's bulging eye, peering out the knothole-sized looking port—a kind of eerie, live turtle egg. The hinges creaked as the door swung partially open and he spotted Jun Min, arms outstretched, as if he were welcoming an old friend.

"Whohooo!" bellowed Jun Min. "What timing! Your absence was starting to worry me. Your debt is past due. Ordinarily I would have one of my warriors pay a visit . . . just to make sure you hadn't skipped town. But, I know you are a smart fellow and won't tempt the fates like that. And, since I like smart people, you're the perfect match for what I have in mind."

Shu Wei was so mesmerized by the outlandish outfit Jun Min wore that he only caught bits and pieces of what the gangster was saying. Jun Min wore a kind of wrap made of interleaved layers of brightly colored fabric. It was secured by a wide leather waistband with a sheathed knife clipped to one side. His headpiece was a creation in the same style as the wrap. Several necklaces of fake gems drooped from his thick neck. Yellow and red plumes shot up from a headband, more North Indian than Chinese. *Opium*, Shu Wei thought. *Too much of the pipe.*

"Follow me," slurred Jun Min. "Ever heard of fantan?"

"Uh . . . sort of," stammered Shu Wei.

The two entered a room with heavy air, infused with cigar smoke and the damp odor of dry rot. Two four-foot-long tables each had a twelve-inch square marked off in the center. The sides of the squares were numbered one, two, three and four. An old man with a wizened face and gnarled hands sat at the head of one table, eyes focused on the proceedings. Jun Min explained that he was the gamekeeper.

A small group of dark-suited men was leaning over the table, poised to place their bets. Others stood behind them, intently awaiting the start of the action. A younger Chinese man sat at one side of the table on a high stool, his shiny queue falling from his pillbox hat and over the back of his silk jacket. The dealer. In front of him was a bag fastened to the table containing buttons. The dealer scooped out a pile of buttons onto the table and covered them with a metal bowl, a *tan koi*. The betting began.

Some of the men chattered madly, others sat placidly, convinced apparently that the gods rewarded silence rather than cacophony. Each bettor placed his wager alongside a chosen number. The dealer lifted the bowl from the pile of buttons.

He methodically took his long bamboo stick with a hook at the end and removed four buttons at a time until only three were left. Hysteria. Those who had bets on the number three won. They broke into broad toothy grins. "*Sàng xīn bìng kuǎng*! Unfair!"

"*Chāng fù*! Bitch!" the others cursed.

"Our boys get a little rowdy," stammered Jun Min. When these poor stiffs win, their take is based on winnings minus our little fee. We get a five percent commission. Get it?"

Shu Wei was aware of Jun Min's increasing lack of stability. He was drifting further into Shu Wei's shoulder, his exhalations more pronounced and laced with a vapor of liquor and opium.

"I SAID DO YOU GET IT?" Jun Min's face was two inches from Shu Wei's, his smile demonic. Spittle oozed from one corner of his quivering mouth. The entire room went quiet. Men stood frozen in their places. Even the scraping noises of the hooked stick on the table and the clacking of the buttons had ceased.

"G-get wha-what?" Shu Wei blurted out.

Jun Min's face relaxed. "It doesn't matter . . ." he replied in a buttery tone, his composure restored. He continued in an almost-whisper, "What matters is you paying attention to me and responding. Sometimes I think no blood is flowing in your veins."

The chatter of the men started up again. The sound of buttons being shuffled on the heavy oak table resumed.

Jun Min seized Shu Wei's sleeve and dragged him around two bends in the hallway to a dead end and unlocked a door. Once inside, sizing up the polished Chinese Mahogany paneling, Shu Wei sensed that this must be the office. A far cry from the simplicity and crudeness of the fantan and lottery rooms, its furnishings were well crafted, expensive. Two antique hongmu wood desks with pearl insets sat on opposite walls. Tall leather-bound books lined three shelves on another. A large scholar's table-top chest with heavy brass hinges and a cylinder lock sat below the shelves. Scrolls with Chinese script were suspended above a low bench that held a joss tub and tea service. A faded picture of the Guangxu Emperor hung, askew, next to a lunar calendar on an opposite wall.

A woven rug covered most of the floor. A section of wood planking beneath it gave slightly underfoot. Maybe, just maybe, this was where the other set of books was kept.

Easing himself into a spindle-backed rosewood chair with ivory inlay, Jun Min propped his slippered feet on the desk, pulled a cigar from a box, and lit it. He sent a small cloud of smoke toward Shu Wei.

Shu Wei reached into his pocket. "H-here. I almost forgot to give you the money," he gushed.

Jun Min took the five silver certificates, turning them over as if they might multiply if he fiddled with them long enough.

"You were late with this!" he barked. "This will not be enough to cover the interest you owe me! But I have a solution. Have you ever heard of a *runner?*"

"Like a runner in a race?" Shu Wei meekly offered.

"You are a *bèn dàn*, a fool, aren't you?" Jun Min sneered. "That's what comes from livin' in a small town. Well, we'll educate you in the ways of the big city.

"A runner is someone who carries money and betting slips between the betting parlors and this headquarters. You, my little *chūn*, my green sprout, will quite suit my needs. You are not known in Chinatown so my copper friends will not be the wiser when you make your pick-ups and deliveries. Of course, I will give you proper introductions. And, beware, there are always black-minded people about."

Yes, and I'm in the company of one of those very people, Shu Wei thought, as he squirmed in his chair. He felt a rising gush of heat in his face, yet his hands were as cold as the ice blocks in the huts along the Little Denjiang River. Clearly, refusing was not an option.

"I've got some business to attend to for the next few days so let's get our little venture—I should say, *adventure*—going in about a week. And, this time, my forgetful friend, be on time. Oh, and by the way, you will not mention any of this to anyone. If you do your little job well you will be compensated. We can discuss the details later."

Jun Min unsheathed his knife and held the point against Shu Wei's chin. "If you don't do your job, my butcher friend, Fang Ju, makes special cuts by request—if you get where I'm going with this. And, while I'm thinking about it, you seem like a smart little Chink-o. I have other things in mind. But we'll get to that next time."

Over the next few weeks Shu Wei lived in two very different worlds. In one, he was an intern at *The Golden Hills' News*; in the other, he was caught up in the dangerous and unpredictable doings of the underworld.

Before he realized his dream as a newspaperman, Shu Wei knew that he would need to rally every ounce of stamina and wit to deal with this dangerous Tong. Switching from one world to another was like turning your soul inside out each time. Even worse, he had to maintain a discipline that kept essential boundaries: a boundary between the two Tong leaders, another boundary between the newspaper and the Hap Tran Tong, and yet another set of boundaries separating himself from his own family and those closest to him. The latter is the one that hurt the most. He lay awake nights trying to sort through the maze of complications.

Shu Wei's next meeting with Yong Qiang was scheduled for the Fish Emporium at ten in the morning on a misty mid-April day. When he arrived, he found Yong Qiang in a foul mood. His sources were unable to develop the film in the camera. He sat on an empty fish barrel, arms folded across his chest, foot tapping. His bowler hat was crumpled from the grip of his tightened fists. He held Shu Wei's camera in his enormous hand while his cigar dropped ash onto his lap.

"So, Chinko-scribe," Yong Qiang began. "My boys were all thumbs tryin' to make pictures outta this device. They had never seen this film stuff before. We're losin' time here. I need answers. NOW!"

Shu Wei's throat constricted. The words tumbled out in fractured sentences. "Only a few years ago . . . Eastman Kodak camera invented . . . needs special processing . . ."

"Stop you *bái mù*, you blathering idiot," cried out Yong Qiang. "I said I need answers, not your fancy talk. Now you take care of it. And those pictures go to me and only me, understand?"

Having little luck in responding with words, Shu Wei nodded his agreement.

"I need these prints back in a week's time," continued Yong Qiang. "Now, get your skinny *hòutíng* out of here!"

"B-but, I'll need more time," pleaded Shu Wei. "I'm doing some things now for Jun Min—things that will help get more information for you. Getting the film developed will take time too."

"Awright, awright, don't cry on me," mocked Yong Qiang. "You can have two weeks. But, along with the prints, you'll need to give me some new dirt on my partner."

Yong Qiang howled in mock laughter, as Shu Wei fled with his camera.

The next day Shu Wei rose early and headed to *The Golden Hills' News*, his camera tucked inside his jacket pocket. He hoped that, by getting in before others arrive, he could process Yong Qiang's film. Arriving by the back alley as usual, he climbed the forty steps and let himself in. No one had arrived yet, giving him a chance to look around. Stacks of sheet paper in one corner were bathed in vermilion stencils of morning light. Shelves above held smudged cans of oils, inks, and blackened rags. The wooden floor still bore fat clumps of cleaning compound from the night before. A pile of manuscripts lay face up on Fan Ching's editorial desk. These had had their initial proofing and were awaiting their final corrections and blessings. Shu Wei was glad he didn't deal with this end of the news business—his English was far from perfect.

He was about to walk away when he glanced at the headline of one of the proofs. It read, "Two members of the Hap Tran Tong kill rivals." He could feel a tenseness come to his muscles and a dryness developing in his throat as he read on:

'*City police apprehended two key members of the Hap Tran Tong after they butchered three members of the Long Zii Tong in front of a joss house on Spofford Street. Bloodied axes were retrieved from trash cans in nearby Church Court. Officers O'Connell and Murphy suggested it was the most brutal attack on a rival Tong they . . .*'

Shu Wei could read no more as a shiver passed through his body like an icy shower. As he stared at the article, the door behind him opened. His head spun around.

Mei Huang closed the door and drew near. She peered over his shoulder. "Sorry, didn't mean to give you a scare," she apologized. "You're up with the chickens, Shu Wei. Couldn't sleep? I see you're reading about our little bloodletting in the neighborhood. I came in on my school holiday to deal with the gory details."

Shu Wei became aware of Mei Huang's delicate perfume. It tempered his unstable state. "Yes, I came in to do some straightening of the shop and ah, came across this story."

"Well, I'm working on this one and, believe me, it is not a pleasant assignment. Even though I love the business, these stories make my stomach turn inside out. The slaughter of a people by their own people. I know it's Tong-to-Tong, but it's still unnerving. These crimes are usually acted out in broad daylight so they become theater. Jun Min has no qualms about making a statement about his enemies. The police are afraid to arrest him. They feel there could be retaliation against them."

Shu Wei's composure was being challenged. On the one hand, standing that close to Mei Huang was stirring something in him: she was slender with hazel eyes that seemed to glisten; her dark hair was brushed back and stowed efficiently in a clip on one side; a small sepia birthmark on her neck was an ornament on her creamy skin. But these feelings couldn't dampen the dreadful news. It hit him. *These Tong barbarians, these yís are, in a way, my employer. No, that's going too far.* And yet, the concept stuck. His was associating with, no . . . *working for*, cold-blooded killers.

He realized he couldn't develop and enlarge his film while she was there. And he certainly couldn't hang the photos to dry. *Great. Another mess.*

"Shu Wei, are you okay? You've been staring at that proof for a while now," Mei Huang broke in, interrupting his thoughts.

"Sorry. I had to read this again. It's so barbaric I'm having trouble digesting it."

"Well, I need to get to my story. Let me know if you need anything—I'll be around."

Shu Wei nodded, then busied himself with cleaning the Mergenthaler linotype machine. In fact, he was preoccupied with his dilemma. If he didn't get the film developed and printed in two weeks, he'd be *pēng hǎi*, boiled into mincemeat sauce. While he was painstakingly brushing out some metal chips from the machine he had an idea—one, he thought, that might just be brilliant. And it involved Mei Huang.

"Mei Huang, do you suppose we could go ahead and develop that film I shot of Bo Cai? I would like to get educated on the process."

"You most certainly can. How about in the next couple of days? I was also working on your notes about the rescue and it would be good timing if we put the photos in some context."

Shu Wei then realized that his own life was now dependent on a roll of film.

CHAPTER TWENTY SIX

Women

When Shu Wei arrived at *The News* offices a few days later, his idea had taken shape. He needed to start learning the basics of processing Yong Qiang's film without revealing his real motive. It was just too complicated to explain.

More and more, he was constantly watching the shadows, sensing he was being followed. If he were to be discovered by his Tong friends going into *The News* offices, his life would certainly be in danger. The discrete entrance to *The News* was down a narrow passageway off Waverly Place, giving access to several other offices and stores. The staff at *The News* had been using it after several threatening encounters with Tong members whose names had appeared in a story in the paper.

As he marched up the well-worn stairs to the third floor that day, Shu Wei could already hear the metallic clinking and clunking of the composing machine. He had grown fascinated by the Mergenthaler. He was in awe of the ability of Jake, the part-time operator of its 90-character keyboard: Jake dumped a silvery stream of molten lead over a line of letter molds that magically sprouted into perfectly formed type. Sometimes Jake let Shu Wei do minor oiling and other maintenance. Shu Wei enjoyed that. He dubbed the machine "Lino-dragon."

Mei Huang was blowing steam away from a cup of tea in the coffee nook. "So, mister cub reporter, shall we begin processing the Bo Cai film?" When they entered the darkroom, she switched on the amber-colored light and motioned for Shu Wei to join her. He was once again enraptured with her silky voice. She pulled on her acid-splotched denim apron and knotted it loosely behind her.

With the door closed, Shu Wei felt the knots in his shoulders slacken for the first time in weeks. He was in a darkened room close to a woman who smelled of the sweetness of forest flowers after rain.

"Shall we get to it?" said Mei Huang. She unfurled the film from its canister labeled 'Bo Cai,' and set it aside. "First, we both need to put on these gloves so our hands don't disappear before our eyes when we place them in these solutions. Going through life without hands is not fun. I'm only kidding—but the chemicals can cause harm to our skin." Lifting an amber-colored jug, she poured some vile-smelling fluid into a pan. Her motions were relaxed, confident.

"I'm used to putting on gloves. My father used many strong glues in his woodworking shop," said Shu Wei. The tautness came back at the thought of his father, only with a particular sharpness. He flipped open his notebook and attempted to refocus.

"Good. Now, we run the film through this developing tray for about a minute-and-a-half. Our second tray is the stop bath." Mei Huang grabbed a pair of tongs from a shelf. She lifted the limp film from the developer. Her slender, yet sinewy fingers were like a piano player's.

"This fluid stops the developing. We want to agitate it for a while. Next, we'll use the fixer solution, moving it side-to-side for several minutes. Once the film is stable it needs a good long rinse in this final tray under the faucet."

"But I still don't see anything yet," said Shu Wei.

"Hold on to your apron," Mei Huang said with a playful slap on Shu Wei's shoulder. "Once this strip of negatives dries, we'll put it in the enlarger over there and make some prints. Then we'll see what we have." Once again gripping the tongs, Mei Huang gingerly plucked the length of film from the frothy water and delicately hung it by a clothespin on a wire.

When the two emerged from the darkroom, the others had left for lunch. "I brought some fresh steamed dumplings with eggplant, garlic, and chives. Will you join me?" asked Mei Huang as she brushed this morning's crumbs from the multi-purpose dining and proofing table. Not waiting for an answer, she took a dented square tin from the shelf and extracted a handful of tea leaves, placing an equal amount in two cups. Pouring a cascade of steaming water over the leaves she said, "Here they call this Imperial. It's my favorite green tea. The *Chulan* flowers give it a soothing scent."

After lunch Mei Huang slid the developed negative strip into a film carrier and inserted it into the enlarger head. She then loosened a knob at the top of the post.

"By sliding the head with the lens up and down on this post we control the size of the image on the paper below."

She placed a piece of sensitized photographic paper in the flat easel with adjustable blades on the base. "Once the enlarger and its light source transfer the image from the negative above to the paper below, we are ready to develop. I do the timing of the enlarger's lamp by feel, but you will need to set a timer the first few times."

The first two prints were taken from the frame easel and run through chemical baths but in different trays. Shu Wei inhaled the compelling mix of the chemicals along with Mei Huang's spicy perfume—a potion of magical depth. "The excitement in this process is watching the image gradually appear," said Mei Huang. "When it looks almost complete, then we run it through the stop and fixer baths. And, again, we give it a good dousing with water. My, these are dramatic images, Shu Wei. Please tell me what goes on here."

Shu Wei described the raid to retrieve Bo Cai. They were now holding two of the processed images. Stunned silence. He felt the immediacy of Mei Huang. Their arms touched, and momentarily stayed in contact, as they held two of the prints. *Did she intentionally touch me? No, probably an accident.* He felt a shiver course through him.

"Amazing," said Mei Huang. "Just amazing. Her sallow complexion and sad eyes alone are proof of her horrific ordeal. I think these pictures would make part of a great story for the paper. And your use of angles and composition is commendable."

Another shiver. After entertaining a burst of romantic thoughts about Mei Huang, Shu Wei's reactive instincts took over. He thought he would be in great danger if he put a story together on Bo Cai's rescue, especially with his increasingly precarious involvement with the Hap Tran Tong. *Someday . . . someday,* he thought. But, if Mei Huang were to help . . ."

For now, he had taken enough notes on the processing of film that his concept seemed more plausible. He could always return for a refresher course from Mei Huang. Spending more time with her doing anything seemed like a good idea.

Two days later, Shu Wei paid another visit to the Occidental Home. As he sat on the tufted bench in the ante room of the chapel, Mother Grace strode in, her Victorian skirt sweeping the floor. An ivory-colored, pleated collar girdled her neck, emphasizing the hard jut of her jaw. The floral pattern on her maroon blouse lightened an otherwise restrained ensemble.

"Ah, my friend, Shu Wei," Grace said, "About your project. You may conduct two one-hour interviews with Bo Cai. You will do them on Fridays or Saturdays, here, in the anteroom off the chapel. The period will be between afternoon tea and chores. The door must remain open at all times, and you will need to honor a break schedule every fifteen minutes. To-day, you can start with a half hour session. Is this all under-stood?"

"Yes, Mother Grace. It is. And, my hope is that you will al-so eventually give me words for the story."

"That will come in due time. Let's work on a hill before we scale a mountain. Now, come in my dear," she said, beckoning to someone hidden.

From around the corner, Bo Cai shuffled numbly over to a chair opposite Shu Wei. She sat down, her movements re-strained, cautious, as though she were back with her captors, anticipating a punishment. She fingered the folds of her white smock into a gnarled mass.

Grace stood, momentarily studying Shu Wei, as if she might change her mind. But then, "Remember, her native tongue is not an easy one to pick up. Her English is rough. You'll have to be attentive. See me, and we can go over your notes afterward."

Shu Wei curled open the pages of his notebook and read-ied his pen. He swallowed, trying hard to quell his own appre-hension.

"Okay, let's start with the basics," he said. Where were you born?"

The look of concern that had occupied Bo Cai's face, faded with relief at the innocence of his question. Her reply was slow and deliberate.

"I . . . I . . . born in Lhasa, Tibet. My father Russian. My mother Chinese. He name Gombojab Tsybikov. Famous man. He first photo-grapher of Tibet and educator in Siberia." Her English, Shu Wei thought, was pretty good considering. He had no trouble at all understanding her.

"He father send him study at Buddhist mona-stery with brother Aleksandr. They not last long. Very, very difficult. Fa-ther's brother, my uncle, he de-depressed, try suicide. Mother,

Akilina, very pretty but no school. After travel in Tibet for long time, father return . . . to Ulan Bator. He study medicine.

"Uncle, mother, Bo Cai live simple life in Lhasa, by Potala Palace. Father never come back. We farm barley, winter wheat, when season good. Sometime work leather factory. When father leave, Aleksandr become mean . . . hit mother and me. Sometime he . . ." She grew silent and continued to twist her dress into a tighter knot of wrinkles.

"I protest but he . . . he . . . say he kill me if I tell. Father find out. He send money so that mother and Bo Cai go Hong Kong. We pack . . . take covered cart, one yak. Other carts too. We cross Himalayas and Ganges, go Bay of Bengal. Conditions most terrible. Mother sick—dysentery—almost dead." Bo Cai paused, drawing a long breath to gain the strength to continue. Shu Wei massaged his fingers, working life back into them where the pen had left an indent.

"At end of trip down to sea . . . find Uncle Aleksandr hiding in supply carriage. He say he go with us on ship to Hong Kong. He gamble whole time . . . rest of father's money gone. So, we live in dirty house Stanley District. Mother and Bo Cai work with fish . . . gut and clean. Uncle get drunk all time. He . . . he even try steal bronze statues from Tin Hau Temple. Police chase him night market. Put him in jail thirty days. When he get out he . . ." Bo Cai broke down again. "He-he attack us . . . every day." Another pause. This time, her head sagged and a tear fell from one eye.

She continued in a trembling voice. "Two year ago, he read about men send young girls to . . . to San Francisco to . . . become slaves. He sell me to Hop Lee in Chinatown. This make him big money. Then Hop Lee sell me to Hap Tran Tong. Hop Lee make even more money. Mother find out. Bo Cai find her . . . dead, in fish factory. May-be she kill herself. May-be he kill her. Next day Bo Cai go with many other girls on boat to America. Two girls die on trip . . ." Bo Cai's face was flushed. Her eyes gushed a stream of tears.

"Let's take a break here, Bo Cai," whispered Shu Wei. "I think this will be all for today." He had sat transfixed, absorbing every word and writing furiously. The more she spoke the more he began to realize that he bore different, yet similar scars. He was currently experiencing a different kind of captivity with the Tong members. "We can continue on Saturday."

He felt the session, as painful as it must have been, had helped Bo Cai. Someone had listened and cared. He'd felt an urge suddenly to hug her, but knew that could be disastrous. Bo Cai might well fear that he was going to attack her. This would also surely mean that he would be banned from coming back to the Home. He thought better of it.

CHAPTER TWENTY SEVEN

Brian O'Grady

Later that week Shu Wei approached Mei Huang at her editing desk. She was a critical partner in his scheme.

"Mei Huang, I don't mean to be a pest *but*, I'm wondering how I might get some developing equipment. You see, I really feel I need to work on my photography . . . and, if I had the equipment at my place in Wu Kang Ho's store, well, then I could practice taking pictures and doing my own printing. Besides, you wouldn't have to worry about having me underfoot in the darkroom. Except, of course, when it makes sense."

"I've never worried about you being underfoot, Shu Wei," said Mei Huang. "In fact, I enjoy your company. But I get what you're saying. Tell you what, I'll look into getting you some trays and the chemicals. Maybe Jake Bradley, our technician, can go to his sources in downtown San Francisco. One thing that we can't provide, though, would be the enlarger. Those are expensive and I'm afraid our budget is already strained."

"Oh, but wait, when we were researching the best way to make prints, we came across a daylight enlarger made by J.J. Griffith and Sons. It's very compact and inexpensive, folds into a small space. You put the negative in a groove at the small end and bromide paper in the large end at the bottom. Then you expose the device to sunlight for a certain time—from a few seconds to a minute or two. It is a little tricky, I'm told, so you would need to try different exposures."

"I like that concept very much!" crowed Shu Wei. "How long do you think it would take Jake to gather up these items?"

"Not sure. But it shouldn't take more than two or three days," replied Mei Huang.

Four days later, Shu Wei brought a large burlap bag to *The News* offices, thinking that the stenciled images of produce would attract the least attention on the street. He bagged up, in small loads, the items that Jake had procured. It took three trips to Wu Kang Ho's store—trips that were anxiety-ridden—to move it all. As he was finishing his third trip of this clandestine operation, he ran into Jun Min.

This rén yāo, this human devil, lives on every street I travel, he thought.

Jun Min seemed to be in an amiable mood. "Aren't you the busy little *hǎi lí?*" he bantered. "Whatcha got . . . buncha bananas for the *hóu zi* you keep?" Jun Min grabbed the bag and looked inside. No monkey. Fortunately, the only items in it were two of the trays for the chemicals.

"Wu Kang Ho needs these for his store displays," stammered Shu Wei.

Jun Min released his grip on the bag. "Betcha eat stuff off of these," he teased and abruptly marched off down the street.

Shu Wei's stomach tightened. He was thankful that he didn't have the bottles of chemicals in the sack this trip. Was their meeting coincidental? *This hóu zi could have been a dead hóu zi,* he speculated had more incriminating evidence been in the bag.

Once back in the store, he worked quickly. After hauling everything to the second-level room, he laid the items out on the floor in the sequence Mei Huang had dictated. Now, the backside of the puppet theater was transformed into a makeshift darkroom. The fit wasn't perfect, but it would have to do.

The curtain, when drawn, gave privacy and proper lighting for his work. A couple of wires, at the back of the proscenium, were perfect for hanging the wet film. The old sink's faucet gurgled, belched, and finally delivered a burst of rusty water. After a couple of minutes the water ran clear.

His biggest challenge was going to be the use of the Griffith enlarger. He already sensed that there was only a brief period during the middle of the day when he would have adequate sunlight on the roof for the transfer of the image to the bromide paper. Other than that, things looked as though they would work. He stood back, a sense of pride building—a pride that even brought a smile to his face.

Over the next couple of days, Shu Wei stretched the limits of his darkroom knowledge. Developing was the easy part. Try after try to use the enlarger on the roof resulted in failure. Finally, on the third day, the sun broke through the midday mists, and he printed two sets of the first two pictures: one set for Yong Qiang and one for himself. *Quality's not great*, he thought, *but, at least the system is taking shape.* Over time, he would perfect things. Making prints satisfied him greatly.

As he was refilling a tray with developer, he thought he heard a squeak. Thinking it must have been the wind pushing against the door to the roof he recomposed himself. Another squeak, this time a definite hinge noise at the bottom of the stairway. He froze momentarily, his heart racing. He grabbed for the largest bottle he had, feeling ridiculous but resourceful. Now, the floorboards on the stairs were creaking. He wished he had closed the door below and locked it from his side—but too late. The creaking grew louder. His mind churned over possible options. There weren't many. *Get out onto the roof? But I'm still trapped.* He cursed his stupidity.

Between the slit in the stage drapery, Shu Wei could see a figure emerging from the shadow at the top of the stairs. "Stop where you are," Shu Wei ordered in a cracking voice, as he stepped into the room. "I have a weapon."

"Some weapon," the figure said. "No need ta engage in bloody battle with me, mate. I'm sure you're gobsmacked ta see me now, arncha?"

Shu Wei recognized the voice. The dim light barely allowed a view of his visitor's face. He took a tighter grip on the bottle as he inched slowly backward. "Brian O'Grady? Is that you? You need to stop right where you are."

"'Tis me lad. The folks in the store said ta look in your room, and I saw the door ta the stairway was open. So, I invited myself up."

"I don't have anything to say to you," said Shu Wei. "Your actions have caused me enough pain."

O'Grady settled, cross-legged, on the rooftop, his back against the wall. "I'm knowin' that and that's why I'm askin' ya ta give me a chance. Your landlord, Mr. Wu Kang Ho has helped ta bring me around. I'm off the drink and he's got me luggin' and loadin' down at the warehouse. Bunch of good chaps there. Miss Caldwell—she's a spunky lady. She's workin' with me. Says my righteous Catholic self could use some reshapin' with her own brand a . . . well, anyway, I'm learnin' ta find another God. I'm even gettin' ta know your Buddhism. Look, Shu Wei, I'm . . . I was in a bad way when I did what I did. Didn't have a settled piece a brain in my head but now . . ."

Shu Wei interrupted, "I'm having a hard time with all of this. People like you just don't change overnight."

"My da went ta prison. I know I was headin' there at some point. That scared the stuffing outta me. Folks are willin' ta work with me. I'm gonna make somethin' a me life again. My da, Daniel O'Grady, stole a bunch a sheep back in County Kerry, Ireland, and they sentenced him ta seven years transportation. Sent him ta Western Australia ta do hard labor. He got his conditional pardon the next year and married a local gal, Phoebe Conway. My ma thought I was better off livin' with papa, so I moved myself ta Australia and settled in with the both of them. He was a hawker on the streets of Newcastle for a couple years. Then he got ta stealin' again and would come home all full a piss and vinegar. He loved to fist it up in the bars. One day I had ta go drag him from the pub before he was done in by the ruffians. Pulled him by his suspenders onta the sidewalk. He ranted and raved, said I was a no good whore and why don't I get lost. Well I took him up on it."

Brian inhaled deeply. The story continued to pour forth in a torrent, as if he were desperate to get it out.

"I found a steamer that was headin' for Hong Kong. Took with me what little money I had. Arrived in Hong Kong but couldn't find work for several weeks. My money was gone along with my pride. I heard San Francisco was jumpin' with money, gals, and good times so I tried ta talk my way into a kitchen job on the *City of Peking*. Didn't work out, but I kept after 'em and told 'em I had some schoolin'. They finally fed me ta the stuffed shirts in the bursar's office. 'Course my history with the bottle got in the way so that didn't last. Guess I'll let the rest a the story come out some other time.

"I know ya don't have ta accept my apologies and maybe they don't hold much meaning at this point anyway. Sorry 'bout your father, by the way. I'd like ta make a new life for myself. A big part a that is ta ask for your and your sister's forgiveness. Gotta make up for my bad behavior."

Neither spoke for a while. Shu Wei looked to the floor, to the bottle he was still holding, and back to the floor. He slowly raised his head and met O'Grady's eyes briefly—long enough to see moisture filming them. Goose bumps traveled the back of Shu Wei's neck.

"In our culture, *Ti-Khuan* is the god that grants forgiveness of sins," Shu Wei said finally. "I suggest we both visit a temple and bring him gifts so that our prayers are heard. This may help in this new start you speak of." He felt this would be a test at least of Brian's will to change.

"I'll need ta pray for the rest a time," suggested O'Grady. "I'm sure that my sins would bedevil the kindest a saints. But, let's go ta this temple-place."

Shu Wei managed a tight smile.

The two walked a short distance down Waverly Place to the Tien Hou Temple. On their way, they picked up a few oranges, Chinese white pears, and some joss sticks.

"Wu Kang Ho introduced me to this temple," said Shu Wei. "And Mother Grace told me it was her favorite, because it is consecrated to the goddess *T'ien Hou* who is revered as the guardian angel of fisherman, seafarers, and women in distress. So now it's my favorite as well."

"I have ta confess, so ta speak, that I have not seen the inside a hall a worship since I was a wee tyke back in County Cork. I don't think I'll know what ta do."

"Don't worry. It's really quite simple. Just follow what I do. There are no priests sitting in little booths where I understand you Catholics have to lay out your sins. And it's not like a chapel service at Mother Grace's Home."

"Believe me, my friend, I have not seen the dark insides a confessional in me home land either. Don't think they would even lend me their bloody ear now."

Arriving at the temple, the two paused for a moment to admire the three-story ornamented facade. Balconies at the upper levels with brightly painted undersides and false columns with Chinese lettering effectively concealed the face of the otherwise bland commercial building. When they reached the hall on the third level, a smoky haze greeted them. O'Grady coughed.

"You'll get used to the incense," explained Shu Wei. "We use it in our rituals to help venerate our ancestors, overthrow the demons, worship our gods, and bring good fortune and wealth."

"We have such things in our religion," said O'Grady, "on a chain that priests swing. Enough ta raise the fear in a lad," he added.

O'Grady drew a breath when they entered. This was no church. Inside, the temple exploded with color. A forest of bright red lanterns with Chinese inscriptions hung from the ceiling. Religious statuettes filled the corners, cloth-covered tables, and chests. Sprays of flowers erupted from a series of vases. Shu Wei added the fruit to a pyramid shape on a table in front of a host of small ceramic deities. He lit his joss stick with another stick in a large copper-colored urn filled with sand and handed it to Brian. Brian, taken aback by his new responsibility, awkwardly followed Shu Wei's mimed instruction and placed it in the urn. Kneeling on a purple silk cushion, Shu Wei put his raised palms together.

In spite of the vibrancy of color and furnishings, the temple had a calming quality. The only sounds were the soft murmurs of the worshipers and the fluttering streamers above, kept in motion by a soft breeze from the balcony window. O'Grady stood, transfixed by the dancing lanterns above that created a subtle theatrical play of light. His reddish-brown hair blended in to the vibrant scene.

He thought about how he had taunted the Chinese—with a few choice off-color words thrown in. But, slowly, he told Shu Wei he was beginning to appreciate their sometimes mysterious customs and lifestyle.

He lowered his lanky frame and knelt on the cushions beside Shu Wei. Even as a boy he'd felt uncomfortable in a church. Here he felt a tranquility, something near serenity. His goal had always been to amass a quick fortune so that . . . what was it that he actually wanted? Whatever it was had always been elusive.

As Brian looked around the temple, he saw a myriad tiny details: small framed photos of everyday people and animals, pictures of Chinese deities and wise men. He was beginning to think that maybe, if he tried a bit harder, he could chart the new course he had pitched to Shu Wei. It was certainly worth a try.

Shu Wei was also lost in his thoughts. In this state, revelation appeared abruptly, in crisp focus. The balm for his anguish could well be sitting right next to him. *Brilliant*, he thought. *But risky, quite risky.*

"O'Grady," started Shu Wei. "If you are serious about getting a grip on your life, I suggest we move over to that alcove and have a little chat."

O'Grady looked at Shu Wei, bewilderment consuming his face at first, then, almost instantly, his curiosity blossomed. Unbending his lanky body, he rose and followed Shu Wei to a curtained niche at the far end of the hall.

Shu Wei's plan involved being absolutely open and frank about his situation and his needs. He badly needed an ally, someone with whom to share information and to give relief to the fast-growing list of headaches and burdens he now shouldered. Of course, that candor frightened him. If that didn't work, he could be writing out his own death order for the *boo how doy,* the hatchet men. Putting that fear aside, he slowly began to tell Brian O'Grady his saga. After the first minute or so, he realized he was in too deep to go back, so he finished the accounting of events. O'Grady didn't budge, didn't move a muscle the whole time.

"Geeminy man, you got yourself in deep, ha'ent ya?" exploded Brian. "We have a sayin' in good ol' Ireland. 'If it's drownin' you're after, don't go tormentin' yourself with shallow water.'

"Ah, lad, I know all about the way a the highbinders. I got my own taste a their kind when I finally got out a the immigration detention—which, by the way, was no grand hotel. The deputy would come in each night and strap our backs just so we wouldn't get too good a night's sleep. When I got out, I booked into the San Quentin House. Jim Gately, the proprietor, took in parolees from San Quentin and got them jobs in the Union Iron Works Rolling Mills at the foot a Irish Hill.

"There musta been some divinity at work the next Sunday when I was sittin' on the porch a the San Quentin House. Out of nowhere along comes Wu Kang Ho. I jumped up and yelled, 'What are ya doin' in this backwater?'

"He said he was lookin' for Irish laborers for his warehouse. Said he wanted ta show that Dennis Kearney guy that he was hiring some a his people. So, I said, 'I'm your guy. I need ta get away from these bloody gang wars and get a real job. I'll put the bottle down. Promise.'

"'If I take ya on,' he said, 'it will only be on the condition that ya get into a program ta dry out. If that works ya can stay on. Only if.'

"Mrs. Grace put me on ta a Christian group at Saint Mary's in Chinatown. Good folks. I go three times a week."

"So, I take it things are still working out for you at the warehouse?"

"So far. The Irish keep to themselves. We were told it's better that way."

Shu Wei said, "I've been thinking . . .you know, *The News* could use some help. Would you be willing to join in?"

O'Grady scratched his stubbly cheek and said, "It'd have ta be after my warehouse work. But, sure. I'll give it a go."

To consummate their new alliance, the two settled in to high back chairs in a teahouse next to the temple. After he gave a brief discourse on Chinese tea culture, Shu Wei proposed that they head to Wu Kang Ho's store. He knew that there was still someone that would need some convincing about Brian O'Grady's transformation.

Back at Wu Kang Ho's store, when Shu Lan-lan laid eyes on Brian, she dropped a piece of knitting she was working on and her jaw went slack. "What are you doing with this piece of sewer scum?" she blurted.

"Whoa! Those are harsh words coming from such a pretty mouth," said O'Grady, holding his hands in the air. "Shu Wei and I have been at the temple and are workin' things out."

"What is there to work out?" demanded Shu Lan-lan. "You have tortured and threatened us."

"Well, I wouldn't exactly say I tortured . . ."

"Mother Grace and Wu Kang Ho have been working with O'Grady," Shu Wei interrupted. "They have been pleased with how it's worked so far. He has apologized for what trouble he has caused and has also offered to help at *The Golden Hills' News*."

"Apologies have no meaning coming from a raving devil. I refuse to hear of this nonsense," said Shu Lan-lan. She started for the door.

Shu Wei grabbed her arm. "Calm yourself, my dear sister. We need to move beyond our hurt just as O'Grady here needs to do some work on his life. I've thought it over and think it could be best for all of us."

Shu Lan-lan's upper lip twitched and her mouth released a whoosh of air. She retrieved her knitting needles from the floor and resettled herself in her chair. Arms crossed, she rubbed her hands against her elbows, pulling at the skin.

Picking up her knitting again, Shu Lan-lan's hands worked furiously. The clacking of the needles filled the awkward silence in the room. When she heard the door close, she exhaled deeply, shaking her head. She recalled the subtle urgings of Auntie Chun Dai: 'Remember child, you were born under the sign of the snake. You have the gift of sympathy and good judgment. Trust your instincts. Men are like rough stones in need of polishing.'

CHAPTER TWENTY EIGHT

Another Interview

A week later, Shu Lan-lan sprawled across her bed reading *The Tale of Fúxī*. She had always enjoyed this mythical tale of a beautiful maiden named Zhū Yīng and the adventures that ensued after she stepped into the footprints of the god of thunder, but her concentration was broken when the door swung open and Shu Wei entered the room.

Exhausted, he leapt onto his bed, the mattress shifting. "What is it that you're reading?" he asked.

Shu Lan-lan pulled her flowered blanket around her and kept on reading. Her supply of patience had run out. She was not about to acknowledge her brother after having endured many weeks of his mysterious ways.

Shu Wei rolled out of his bed and pranced on tiptoes over to his sister, like the fox he used to mimic when they were children. The performance always served as a tonic when Shu Lan-lan had a bout of melancholy or was mad at him. This time, however, the effort was futile. Shu Lan-lan only inched further toward the wall.

"My dear Shu Lan-lan," coaxed Shu Wei, "please speak to me. I don't need the silent treatment. Would it make a difference if I said I love you and that I know I haven't been a good brother lately? Things have been very difficult for me."

At that, Shu Lan-lan unleashed a downpour of tears and embraced her brother. "I have been sick with concern for you," she moaned. "Your behavior these days is beyond baffling. I feel as though I don't know you anymore. Fan Ching and everyone at *The News* say they hardly see you. Now you have some crazy apparatus set up in the puppet theater upstairs."

"That apparatus is my dark room. I use it to practice making prints for use at *The News*. I'm so sorry if this seems peculiar . . ."

"Peculiar?" Shu Lan-lan interrupted. "The really peculiar part is that you don't seem to care about those around you anymore. You need to know that Bo Cai was asking about you. She wondered when the next part of the interview would be."

Holding his sister's hands, Shu Wei implored, "I can only say that, one day, all things that seem upside down now will be right side up. Until then, it is in both of our interests that things go along as they are. Now, shall we go next door to our favorite noodle shop?" Shu Lan-lan, sniffling, rose reluctantly to join him.

The next day, Shu Wei and Shu Lan-lan went to the Occidental Home. They were told by the doorkeepers that the girls were in chapel, but they were welcome to join the service. They quietly slid into chairs at the rear. Mother Grace paused in her delivery of the day's final blessing. Continuing, her firm voice rose and fell as the girls squirmed in their seats.

"The Lord shall preserve thee from all evil; he shall preserve thy soul. Now, may the God of Hope fill you with all joy and peace in believing, that ye may abound in hope, through the power of the Holy Ghost. Amen."

A scattering of *Amens* rippled through the small room. Chair legs and shoes scuffed on the newly polished floor. Animated chatter broke out. As they filed out, the bobbing sea of white scarves covering the girls' bowed heads made them look like a flock of sheep to Shu Lan-lan. Bo Cai worked her way over to Shu Wei.

"How've you been," probed Shu Wei. "I've been wondering how you're doing."

Bo Cai dropped her eyes and smoothed invisible wrinkles in her ruffled gown. "Bo Cai still have bad nightmares. The devils chase, I scream . . . wake up. I make . . . other girls scare."

"Would you be willing to resume our little discussion?" Shu Wei asked tentatively. "We can take it slowly and break it off anytime you are uncomfortable."

"Yes, good to talk. Not good hold things aside."

Shu Wei nodded in sympathy. "We could continue where we left off, if that's all right."

Settling into chairs in the chapel anteroom, Shu Wei tugged at the drawstrings on his satchel and pulled out his notebook.

"Tell me, after you got to San Francisco, what happened then?" he prodded.

After a prolonged pause, Bo Cai said: "They take me special area . . . away . . . not main immigration hall. They take to place say 'assigned immigrants.' I go with eight other girls to alley home, Chinatown. This where, I think they call, auc—tions take place."

"Auctions? You mean people were actually bidding on girls for a price?"

"Yes. When I get to building, we go up dark stairway to big room. Much opium smoke. Many guards. Man from Hap Tran Tong main slave dealer. He very large, ugly man. Face have many small . . . scars. His long braid oily. Has eyes of pig. Eyes move a lot, ve-e-ry nervous man.

"Bo Cai second girl auc—auctioned. Bo Cai sold to short Chinese man. One stub arm, large hump on back. Price twelve-hundred dollar."

"Twelve-hundred dollars! That is more than I will make in my lifetime."

"Must sign contract; can't read—no one help. Later, find out Bo Cai have to work entire life in man's house. Can buy freedom—cost six-thousand dollar."

"Clearly impossible," broke in Shu Wei. "I can see why Mother Grace has to use the tactics she does."

"At first, chores only: clean, fix meals, wax floors, dust. Man have wife . . . she do nothing. She much older than man. She not Chinese. Maybe Russian. Also, large and fat and smell bad. Too much powder. Make sickening gestures to Bo Cai.

"Bo Cai fifteen when start work. First six months—twelve hours day. Sleep on mattress, floor of closet. Have oil lamp. Many fumes. Sometime make me sick. Only use few minutes. Bo Cai locked in closet. Cockroaches, insects. Twice get bad scars from bugs in mattress. People tell me I bring bugs—bugs punish me. People hold fat cockroach to Bo Cai's face. They yell 'zhanglang! You . . . cockroach!'

"High window in closet. Face onto yard. Sometime I look—see birds in tree. Wings give freedom. I think: someday. Someday. Bo Cai has old newspaper from immigration center. Start to read—how you say—right-side up, then up-side down. Try not go crazy. People grab from me, tear up, put down my blouse. I tuck paper away. Make songs from stories . . . like nursery songs when Bo Cai young." Bo Cai's head bobbed from side to side as if hearing the notes of the rhymes that quite possibly saved her sanity.

"Next six months, things worse. Clean same things over and over—sometime six time. Never clean enough. Sometime use toothbrush. Bo Cai fix food. At first, people like. But later scrape off food, throw it me. Say taste like dog pooey. Once throw whole bowl. Knock me out. I wake, they yell and poke Bo Cai. Say get back work. Head hurt—big cut, bruise."

"Bo Cai, Bo Cai, let's stop here and take a break. I can tell why this would be hard for you."

Bo Cai ground her palms together, as if trying to ban the memories she was painfully reliving. She stretched her arms and grabbed her knees, head drooping as though there were a hinge at the back of her neck.

Eventually, with a shaky voice she continued, "When I work, people do bad things to Bo Cai. Hard for me say . . . can't say."

Bo Cai slouched further into the chair, her lips quivering. One arm clutched her other to stabilize the shaking.

"Did you ever fight them or challenge their orders?" probed Shu Wei.

"Did one time. Tie me with clothes line. Shove me into closet long time. No food. No water. Just bucket for toilet. When they bring me out lips very sore. Could not drink from glass. Bo Cai lean on chair, table. Very, very weak."

"How did Mother Grace discover you? How did she know where you were?"

"Life get so bad. Maybe people feel they do what want after pay big money. Worst time, they ask two boys . . . from next door over. Maybe ten, twelve year old. People give them broom stick. Older boy hit me. Younger boy not hit, he cry. Bo Cai bleed on kitchen floor, get sick. Younger boy scared, run away. Maybe tell his mother. Few days later man come to door . . . Detective Kwong. People only open door little bit. But Bo Cai make sure man see me. Body full of scars . . . sores when man come. Think maybe I lose mind. Think about taking life. No want more beating. Tired of living."

Shu Wei crossed his hands in the air—a signal to cease. They both were drained emotionally. At first, Shu Wei found himself speechless, unable to even look at Bo Cai. She began to shudder and cry softly.

Shu Wei quietly folded his notepad and tucked away his favorite Chinese yellow pencils. Bo Cai's smock was damp around the neck with perspiration.

"You are a strong and courageous young woman, Bo Cai. Thank you for allowing me the chance to record your story. I hope to bring attention to your experience so that other girls can avoid such traumas in the future."

"I want survive," said Bo Cai in an unsteady voice. "Maybe now can start over."

Light streaming through a stained-glass window laid a lavender film over one side of Bo Cai's face. Shu Wei was struck by the accidental magic; he knew that this color was associated with an ancient Taoist symbol of divine presence. Bo Cai's eyes flickered as she tilted her head toward the luminous window.

Shu Wei contemplated his session with Bo Cai on his walk to *The Golden Hills' News*. His heart swelled with two emotions: anger and sorrow. Given his own state of mind, how much solace could he really offer? The anger, however, he could do something about.

CHAPTER TWENTY NINE

Jack London

That afternoon, Mei Huang sat at the editing desk, hunched over a proof copy of the next day's edition of *The News*. "Well, look who blew in off the street," she cried. "I thought maybe you had gone back to China."

"I've been . . . well . . . ah, caught up in different things," Shu Wei said with a tight throat.

He gingerly pulled the stack of his notes on Bo Cai from a crumpled black bag. "I don't know what to do with all of this, but it seems like it's time to start trying to making something of it."

"I would recommend getting it into a draft and even including a few of the pictures you took," suggested Mei Huang. "I can help with that. When the time is right, we can publish it."

Shu Wei was delighted that a piece he worked on might make it into *The News*. The part that concerned him greatly was the potential for the Hap Tran Tong to figure out that he was behind the article.

"Mei Huang, for reasons I can't explain right now, it would be best if my name or Bo Cai's didn't appear anywhere in the article."

"That's probably wise, given the possible retribution by the Tong," replied Mei Huang. "But that decision will rest with your editor, Fan Ching. By the way, I have someone that I'd like you to meet. His name is Jack London, a poor struggling writer just like you. I think he's only a few years older than you. Do you mind me asking your age, Shu Wei?"

Shu Wei shrugged and jotted the Chinese characters for seventeen on a scrap of paper and handed it to her.

"Ah! Then Mr. London is not far from your age. He's twenty-two. When we spoke the other day I found him very approachable. We talked photography and writing for hours. And he lives in Oakland right on Lake Merritt. I got him to agree to come by in a few days and spend some time with you. What do you think?"

Shu Wei had no idea what or where Oakland was, but he liked the idea of meeting a writer that was close to him in age.

"You are very kind," Shu Wei said in a voice barely heard over the linotype machine. His fondness for Mei Huang as a mentor and collaborator was growing. "I would enjoy that very much."

"Good, we'll see when Mr. London can get together with us. In the meantime, you need to stop by more often. We're beginning to think you don't like us anymore."

Shu Wei mumbled his response, "No, it's not that at all, believe me. It's just that . . . well, as I said, I have a lot of . . . things on my mind right now." Shifting awkwardly from foot to foot, Shu Wei realized that a frown of concern had settled over Mei Huang's brow.

"Shu Wei, promise me," Mei Huang said, leaning toward him, "that you not forget we are friends first, coworkers second. And from the friend's perspective, you are welcome—in fact, required—to come to me with any issue. Any issue. Is that clear?"

The words "friends and coworkers" wrapped around Shu Wei's body like a warm blanket. He couldn't decide which one he favored the most. The pleasant rush he experienced told him that either one would do.

Three days later, Mei Huang ushered her guest around *The News's* offices. Strikingly handsome, the young man's fine chiseled face wore marks from his recent stay in the brutal elements of the Yukon region during the Klondike gold rush. The ravages of scurvy contracted at the camps had swelled his gums. "Hi, I'm Jack London," he said to Shu Wei, extending a scarred, well-calloused hand.

"Mei Huang tells me you've had a tough go of things in the last few months. But I understand you both are making good progress on some exciting stories for the paper. She says you're wanting to be a . . . what's the word these days? An investigative reporter, or something like that."

"Yes, sir, that's my intention. I've got a long way to go, but Mei Huang and Fan Ching are helping me."

"Well, learning in the streets is the best way. I know. I had no easy time growing up either. My parents split up after I was born—basically learned to educate myself. When I was ten I used to take my books down to the waterfront in Oakland to study at a saloon. Spent many an hour at a table in the back until the place got too busy. The bartender would look after me. Almost like a father to me. Like books, Shu Wei?"

"Yes, very much. But I don't get much of a chance to read these days."

"Books gave me a lot of inspiration. When I was only nine, I picked up a book called *Signa*. Hear of it?"

"No, sir, I haven't."

"It's a novel by Maria Louise Ramé. Her pen name was "Ouida." Boy, that woman could write. It's a moving story about an orphan boy. You might want to read it some day.

That book, I like to say, was my inspiration, my muse. Everyone needs a muse."

"What are you writing now, Mr. London?"

"Oh, please, not so formal, just call me Jack. I'm working on several things but, for me, it's always been a struggle. I've gotten short stories published in magazines, but my real love is writing novels. So far, can't get anyone stirred up about my latest novel, *Call of the Wild*. My time in the Yukon gave me lots of material: hardy prospectors, hunters, gamblers, prostitutes, ruffians, preachers. That's the thing, write from your heart, your own personal experiences. But hey, enough yammering about me. How can I be of some assistance?"

"I showed Mr. London your notes on Bo Cai," Mei Huang said. "He's willing to help you in writing a draft of the story. I've already developed your roll of film and printed a few pictures. Maybe we can get Jake in our office to make an engraving or letterpress version of one for the article."

"You know, you've got a real story here," said Jack. "I got pretty worked up about the whole affair. In fact, there are things in your notes—parts of Bo Cai's story—that might just shape a character in my book. See, we both get something out of it. How 'bout we settle in to this comfy sofa over here and go over your notes in more detail?"

A warmth settled over Shu Wei. Was it "collaboration?" Yes, he thought that was the word that Mei Huang used the other day.

"Say, Shu Wei, maybe I'll come back and have you take a look at the manuscript of my book. What do you think of that?"

Shu Wei could only nod. He was captivated by the dashing London. He contemplated that other word he had learned that day: muse. Maybe Jack London would be his muse.

Two days later, Shu Wei stood beaming alongside Jack London and Mei Huang in Fan Ching's office. "Well, I think we have a strong story here," Jack pronounced. "Shu Wei's detailed notes brought this poor girl's story alive. It's a story that should be told—even though I know you're uneasy about the potential retribution from your Tong friends."

"What was it that the clergyman Henry Ward Beecher said?" asked Fan Ching, rhetorically. "'Newspapers are the schoolmasters of the common people.' We have a duty to educate the people of this city about the heinous wrongs being committed right in front of our noses. Even at the possible risk of backlash by those lowlifes who commit these wrongs."

"Indeed," said Jack as he grabbed his hat. "And now, I'm off for a drink. Anyone want to join me?"

CHAPTER THIRTY

Runner

During the following two weeks, while Shu Wei frantically worked to satisfy the demands of Yong Qiang's request for prints, his obligations to Jun Min as a runner brought him to a state of near-exhaustion. On the other hand, the session with Jack London had thoroughly inspired him. He wanted to dig further into this world of seamy back-room betting parlors. A deep-seated passion to observe and record gripped him, and the opportunities to satisfy that passion were seemingly endless.

One of those 'opportunities' had involved regularly returning the betting payout and picking up white pigeon tickets at a cigar factory on Pacific Street, near Pacific Alley, not far from where Bo Cai was rescued. Shu Wei never quite got used to it. He dreaded every second of the exchange.

As usual on this day, inside the front door, two men at the front counter sat on stools in opium-induced trances. One normally held a sickly cat with a bushy tail. They were expressionless, eyes staring straight ahead as Shu Wei passed. Shu Wei never learned to tolerate the odor of the factory: the smell of wet leaf tobacco lying in heaps on the floor of the main room, a few steps up from the entry. Everything was damp and greasy. Dried meat hung on the walls and several wooden cigar molds lay on top of a pile of dirty rags and clothing.

Shu Wei climbed a vertical ladder, through an opening in the ceiling, to the factory proper. Five or six workers sat at each of three long tables. Two of the men were racked with frequent consumptive coughing. Some made the filling, and some wrapped the uninjured leaves around it. Salt-cellars, butter-chips, and small medicine jars held the paste used by the wrappers. Holding the point of the cigar in his mouth, the cutter rolled, pinched, and pasted it with slender and deft fingers.

One of the cutters, a man of broad girth with thick inflamed lips and a mantle of lesions on his bald head, was Shu Wei's contact. The man's sinister gaze never failed to unsettle Shu Wei, who handed the man the payout of the morning's lottery and, with a shaking hand, retrieved the marked-up afternoon tickets. The man ignored the company-provided knife beside him, placing the pointed end of a cigar in his mouth, biting off the end leaf and rolling the cigar around, wetting it thoroughly, giving a handsome luster to its wrapping.

Leafing through the money, the man's fist slammed onto his work table, sending several cigars flying. He fondled the knife, taunting Shu Wei, then threw it forcefully into the wall, sailing by just inches from Shu Wei's head.

"You *zázhǒng*, you worthless half-breed!" he snorted through his thick lips. "Your people have shorted me. Next time that knife will land in that soft brain of yours—if the gods gave you one."

"I-I . . . I'm sorry," pleaded Shu Wei. "You have my w-word. I had no idea . . ."

Grabbing Shu Wei by his delivery bag, the large man threw him to the floor, where he landed close to the ladder opening.

"Tell your bunch of *gōnggongs,* those eunuchs, that I will come down and remove their personal parts the next time this happens!"

Shu Wei slithered to the ladder, clawing his way down the rungs backward and landing hard, the jolt from the impact running up his spine. The two men at the counter didn't look up as he gathered himself and scrambled for the door. *It was stupid of me not to count the payout before I delivered it. What is Jun Min doing? Trying to kill me? Maybe he suspects something.*

That evening, as was his custom, Shu Wei recorded the day's observations in his notebook. Every day he documented life and corruption, as he saw it in Chinatown. He hoped it would be the basis for more writing opportunities at *The News*. His real goal was to use his pen to help banish evil—exposing the perpetrators of the vile tragedy in his hometown along with the restoration of his and his family's name. Big dreams, maybe too big. A long way to go.

The next day Shu Wei visited a new contact, this one a chicken breeder. He couldn't fathom how one could raise chickens in Chinatown. In Sanhou, his hometown, their neighbor up the road kept a flock of chicks and pullets in outdoor cages with fresh air and sunshine. Here the chickens were all inside.

The sour odor of bird droppings and damp tobacco leaves hit Shu Wei the minute he opened the door to Sam Hong's place on Commercial Street. Sam was a frail but agile proprietor who dressed like a pauper: overalls torn and greasy, a hat full of moth holes, and no shoes. He sat in a doorway, plucking feathers from a goose. These would later be sold downtown for goose-quill pens or for ladies' hats in a millinery.

Near Sam's back door, a malodorous sink full of chickens' feet and decaying vegetables vied with the stench up front. A coop full of chickens stood next to drying tobacco leaves on the floor. *Is everyone in the tobacco business in this town?* Shu Wei wondered. He later discovered that, in fact, there were between three and four hundred cigar factories just in Chinatown. The account in *The San Francisco Call* he had read reported that only two hundred of those were licensed. Shu Wei figured Sam's establishment was avoiding the tax man and, possibly, the health department as well.

Old Sam ushered Shu Wei down a steep ladder to a warren of musty rooms, lit, as far as Shu Wei could tell, only by candlelight. Silhouettes of human forms, formed by the soft tapers' glow in those tiny cells, danced across wall and ceiling. Groans and muffled screams of delight pulsed from the rooms. He shivered.

The shoeless man stomped across a moldering bed of straw and chicken feed, stooping to avoid an empty bird cage overhead, brimming with excrement. Shu Wei couldn't help but ponder the possible fates of the missing birds.

The old man folded himself into a rickety chair and motioned, with a tangle of deformed fingers, for Shu Wei to join him. Seeing no chair and dismissing the alternative of sitting on the gummy floor, Shu Wei perched on a stack of straw bundles that reeked of chicken droppings. Sam reached out with a withered hand and squeezed Shu Wei's forearm, watery eyes locking on the young boy.

"*Koŭ mì fù jiàn*," muttered Old Sam. "Jun Min have mouth of honey, heart of daggers. No can trust. Much money he take—no get back. No more bet. Can't trust. No more deal." As his voice rose to a crescendo, saliva bubbles formed at the corners of a mouth now twisted in anger.

Shu Wei squirmed on his straw perch, trying desperately to appear composed. As he prepared to rise, he caught sight of a dark form writhing snake-like along the floor. Before he could react, a young girl clad only in a filmy wrap held one of his legs in a vice-like grip. Her motions were deft, practiced.

"You pay Sam Hong now for good time," the wizened man croaked.

Every fiber in Shu Wei's body came alive at once. Wresting loose from the girl, he lunged for the ladder. His foot slipped from the first rung and he felt a hand on his heel. The ladder rose like a forty-foot high cliff before him. Clutching the grimy railing, he bolted up to the main level, his feet barely touching the rungs. Reaching the street, Shu Wei's breath came in rapid bursts, calming only when he reached the refuge of Wu Kang Ho's store.

The next day it was time for Shu Wei to meet with Yong Qiang again. In spite of his recent confrontations in his job as a runner, he sensed a settling of the nerves—maybe even a guarded confidence that he could actually deal with sinister people. After all, he'd come to the conclusion that these Tong thugs weren't really all that bright. Sinister and cold-blooded killers for sure, but not intelligent. Maybe all killers had those traits. Now, if he could just keep his cool.

That confidence, that cool, faded as he approached the Fish Emporium. Yong Qiang threw open the door just as Shu Wei reached for the handle.

"What's my little *niángpào*, my girly-boy, been up to?" asked Yong Qiang.

Shu Wei swept past his heckler and dumped the package of prints on the scaling table. "This is what I've been up to," he blurted out, wishing he hadn't been quite so aggressive in his tone.

"My, my, sounds like you're getting a bit grumpy," Yong Qiang jibed. "Haw, haw! What's that expression? *Zhǐ huì yòng gōng bù wán shuǎ, cōng míng hái zi yě biàn shǎ.* All work and no play makes Jack a dull boy. Let me see what your nimble little fingers have come up with."

Yong Qiang fanned through the prints, plucking two from the pile and studying them. "Not bad, pretty boy. Not bad. Got some talent there. Now, we need to keep going with our little project. I'm thinking my partner is hiding more than I thought. Just don't know where."

Yong Qiang suddenly burst from the chair, his arms pumping up and down, causing Shu Wei to cower backward and instinctively raise an arm. "Don't just sit there, you *yǎ zi*, half brain! I need results. Results! I need results!" Yong Qiang pivoted abruptly. He stopped to pick up a cleaver still caked with a film of fish blood and ran his finger along the blade and studied Shu Wei, before releasing another wicked laugh. "Didn't I say '*results*'?" he hollered. "Well, go get them!"

CHAPTER THIRTY ONE

The Book

Several days later, Shu Wei realized he was growing overwhelmed with his various obligations. But he knew he must persist if he wanted to keep up his investigations. Investigations. He was doing *investigations*. Rolling that thought over in his mind, he almost missed Jun Min's approach as he sat in the front lounge of the Hap Tran's headquarters, while he examined a red and yellow jar with a dragon and sea life wrapping its circumference; a bad copy of the Ming version.

"So, my favorite *lǎo piáo* graces us with his presence, " Jun Min sneered. "Come, let us get to work."

The two wound their way down the crooked corridor, past the frantic shouts in the lottery and fantan rooms.

"Today, I have special treat," Jun Min announced in a parody of his Chinese accent. "You like velly much. You clean opium rooms. Make nice-y nice-y. Make sure supply good."

Shu Wei stood, stunned that a fellow Chinese would openly mock his own people. These Hap Tran Tong people, he concluded, were born perverse. They were bullies and freaks—*guài dàns*. He'd certainly had his fill of them. Descending into the dank basement, memories came racing back to Shu Wei. His first pull on an opium pipe. The first glimpse of the vacant eyes of the limp bodies sprawled in contorted masses.

Demeaning. The word struck Shu Wei. *I am now the lowest of the low. I service the users. The addicts. The wasted ones.*

"Now, be a good little Chink and do as I say. Jun Min has some business to attend to upstairs. Important business. I'll be back to check on things."

Shu Wei tidied the items in the opium storage room, each one bearing a coating of sticky opium residue. He was stunned by the variety of smoker's lamps, pipe bowls, wicks, small opium jars and cans, vials, alcohol bowls, hollowed-out scales, and pipe stems. He did his best to clean out the glass and tin items resting in a rancid sludge on the bottom of the sink—a sink that had not been touched by a cleaning agent in years. A nearby table was equally stained with congealed layers of brown and black grime.

He adjusted the flame of his kerosene lamp, bringing eerie shadows to the dank room. The top shelf was barely within reach. Standing tiptoe he leaned on a shelf for balance. The shelves all moved slightly—at once. He pushed a little harder. A metallic crack. They moved even more.

Shu Wei paused, took a breath and gathered his wits. If this was a secret door, it certainly wasn't secured. Just as he thought this, he noticed a keyhole in the middle of the backing boards. He figured that someone had forgotten to turn the key in the lock. As he pushed the door with the shelves around to its fully open position, the source of the cracking noise became clear. Moisture in this perpetually damp environment had corroded the metal bar of the locking mechanism of the door. Shu Wei's earlier pressure must have been just enough to make it fail.

A drip from the ceiling snaked its way down his queue. A shiver coursed up and down his spine as he faced his new dilemma: whether to probe further or turn back and replace the shelf-door as if nothing had happened. Something, a hunch, an innate curiosity—a curiosity that he realized had bedeviled him before—nudged him on. The swaying lantern he held threw smudges of hazy golden light on the darkened surfaces. Fumes from the lamp oil thickened the air in the cramped space. He painstakingly closed the shelf-door behind him.

The flickering lamplight bounced crazily down a narrow stairway that plunged toward endless murkiness. Shu Wei's resolve wavered. Sweat now beaded on his brow. His slippered feet glided silently down the steps. Even so, the wooden treads groaned. At the stairway bottom he could barely make out the walls of a low-ceilinged corridor braced with heavy wood posts; the handiwork of someone gifted in the art of square-set timbering.

Shu Wei plunged further into the ink-black passageway. He was about to turn around when his groping hand felt a small indent in the adjacent wall. Raising the lantern, he could make out the edges of an enameled metal box resting in a deep square niche.

Glancing back toward the still-closed shelf-door of the storage room, he listened for any audible signs of activity. Suddenly, a skitter. A furry, whiskered rodent sniffed Shu Wei's slippers and bolted away, as if on an advanced mission to inspect this intruder. Shu Wei could almost hear the echoes of his heartbeat off the slimy walls. He covered his mouth while he exhaled three deep calming breaths.

Gently raising the lid on the box, he discovered a thick pebbled leather book with a bronze clasp. He set the lantern down and carefully folded back the cover. As he scanned the first few pages, the cadence of his pulse grew increasingly ragged. He stiffened, his quick spurts of breath forming feathery puffs in the humid air. The lantern clanged against the wall as he raised it to throw light on the pages. Another skitter. A tightening of the jaw.

The inky flourish of the Chinese characters on the first pages offered few clues at first. But then, Shu Wei's stomach clenched. The next few passages disclosed one revelation after another. He was ecstatic at the find. This would provide substantial evidence against the Hap Tran Tong. Shu Wei cradled the mildewed volume like a newborn.

His heart galloping again, he stood and eased the collapsible camera from its special pocket in his tunic. Just as he raised the camera into position for the first shot, the wick inside the lamp flared like a dying comet and died. The kerosene was gone.

Now what? He could replace the book, retrace his steps back to the opium storage room, or . . . take the book and continue to grope his way through the dark, hopefully to a safe haven. *It's all or nothing. I can't afford to pass up this chance.*

Shu Wei began his slow, deliberate slog along the tunnel. The dampness entered his bones. A fine silty powder drifted down and carpeted his head and shoulders. His hands waved at cobwebs in broad sweeps as if he were warding off the spirits.

Now the tunnel turned and seemed to slope upward, a promising sign. His foot landed on something soft, lumpy. A cacophony of squeals. Furious scuffling. Shu Wei had disturbed a nursery of baby rodents—no doubt the offspring of the furry inquisitor he had encountered earlier. He pushed on, quickening his pace.

Another turn in the narrowing chute. A steeper incline. The ceiling was now ominously close, pressing down. No time for claustrophobia. And then, a faint shimmering ahead, lower down. His pace quickened into a clumsy stagger. As he approached, the ever-brightening ray of light appeared to be leaking from the base of a door. He stopped in a panic. Currents of icy fear. *What if Jun Min is waiting on the other side of that door?* He took two steps back. But he knew he had come too far to retreat now. Inching toward the door he heard muted voices. More anxious tremors. He pulled up on a rust-encrusted lever and pushed on the door. Nothing. He pushed again, harder.

The door gave slightly. This time he drove his shoulder into it. Liberation! He was showered with reflected light from a nearby window. Pulling the door closed so that it latched, he looked around furtively. But where was he?

His legs became rubbery. Shu Wei fought to regain his composure. Then he heard the high-pitched vocals. The tinny pleading of the *suǒnà*, the double-reeded horn. This had to be the Chinese Opera House. Clutching the book as though it were some ancient artifact, he began a headlong dash down the lane that led to tiny Adler Street. Fully expecting to encounter Jun Min, Shu Wei's legs churned like the spokes of a water wheel, his feet barely grazing the ground. He turned onto Dupont Street, frantically zigzagging to avoid pushcarts, sidewalk merchandise, and idlers poring over notices on a brick wall. A band of pigeons, feeding on curbside leftovers, exploded in flight.

All the air was driven from his overheated lungs as he finally arrived at *The News* offices. When he charged through the door, Fan Ching and Mei Huang flew from their chairs and flattened themselves against the wall, thinking their lives were about to end.

"What in the name of the Eight Immortals is going on?" blurted Mei Huang.

Shu Wei, red-faced and out of breath, retrieved the book from inside his tunic and slammed it onto the table. "Here . . . found this in a niche in a secret tunnel at the Hap Tran Tong headquarters. I stole it and then had to fight my way through rats and then found a door and raced here and . . ." panted Shu Wei.

"Maybe if you could slow down and tell us exactly what happened we might comprehend what you're saying," implored Fan Ching.

Shu Wei launched into a detailed account of his discovery and the contents of the book. Mei Huang and Fan Ching exchanged knowing glances as they slowly absorbed the significance of the find. They knew that once the Bo Cai story and other evidence of the Tong's criminal activities were released, it would most likely be the undoing of the Tong. But, they also faced the imminent threat that came with it: the risk to their own lives.

"I don't know if my friends at the Tong headquarters discovered that their book is missing yet," said Shu Wei. "It may take them a while. In the meantime, I need to make my visit to the Globe Hotel before it's too late to hopefully discover the identity of Marie Banier's killer."

"Whoa, whoa, let's take one thing at a time," insisted Mei Huang. "Before you scared the wits from us just now, we were discussing the dangers we face."

"First, it would be prudent for all of us to stay as far underground as we can from now on," advised Fan Ching. "We are at the point where we need to make ourselves less visible and take other precautions. Toward that end, I have already arranged for alternative living quarters for each of us. Shu Wei, you will now be staying in a room over a Chinese tea warehouse on Sacramento Street. Also, we will need to walk about in twos whenever we go out.

"I have had inspections made of our building fire escape to ensure it's safe for quick exits. But, nonetheless, we have to still put out a paper. Now, let's look at what this book is all about. By the way, Shu Wei, I would like you to photograph key pages immediately—as a backup copy."

Fan Ching locked the entry door and threw the new heavy security bar. The three began looking through the book with a focused intensity. The warmth of the room intensified the book's moldy odor. A fine dusty grime stiffened the sheets.

"It looks like the last entry was two weeks ago," observed Fan Ching. "So, chances are, Shu Wei, that the missing book won't be discovered for a while. But, of course, we don't know that."

The second page displayed the signatures of the two primary principals of the Tong, Jun Min and Yong Qiang. Their name seals bore images of serpents, dragons, and swords.

"Oh my," said Mei Huang, "this is startling."

Three full pages of girls' names listed original purchase prices, sales prices, names of purchasers, points of sale and entries to the country, personal details with rankings for beauty and desirability, and ultimate destination. Most were assigned to San Francisco Chinatown "clients," but a good many ended up in mining towns and farms. Bo Cai was number thirty five on the list.

Records of opium sales filled ten pages. Details spelled out suppliers, distributors, points of sale, ports of origin and delivery, income, and profit. Johnny Two-Fingers accounted for roughly one sixth of all transactions.

Gambling consumed the majority of the book. Some twenty-five pages detailed monthly takes at the booking outlets, transfers to local "banks," names of dealers, gamekeepers, brokers, and "special operatives."

One category covered "protection transactions" between the Hap Tran Tong and merchants, benevolent associations, and individuals. Some entries were labeled "uncooperative," "troublesome," or "needs special visit."

The next to last section of pages in the book brought universal scowls and looks of consternation to all three. Titled, "Main Enemies of the Hap Tran Tong," the listings were entered in various ink colors apparently denoting levels of perceived threats. Those in red, the highest target level, included certain newspapers, schools, and individuals. Among these, *The Golden Hills' News*, Grace Caldwell, and the Occidental Home, were underscored with two heavy lines that almost pierced the thick parchment.

"Well, I guess we know where we stand," said Mei Huang. "If we're on their list, we must be doing something right."

Shu Wei shot her a puzzled look. She nudged him playfully, as if to invoke humor as a balm. The pained look on Shu Wei's face slowly dissolved into a reluctant half-grin.

"Remember what I said, Shu Wei," broke in Mei Huang, "you and I are in this together. When you get to it, I would be happy to go with you to the Globe Hotel."

"My, oh my, no!" Shu Wei cried out. "I wouldn't want you in harm's way. I have already enlisted my new friend, Brian O'Grady."

"Isn't that the same one that caused you so much grief before?" quizzed Fan Ching.

"Correct. But we have . . . well, we have reached an understanding—even though my sister is still highly suspicious of his motives."

Finally, flipping to the last pages of the book, Shu Wei's eyes grew as large as marbles. He held his left hand to his mouth and let out a breath that was half whistle. "Now I know why my instincts said to take the risk with this book," he said. "This is truly amazing!"

Depicted in a rough schematic diagram beneath the title "Society Members," was an array of the Tong's international players and syndicates. Prominently placed at the top was Yong Qiang and his operations in Hong Kong, Sichuan, Yunnan, and lastly, Sanhou. The Fiery Dragon had many tails.

CHAPTER THIRTY TWO

The Globe Hotel

Emboldened by his coup of retrieving the book exposing the Hap Tran Tong's illegal dealings, Shu Wei decided to press on with his investigation of the Globe Hotel. He knew that he had limited time. Jun Min was no doubt wondering where he had gone after his half-finished cleanup assignment in the opium den.

The next day, before the shopkeepers had opened their window shutters, Shu Wei waited in the cramped lobby of his temporary residence on Sacramento Street. He had the collar turned up on his pea coat that Brian had loaned him. A black bowler, pulled low, was parked over one eyebrow. Brian made eye contact as he went past and Shu Wei hurried to join him. The two strode briskly toward the Globe through shadowy back alleys and passageways.

As the two approached the hotel, Shu Wei's throat tightened. The few leads for the possible killer of Marie Banier that he got from Sergeant Growman were sketchy, at best.

The four-story hotel stood at the corner of Dupont and Jackson Streets. A German named Schaeffer had built it in 1860 as a "fine house" for the entertainment of German guests. An exhausted pile of weather-beaten brick, its facades still hinted at a dressy pedigree of an earlier age.

Fan Ching had told Shu Wei that the lodgings on the upper floors provided a view of the towers of St. Francis Assissium and the spires of Señora de Guadeloupe at the northern edges of Chinatown, but from what Shu Wei could tell, the grimy windows wouldn't allow many views at all.

The two had to step gingerly past two squatting men who had commandeered the steps to the main entrance. Opening the front door, they were greeted with a musty and putrid stench that took their breath away. "This will take some gettin' used ta," said Brian. "My sniffer has its limits."

As they made their way to the reception desk, a scrawny rat scampered between Shu Wei's legs, causing him to jump. Water stains gave the striped wallpaper behind the desk the appearance of an ancient Chinese brush painting. Debris littered the cracked marble floor and a battered spittoon lay on its side, its contents trickling out. A snoring man was curled up on a sagging purple couch, his long shaggy beard fluttering with each exhalation. A squadron of flies was practicing takeoffs and landings on a nearby trash barrel.

A disinterested older Chinese man sat at the reception desk, feet propped on an overturned packing crate, his head buried in a crinkled newspaper. His mouth released a projectile of seeds at regular intervals.

"Yeah, what the devil brings you two to our glorious palace?" barked the man.

"Are you Jimmy Sun?" asked Shu Wei.

"Yep. You must be the two from *The News*. No one else in their right mind would show up here."

Jimmy said that the building had been condemned by the city, but the new owners had refused to comply with a court order. The City was seeking a new injunction.

"You might want to watch your step. Other day one of our residents put his foot through a pair of rotting floor planks in a hallway and damn near tore his leg off. No cop or ambulance attendant will set foot in here, so the poor soul had to drag his torn limb for four blocks until a guy in a carriage took him to the hospital. Heard he died of shock."

Shu Wei and Brian looked at one another with equal amounts of bewilderment and concern, not sure if the old man meant this as a scare tactic or a legitimate warning. Barely looking up from his newspaper, Jimmy handed the two a crumpled piece of paper with some names and room numbers.

Brian had suggested he be the one to stay in the staircase and be available if needed. Shu Wei was to yell out for him in case he was in trouble. He told Brian that his only concern was being locked in a room with a maniac.

"Ya just cut your worryin' mate," Brian replied, "I've got a lotta shoulder and these doors here don't look like they'd take much ta splinter 'em."

"Let's get going then," suggested Shu Wei. "I want to make quick work of this. The less time we spend in this cursed place the better."

Brian borrowed a wobbly three-legged stool from a corner of the lobby. As they made their way on to the stairs, they encountered their first obstacle: a man sat crouched in a corner, shoveling food from a carton into his toothless mouth with chopsticks. His earnest grin widened as they attempted to maneuver around him. He muttered, "You sit, you eat, you like . . . be friend." They delicately stepped over an outstretched leg.

Further up, at the second landing, an emaciated black cat, bared its fang-like teeth and spit out a breathy growl. Arching its back, it huddled over its treasure: three lifeless rats with beaded eyes and festering sores from puncture wounds.

A wall-mounted gas fixture spurted chalky light, revealing decaying wooden banisters and steps strewn with decaying magazines and newspapers. The air was a damp potpourri of pungent cigars, cheap liquor, and opium vapors.

"How 'bout ya stay in the stairway and I go do the interviews," suggested Brian.

"When you get good at the stairs thing then we'll talk about other options," responded Shu Wei with a half-smile and a gentle slap to the back of Brian's head. "You need to work from the ground up."

Brian's shoulders drooped in mock devastation. "You're a hard lad ta work for, know that?"

When they reached the third floor Brian settled in on his stool and Shu Wei went in search of room 308. Shu Wei had just left the stairwell when a man with a nightshirt loosely draped over his gaunt frame bounced past, skipping every other step and chanting something in what Brian assumed was Chinese. His coal-black hair was arrayed in great plumes, bird like. Brian guessed it was some kind of ritual. After twenty repetitions up and down the stairs, the man disappeared with a final "Who-o-o-p." Brian breathed heavily and slumped back against the wall wondering when the next freakish soul would appear.

Shu Wei stood in front of room 308 unmoving, gripping his notebook and thinking what pathetic protection it would offer. His knock was gentle. Hearing nothing from inside, he knocked more firmly, the thin wood giving slightly. Finally a faint "Come in." Shu Wei eased the door open. The small room was cell-like. A badly-stained mattress lay on the floor, partly covered by an olive-colored wool blanket with ragged holes and singed edges. A clothesline attached to a hook on the window jamb extended diagonally to a nail in another corner. Sweat-stained undershirts and pants, thin from wear, decorated the line. A single bulb hung from the ceiling of rotting plaster.

Shu Wei looked warily around, glad that he had left the door ajar. Then he was grabbed from behind.

"Hey, lookin' fer me? Visitors good. Always give warm welcome. Call me jokester 'round here. Some say you need talk."

Gwong Fen had skin that could be mistaken for aged horsehide. His fingers nested into one another, arthritically. The whites of his eyes overwhelmed his small penetrating hazel pupils. A faded denim work shirt engulfed his bony body, nearly obscuring his filthy tan pants. Shu Wei stood while his interviewee settled onto the mattress after extracting his opium paraphernalia from a tattered leather bag.

"Thank you for speaking with me," began Shu Wei. "I will be brief. Did you know Marie Banier? Did anyone you know speak of her?"

"Ha, Everyone know Marie. She very nice lady. Brought fruit to hotel. One time see me sleeping on sidewalk—on newspaper. She give money. I say couldn't take. She give anyway."

Gwong Fen launched into a fusillade of words. "Many years working railroad. Central Pacific. Other men steal Gwong Fen food, even money then. Lots danger. Rocks fall on Gwong Fen. Still have scars.

While Gwong Fen continued his diatribe, Shu Wei was assessing this man as a potential killer. His stories painted a picture of a man who knew hard labor and had little money. No money was taken from Marie at the time of her murder. It seemed more of a revenge killing. Shu Wei had already guessed that this man was probably not involved with Marie in a romantic way. Her standards were considerably higher than an eccentric laborer.

"Did you know of Marie's death?"

"Ah. Yes. Sad day. Everybody know. Gwong Fen sick like dog that day. Neighbor friend, Clever Jimmy, he bring soup to me. He say 'you look like boiled rabbit.' Ha! Jimmy always funny."

Shu Wei was anxious to move on. He thanked Gwong Fen and backed from the room, keeping a wary eye on his subject.

Brian jumped nervously from his stool on the landing as Shu Wei opened the door.

"Rough time on the stairs?" Shu Wei kidded.

"My lad, an entire tribe a weirdos and wackos has passed through my portal. Problem was I was anchored at my station. One chubby half-brainer tried ta visit my lap. Had ta say I'm waitin' on my boyfriend—he'll be comin' along shortly. He moved on kinda sad-eyed."

"Well, while you were having your fun, I didn't get very far in the first round. Gwong Fen seemed like he had a pretty sturdy alibi. Don't think it's worth pursuing."

"Shall we move on then? Who's up next?"

"It looks like Gip Sung-Jiang in 210. I'll try to get through this one before noon and then I think we regroup. I feel like it's kind of like finding a . . . what's the expression?"

"A needle," prompted Brian, "a needle in a haystack."

"Right. Another one of your Anglo-Celtic concoctions I'm guessing."

"Ah, lad, you've only begun ta know the lot a those."

Brian resumed his post, this time on the second floor stairway landing, while Shu Wei headed for room 210. As Brian stabilized his rickety seat, he could hear a loud argument in progress somewhere in the building. He only hoped the participants would keep their distance.

Gip Sung-Jiang's quarters in 210 were even smaller than Gwong Fen's. The man had no mattress. He appeared to sleep on a heap of mildewed clothing. Fish head remains, pieces of rotting fruit, and discarded jars with mysterious contents were strewn about. Shu Wei came close to gagging when he first entered the room. He focused on the task at hand.

Gip Sung-Jiang squatted and leaped about the room nervously. His hair grew in tufts. His skin was littered with sores. One eye glowed a deep scarlet. Shoeless, his feet wore a film of dirt. Fingers were permanently calloused with knobby joints. One cheek pulsed with a tic at regular intervals.

Shu Wei began unfurling his notebook as he lowered himself on one of the few scraps of flooring that was free of debris. His inner self was beginning to send out prompts. *Could be the killer. Erratic behavior. Unstable.* On the other hand, he had nothing solid to go by yet. And, if he applied the revenge-from-a-lover-spurned theory, that seemed highly unlikely. Unless Marie had also lost her senses by then, which he knew wasn't the case. While Gip Sung-Jiang continued to vault from corner to corner, Shu Wei started his questioning. What brought him to the Globe Hotel? When did he meet Marie and how? Had he heard about her murder?

Meanwhile, Brian had just resettled himself on his stool on the second floor landing, leaving the door to the hallway ajar. He was thinking how civilized and quiet the confines of the stairs had become when a shuffling noise arose from somewhere below him. At first, he thought it was a large rodent but then, gradually, an enfeebled man emerged at the lower landing, clutching the splinter-ridden handrail, hand over hand, as if he were rope-soloing up a rock face. The vapors of intoxication leaked upward to Brian's post.

Small growths of ivory hair on the man's head lay like fluffy snow drifts. Half-closed eyes were pocketed in an ashen angular face. A walrus mustache sagged over his upper lip, retaining specks of uncertain origin. An ascot lay in disarray beneath a high white collar. A red carnation, brown at the edges, drooped from one of the stained lapels of a satin-lapeled overcoat. Faded checkered pants, appeared to hold remnants of previous meals. When he finally noticed Brian, the haggard man paused abruptly and leaned, warily, on his black hickory cane.

"Whatsch thisch, a policeshman?" warbled the inebriated older man. He cocked his head like a bird listening on a wire. Or did you jush finish milkin' your cow? Har, har, har!"

"No, no, just waiting for me friend," replied Brian, glancing down at the stool he was sitting on.

"Shum friend. Leavin' you in the stairwell. Musht've been a fight or shumthin. Had to shtay in the shtair 'til things coo . . . cooled down, eh?"

"No, my friend is talking ta people in the building. We're with the local newspaper."

"Newshpaper? Didn't know we shtill had one round here. Mind if I sit down? Been doin' some tippin' o' the ol' bottle with a friend on the firsht floor. Nysh fellow but he drinksh too much. Talkin' over lotsch about women. Ashk me, they're all trouble. Shay, name's Clyde Bommer. Whatsch yours?"

"I go by Brian. Brian O'Grady."

"Nysh Italian name. Yoush to know shum of your folks. They were a shlippery bunch. Shold me shum bad shpikes for the railroad. I went after . . ."

"I'm Irish," interrupted Brian. "Come from County Kerry. By the way, what is a shpike?"

Clyde made a hammer-like motion. In doing so, he sagged into Brian's leg. Brian twisted sideways on the stool, keeping his distance.

"Lookit, you sheem like a nysh chap, how'd you and your friend like to come vishit me in my room. Got shum nysh rum, maybe shum vodka. Room 412. Nysh to have vishtors." With great effort, Clyde raised his lanky frame and made his way up the stairs, careening from wall to banister and back again.

Brian's mind had been at work while this human construct of oddness prattled on. A fop? A dandy? He couldn't quite put his finger on the right term. But, in any case, he was intrigued. He thought it was worth a mention to Shu Wei. And maybe a stop at Room 412.

Just as Shu Wei was exiting Gip Sung-Jiang's room, Brian came bursting around the corner. "How'd it go bud? Did ya have any luck?"

"No. I barely got him to stay still long enough to question him. When I did, he told me he never knew Marie and then he got angry and told me to leave. I guess it was the knife that convinced me that he meant business. This newspaper business gets riskier by the hour."

"Gave ya a lot a guff now, did he? Well, no sense in steppin' back when you're at the edge a the cliff. But, I might have a bloke of interest ta us. Came up the stairs a shambles—plastered, he was. But, somethin' about him got me ta thinkin'. The man had some fancy clothes—okay, they were fancy in their time. But he also made a knock about women. Now, it's not much, but might be worth checkin' inta."

"Alright Mr. Sherlock Holmes, just how do you suggest we approach this drunkard? Knock on all the doors until the right drunkard appears?"

"No, indeed. The very lush a which I speak has given us an invite ta his room. I know you're not inta sippin' the cordial and I'm on the wagon but we might, well . . . just for the sake a the chase, touch a glass with the polluted soul."

"Brian, I don't know why I would agree to this. He's not even on our list. I'm tired and hungry. Let's just get out of here."

The two made their way back to the stairs and were starting their descent when they heard, "Sha-a-y, ish thash your friend, Mr. Italiano?" Clyde had made it no further than the next landing up from where Brian had left him. "Whynsh ya come on up to my playsh. Got plenty of shpirits. No, no, not ghostshs. Har. Har."

"That's Clyde," said Brian. "He thinks I'm Italian. Couldn't convince him otherwise."

Shu Wei stared at this doddering creature. Shaking his head, he said "Well, what have we got to lose?"

Brian and Shu Wei jointly hoisted the soggy hulk off the staircase and guided him to the fourth floor. Shu Wei turned his head to avoid the fumes as they half-dragged him, his arms over their shoulders, to his door.

"Make yourshelves comfort—comfortable, hic," Clyde directed, pointing to a frayed daybed. "I'm jusht going to fresh—freshen up a bit."

Shu Wei looked around. He saw that the main room was by far larger, more tidy and organized than the other two he had visited. A wool blanket was neatly tucked beneath a mattress that rested on a carved oak frame. Ordered stacks of playing cards, paperbacks and cigar boxes, along with small figurines, all rested on a low teak table. Brian was right. There *was* something about this man that tugged at his curiosity. Some of the objects in the room were clearly antiques of value, items that suggested a former life well-lived. Possibly someone who could have traveled in Marie's society circles.

When Clyde returned to the room, he had clearly made some genuine, but mostly futile attempts, at restoring some parity between dishevelment and order. His hair had been forced into submission and his ascot was moored once again beneath his vest. Some of the bits had been combed from his mustache.

Landing heavily in a high back birch chair with velour cushions, Clyde exhaled a mighty push of air, sending his eyebrows in a turmoil. "Sho, you boysh are from a newshpaper. Whish one?"

"*The Golden Hills' News*," Shu Wei managed to spew out, wondering afterward if he should have been so open.

"Oh wait, I promised a nip to the Italianian here," Clyde said as he rose unsteadily and opened a cabinet with a mesh frame. "What do you boysh like? Brandy? Vodka?"

"I think we're just fine," responded Shu Wei, shooting a quick nervous glance at Brian.

"Good. Good. Brandy lovers, eh?" Clyde proceeded to pour healthy shots into three short cut-glass whiskey glasses.

Half the amber liquid ended up on the cabinet's top. After distributing the dripping vessels to Brian and Shu Wei, Clyde lumbered over to his chair, cane thudding, and once again launched himself backward into his chair. "Shorry if I misshed your names boys. You shay you're with the Golden Shtate News?"

"I'm Shu Wei and this is Brian. We're working on a story about Marie Banier for *The Golden Hills' News* and would like to ask a few questions."

At the mention of Marie's name Clyde froze, a great whoosh of brandy fled from his mouth, and his brandy glass went crashing to the floor.

"Good blazes in hell!" he snorted. "You have a demon's nerve to even menshen that bloody witch's name. That wash a woman that got what she desherves."

"Do you know about her death?" quizzed Shu Wei. "Anything at all? Any friend that would know something?"

"You're here to interro-terrogate me, arnsha you two shniveling good-for-nothings. Well, I'll have nothing of it! You can jush get out of here before I cane you both."

Clyde's lower lip trembled. His hand gripped his cane with an intensity that drew the color from his skin. He began slamming it into his palm, harder and harder. As the old inebriate began extracting himself from his chair, Brian and Shu Wei were stumbling toward the door, sensing a quick exit was the best course.

"No! no!" bellowed Clyde. "Wait. Shtop. Don't go. This ishn't right, leaving it like thish." He crashed back into his chair and threw his cane into the corner, knocking over a ceramic jug, creating more jagged shards on the floor. Shu Wei and Brian paused and cautiously turned around. This man, who seemed a harmless alcoholic a few minutes ago, proved to clearly have a volatile side as well. Shu Wei stood, unmoving, his mind swirling with possible outcomes should they stay. He decided to stay; he signaled that to Brian with his eyes.

"Sit down fellash. Thish is going to be hard for me. I've held onto . . ." Before he could finish his sentence, Clyde stiffened and let loose a barrage of sobbing. Shu Wei was transfixed. He'd never seen a man of Clyde's age so filled with raging sorrow. Shu Wei and Brian slowly lowered themselves back into their chairs.

Still shuddering but now reduced to pathetic sniffles, Clyde continued. He unraveled his ascot from around his neck and tossed it aside. "I've held onto my dirty sheecret too long. Firsht of all, my real name is Claude Parkford, not Clyde Bommer."

Shu Wei sat up board straight, as it suddenly came to him that this must be the very Claude Parkford, spouse of Evelyn Parkford. Incredible. *What on earth is he doing here in this rat hole?* he thought.

"Itsh time I cleanshed my soul. You shee, I've been hiding the truth—even from myshelf—for many yearsh. I . . .I wash the one who killed Marie Banier. The drink ish my only friend now."

Shu Wei's and Brian's hands reflexively shot up and covered their mouths, almost simultaneously. Shu Wei was now certain he would either get the story he was looking for or they would not make it out of the room alive.

"You shee," blabbered Claude, "I am a very shick man and my doc tellsh me my daysh are limited. I have a deathly brew of cancer and cirrhosis. As Leonardo da Vinci once shaid, 'While I thought that I wash learning how to live, I have been learning how to die.' In what little time I have left I want to lay my blackesht deedsh before my Maker to give him a chance to find forgivenesh."

Shu Wei delicately extracted his notebook. His eyes drifted to a small bronze cross on the wall with an embossed figure of

Jesus, his torso partially draped, arms splayed out and his head bent aside, eyes closed. He wondered if this were the "Maker" that Claude spoke of. *Just how does this Maker person give forgiveness in this case?*

As Claude's head dropped, the tufts of white hair bobbed in cadence with his trembling body.

"I wash never one to find marriage a shacred inshtitution. It sheemed too confining, too reshtrictive. For me, the purshuit of women grew into an obsesshion. My wife, Evelyn, knew about my lusht to wander from the beginning. At firsht, she thought I wash shimply shpending time on my business. But then she began picking up on those little loose hairsh on my coatsh, and lipstick smearsh on perfumed shirts. I couldn't shtop though. My cravings were endless."

Shu Wei had settled his nerves by now, searching for the chance to probe further. Brian sat composed, unwilling to enter the conversation.

"Can I ask how you met Marie?" ventured Shu Wei, sensing a point of entry.

"I met Marie at one of thoshe fancy partiesh up in Pacific Heights. She glowed. She was like no one I had ever met. Kind in her nature but full of shpunk. Asshertive. Very attractive. And, like me, had money." Claude reached for another glass and poured a new supply of brandy, swirling it with abandon until it overflowed onto his pants.

"We began sheeing each other in dishcrete places. Then, boldly, one day, we met at her houshe. Shtarted developing into a habit—middaysh, sometimes eveningsh. One of Evelyn's friends happened by one night as I wash leaving her home." Claude raised a new refilled glass to his lips, lowered it again, tugging at his shirt collar.

Claude sputtered on. "Well, I knew the cat wash out of the bag. Sure enough, Evelyn confronted me the nexsht evening. Shaid she would be filing for a divorce. Then she confronted

Marie. Marie didn't take kindly to the inquishition. She felt her privacy had been invaded and, worshe, her standing in shocial circles was at risk. That'sh when things shtarted getting ugly. Marie shtarted circulating rumorsh about me; that I wash a homoshexual, a drug addict, an alcoholic. None of these wash true of courshe, at the time.

"The rumorsh began to shtick and affect my bushiness affairs. Orders for the railroad project dropped dramatically. That'sh when the heavy drinking began. In a befuddled state at a bar one night, I decided on a drastic measure. Marie would have to go."

Shu Wei's fingers tightened on his pen. He stole a glance at Brian who had downed his glass of brandy but was still clutching it mid-air, his eyes fixated on Claude.

Claude rocked back and forth like a child contemplating admitting guilt to his parents. The sobbing began again. It slowed. The glass rose to his mouth. This time he flung it against a wall. More shards. The brown liquid made a vein-like tracery on the wall. Claude watched, mesmerized by its tedious trickle.

"I never would have had the courage to do it myshelf. I hired a Tong member. From the Hap Tran Tong. I shpent nearly what wash left of my money. He wash a willing chap, with a heart of shtone. I never knew the details, jusht the outcome. He and I never shpoke again, or shaw each other. He died in a Tong fight five yearsh later. They never traced it back to me. Well, many had sushpicions but they had no sholid proof. I shpent a few yearsh trying to regain my footing in the bishness but it wash of no yoush. People avoided me. That'sh when I moved up to the Shierras into a cabin for a few yearsh. Came back and shettled into the Globe after a mad bloke came after me wisch a cleaver."

Still reeling from the mention of the Tong, Shu Wei steeled himself and jumped in. "I heard there was a one-year-

223

old child living in the room next to Marie who was spared. Were you aware of this at the time of the murder?"

"No. Jusht ash well. My grief got to be heavy enough once the deed wash done. I hadn't sheen Marie for a year-and-a-half before that. At least they couldn't shay the baby wash mine.

"You two are the one and only reposhitory of my grief and my confesshion. Undershtand that I acted under exshtreme emotional distress. I wasn't myshelf. Of course, I realize I'll pay the penalty for all of this but, I jusht want to bring an end to the mental anguish, the unending nightmares, shpecially when I have a limited time left."

Shu Wei closed his notebook and folded his hands in his lap. Brian's head was wagging back and forth in disbelief. The two squirmed in their seats in unison, both relying on controlled breathing to deal with what they had just heard.

Claude rose from his chair abruptly and located another glass, filling it to the rim. A ray of light from a window twinkled off the cut-glass. "I shuppose thish should be a kind of toasht," he began. "A toasht to the shedding of sins. A toasht to the finality of all this incessant madness. And, to you boysh, you got what you came for. Now, get the hell out, and run back to your newshpaper, whatever the name of that rag ish."

Shu Wei and Brian crept toward the door, sidestepping broken glass. Their steps were leaden, deliberate. While they retreated, Shu Wei didn't feel they'd heard the last of Claude. He was right.

"Whoa, you two!" commanded Claude. "One lasht thing. Are you fellash any good at writing obituaries?"

CHAPTER THIRTY THREE

Another Fire

Following the emotional interview with Claude Parkford, Shu Wei and Brian walked briskly toward *The News* offices. Shu Wei kept his head down and pulled his bulky hat to his eyebrows. While he was giddy with the uncovering of Marie Banier's killer and the grand story it would make, he was filled with grief for Perrier, and a heightened fear regarding his own precarious future. Yet another psychopath. *How many more can I encounter? Surely, there's a limit.* Claude's particular brand of delirium was energized by revenge. But wasn't he himself on his own mission of revenge? Yes, but he was convinced that his type of revenge was of a whole different variety. His was revenge aimed more at acts of moral turpitude.

Shu Wei was oblivious to the darkening scene as the two quickly worked their way from Shu Wei's temporary residence on Sacramento Street. As the light was drawn from the streets, merchants were lowering wrought iron bars across the wooden planks of their storefronts. A cat with prominent ribs looked up momentarily and then continued nonchalantly bathing his outstretched rear leg.

Next to Shu Wei, Brian was giddy with his new status: a contributing member of the team. Breaking through his companion's trance, he blurted, "Well, my pal, looks like we're lookin' at some real *comhaltas*. That's jargon in my homeland for the power of workin' together."

Shu Wei nodded. His mind was at work, not on Brian, but on introducing another element to his friendship with Mei Huang. For now, it seemed right. He brought his arm around Brian's broad shoulders.

The pair turned the corner onto Dupont Street. Dark shadows lazed across the cobbled street, appearing as a field of lumpy coal. As the two passed by Long Bin's Toy Emporium something caught Brian's eye.

"Take a gander . . . over there." Brian pointed to a news rack in front of the toy store. It held the latest edition of *The Golden Hills' News.* Shu Wei let out a smothered gasp, a toxic mix of dread and shock foaming up in his stomach. He scanned the front page headlining the story of the rescue of Bo Cai, along with her picture and credits to Shu Wei and Mei Huang. Shu Wei ripped the paper from its stand and stood huddled in a doorway, shaking. As he read further, his irritation at Fan Ching for releasing the story slowly faded. Isn't this what he'd been working toward? He needed to learn to live with these added dangers. *Just think what that poor girl went through*, he thought with a shiver.

"Come along, mate," urged Brian. "You're startin' ta burn a hole in that sidewalk. We need ta keep on the go."

It seemed to Shu Wei like the shadows had grown meaner, more sinister, his safety now more in question than ever, as he and Brian finally turned down the back alley toward the stair-way to *The News.*

Reaching the newly reinforced door of *The News* offices, Shu Wei rapped out their new code. *How pathetic*, he thought. Why would the Tong even bother with knocking? Fan Ching opened the peephole. A few moments later the door swung open. The staff was relaxing around the large table in the center of the room after just having printed the next day's paper.

Shu Wei tossed his notebook and the rumpled newspaper onto a corner of the table. Perrier was in the process of pouring cognac into two cut-glass tumblers. Two steaming cups of tea sat before Jake Bradley and Mei Huang who lounged at the big oak proofing table, arms draped over their chairs.

"Well, it's the hardened street reporter duo returning from the field of battle," said Perrier as he saluted the two with his glass.

Ignoring Perrier's comment, Shu Wei said in a clearly anguished tone, peering at Fan Ching, "I didn't think you were going to use my name on this article! I guess you know that the entire Hap Tran Tong will now be after me."

"Correction; after us," Fan Ching pointed out. "I never *promised* I would publish without a source," he said. "Besides, I decided that you and Mei Huang put together such a good story that the world out there ought to know who's responsible. Our little community newspaper needs to build up our image. We're printing fact-based stories with broad relevance and not just for our own edification. Now, let's see what you learned at the Globe."

Shu Wei was momentarily distracted by the casual nature of Fan Ching's request. He provocatively leafed through the pages of his notebook. Brian grinned broadly as he idly stuffed his hands in his back pockets.

Refills of tea and cognac were poured. The room grew increasingly quiet as Shu Wei began reading from his interview notes. Fan Ching nervously tapped his fingers on the table. When Shu Wei had finished relating the last details of Claude's confession, only the horse carts and vendors hawking their wares on the street below could be heard.

The group at the table sat stunned, still trying to comprehend the gravity of Shu Wei's words. Finally, Fan Ching blurted out, "Oh, my heavens! Are you sure? What a phenomenal story! This is the stuff of national interest. You have caught the story of the year. This is extraordinary! We must celebrate!"

Perrier was clearly stirred by the revelations. When the commotion had faded, he spoke in a somber tone. "Shu Wei, I am deeply moved by your initiative to go into this hotel and uncover what has troubled me for so many years. And a special thanks as well to Brian for his allegiance to the cause. You both are to be commended.

"We will never know whether this demonic man has felt any remorse over his deeds these many years. But this would be a minor punishment in comparison to my agony. With his confession, he has lifted the mystery for me and has given me a degree of closure that I never thought possible. Whether his confession is conscience-driven or because of the inevitability of his demise, I care not. The courts will write that final chapter. As for the issue of my father's identity, I don't pretend to have more than speculation myself. I will leave it at that for the time being. I am too weary of it all to pursue that course any further."

Shu Wei added, "I am all too afraid of breaking the news to Evelyn Parkford. She is somewhat frail and will need some comfort. It will come as a shock."

"Indeed, a sensitive issue, to say the least," offered Fan Ching. "At least she too, will get closure on her troubled marriage and Claude's dalliances. Isn't it odd how messy the world can be sometimes? This story will no doubt put our little paper on the map, so to speak. But, of course, Claude's confession will need to be corroborated and documented by our police friends. He will no doubt be brought into custody. For now, let's raise a glass to our brilliant staff, shall we? Brian, this now includes you as well.

"After we celebrate, I would like us all to huddle around and plot our strategy for getting this story into print. My guess is that it will take several days. Mei Huang, I'll need you to help Shu Wei get his notes in order. And, let us remember that we all need to stay alert. Our friends at the Tong will not stand idly by in the meantime."

The next morning, while *The News*'s story of Bo Cai spread through Chinatown, Perrier and Fan Ching sequestered themselves with the police and went over the story of Claude's confession, along with the copy of the Tong's ledger book and other revelations from Shu Wei's notebook.

"You folks have finally led us to what we've been tryin' to get hard proof on for years," clucked Sergeant Growman. "I'll have my men digest all this and put together a summary document. That will get us close to having papers for the property searches and indictment.

"Tell you what: You and your staff, Fan Ching, will now be subject to every nasty trick in the book by the Tong. I'm short on men so I can't be givin' you personal protection, maybe an occasional escort. But, I can offer you access to me around the clock through the gals at the switchboard on Washington Street. I have a feeling things are about to get real hot around here."

Later that evening, around eight o'clock, Brian and Shu Wei were still at *The News* offices. They pleaded exhaustion and said goodnight to Jake Bradley who was dealing with a stuck button on the Mergenthaler keyboard. Perrier, Fan Ching, and Mei Huang had left under the escort of one of Sergeant Growman's men dressed in street clothes. "Don't stay late, Jake," admonished Shu Wei, "and make certain you be aware of your surroundings."

Wearing another one of Brian's stock of navy pea coats and matching caps he kept at *The News* offices, Shu Wei was almost invisible on the darkened streets. Brian walked five paces behind Shu Wei, constantly sizing up the flow of the crowds along Dupont Street. Forcing airs of nonchalance, they both paused often to peer into store windows.

As Shu Wei turned left down Sacramento Street, Brian suddenly ran to him and whispered a desperate, "*Luàn zi!,*" one of several Chinese words for trouble he had learned from Shu Wei. Heat surged through Shu Wei's body like a furnace. He felt as though he might swallow his heart whole at the signal from Brian. Brian led him by the elbow into an alley.

"Someone behind me on Dupont Street yelled 'Fire!'" Brian breathed loudly into Shu Wei's ear. "I looked up and ... and saw smoke about where *The News* offices are. We need ta go back. Jake may be in trouble. The Tong must have seen us leave."

Shu Wei could only stare numbly at his companion at this revelation. Repressed images of the fire at his father's business in Sanhou leaped back into his mind. Memories of the snapping embers, acrid smoke and hungry fingers of flame were still very much embedded in his subconscious. The same jolt of fear and panic he'd felt on that fiery night settled over him. But he had to act. He owed it to *The News* and to Jake. They couldn't afford to delay.

As Shu Wei and Brian approached *The News* building, small wisps of smoke leaked from around the window sash on the third floor. A flickering glow erupted behind one of the window panes. Two figures were backlit by a streetlight as they passed beneath a canopy near the rear door off the alley. Shu Wei knew that distinctive bend in the profile of one. Yong Qiang. Shu Wei wrestled his camera from an inner pocket of the pea coat and snapped off two pictures.

"Forget them!" urged Brian. "We're gonna have ta get on with the business at hand. C'mon, let's see what gives upstairs."

Shu Wei followed, terror mounting. He froze when he encountered an ax buried in the splintered boards of the door leading to the back stairs. He eased the ax from the door. He and Brian scrambled up the stairs, smoke slowly biting their lungs. The press room was a nightmare of destruction. A growing knot of flames in the corner was quickly devouring a stack of proofs.

"Quick, Shu Wei, grab that and give it ta me!" Brian yelled, pointing to a wool blanket on the floor. It normally covered the press. Taking it, Brian dampened the worst of the small fire in a corner where the stack of proofs had combusted. The clanging bell of the arriving fire cart echoed off the buildings, the horses spouting steamy snorts as their hooves clattered on the stony street.

Shu Wei assessed the damage. The linotype machine had been attacked with an enormous iron bar that now lay in a bed of bent and tortured parts. Spring screws, rail levers, dowels, and threaded shanks lay strewn about on the floor. The motor had been levered from its seat and mutilated, oil poured uniformly over the machine. Developing and fixing fluids were sprinkled over everything in the room.

The small cylinder press stood intact except for the defacing of its drum, some of the gear cams and cranks, and the upper bed. As he bent to examine a tray of printing inks that had been smashed he heard Brian call out. "Over here! Hurry!"

Stumbling over debris, Shu Wei instinctively clamped his hand over his mouth when he reached the darkroom. Jake Bradley was writhing in a corner, hands shackled by cords. Heavy tape covered his mouth. More tape encircled his eyes and head. Scarlet scratches and nicks covered his forearms and hands, testament to a struggle. To his right, a large knife pinned a pile of Shu Wei's notes and story drafts to the floor boards. Lying alongside was a note written in Chinese. It said: "No more stories. Death to the *The News*. Death to the fools who print lies. *The Hap Tran Tong*."

It was another horrific flashback for Shu Wei but this man was alive, thank goodness. He grabbed a knife from the work table and cut Jake loose. He carefully unwound the tape from his constricted jaw and eyes. In raspy bursts Jake spurted, "I . . .

I heard a horrible racket. These men chopped their way through the main door. They were on me in no time. One was carrying a large knife. He came at me and pulled my hands behind my back. He had a mask on so I couldn't see his face. I did see a scar on his left hand and he had a large ring with two serpents on his right hand. He walked with a limp."

At that moment, firemen burst through the door carrying hoses and axes. They immediately doused the still-glowing pile of embers in the corner. Right behind them were Fan Ching, Perrier, and Mei Huang. "Our neighbor in the restaurant next door heard the racket and came over and got me," blurted Fan Ching. "This is a horrible thing for us all. Are you okay, Jake?"

"I'll live to see another day, but my arms and head ache," moaned Jake. "I guess I'm lucky they weren't *really* angry. My parts might've ended up on the floor with all the rest."

"How are you two?" quizzed Mei Huang, looking in the direction of Shu Wei and Brian.

"We're fine," said Brian. "'Tis a bloody shame we didn't get here sooner though. These hoodlums must have watched us leave earlier. So much for the secret entrance."

"This may put us out of business," suggested Fan Ching. "We won't know until we assess all the damage. This was old equipment to begin with, but it still had some years left. I hadn't planned on replacing it until our circulation went up. Our insurance carriers dropped us last year when we couldn't keep up with the payments."

Brian broke in, "We'll get her up and going, don't you fret lads. Shu Wei and I . . ."

"I appreciate your spirit," said Fan Ching, "but you two already have your hands full. I'm not sure how we'll cover it, but we'll find a way. The Tong is hoping we'll just give up and quit."

Sergeant Growman and Wu Kang Ho clambered up the stairs and joined the group, pausing to catch their breath. "Holy saints above!" spat the Sergeant. "The slimy despicable louses who did this will be caught—I swear on the sacred cross of Saint Patrick."

"Shu Wei, I'd like you to take pictures of this mess," said the sergeant. "Then, if you'll lend me your camera overnight, I can have my police lab develop them so we can use them for evidence."

Wu Kang Ho said, "I am truly sorry for this awful situation Fan Ching. If there is anything I can do . . ."

"Your simply being here is a start—and that goes for all of you."

The firemen shoveled the reeking charcoal pile into some metal wastebaskets. "Looks like we've got it covered here, Sergeant," one of them said. "We'll get this down to the sidewalk so there won't be any chance of a flare up."

"Shu Wei, if you'll help me nail a few boards up for a front door when we leave, we can at least get home to get some rest," said Jake. "I don't think sleep will be easy tonight for any of us."

Word about the calamity at *The News* offices spread quickly. In the next few days, the outpouring of support was staggeringly generous, particularly from *The San Francisco Call*. *The Call* lent their presses on off-hours and helped in setting type. It was an opportunity for the staff of *The Golden Hills' News* to work in their brand-new building at Market and Third Streets, a stunning fifteen-story edifice of granite and white marble. Shu Wei and Shu Lan-lan had made note of its large dome on their trip from the immigration center.

While Brian and Jake were back at *The News* cleaning up and making repairs, Shu Wei was enjoying a respite from the mind-rattling chaos in Chinatown. He and Mei Huang were huddled over a table piled high with notes and proofs in a spacious room on the third floor of the new *Call* building, the temporary command center for *The Golden Hills' News*.

"We're fortunate that Fan Ching had the foresight to stash these papers and photos in the safe before our friends arrived the other night," said Mei Huang. "They probably thought they had put our lights out for good."

Shu Wei was daydreaming. His wits were frayed, but just working again with Mei Huang was restorative. What was that word again? Colleague. But more than a colleague. A bright attractive partner. He smiled inwardly.

"Shu Wei? Are you with me?" Mei Huang waved a hand in front of Shu Wei and snapped her fingers.

Shu Wei winced and his head jerked up. "Oh, sorry, I guess I haven't had time to clear my mind lately. I was thinking how I miss my sister. She probably heard about the raid on the paper and no doubt is worried about me. It was selfish of me to not think of that."

"Your sister knows," half-shouted Wu Kang Ho from across the room. "I have been keeping her up-to-date on things. She says you owe her a seat at the mulberry tree, whatever that means."

"It's an ancient . . ." Shu Wei began. He didn't finish, suddenly distracted by an imposing figure entering the room, followed by Fan Ching and Perrier. The man, of medium height, was wearing a rumpled cream-colored three-piece suit. He half-shuffled his way toward Shu Wei and Mei Huang. A wavy haystack of white hair contrasted with his ruddy complexion. His salt and pepper eyebrows branched out wildly over his eye sockets like cliffs of dune grass. His furry mustache spilled over his upper lip like an untrimmed hedge. A peach tie was anchored within a stiff collar and nested beneath his buttoned vest. His left hand fidgeted with a banded cigar.

"Name's Mark Twain," the stranger growled. "How y'all doin'? Mind if I join in?"

"Mr. Twain is in town for a few days and heard about our little incident," explained Fan Ching. "He wanted to give us some words of encouragement."

"Good to see you folks are not givin' up," rumbled the older man. "Know what they say? 'It's not the size of a dog in a fight, it's the size of the fight in a dog.' You folks are carryin' on like a big dog. I'm likin' that.

"So, you know, I did a bunch of writin' in my day for *The Call* here. Was the only reporter for a while, back in the sixties. Different issues back then. From what I hear, y'all got yourself some doozies here."

Twain's piercing chestnut eyes settled on Shu Wei's like a doctor probing a patient. "Understand you lost some loved ones, young man," he said. "Had some hard times. But I always tell people, 'Don't go around saying the world owes you a living. The world owes you nothing. It was here first.' So you gotta make your own way. I know you'll do it. Keep up the good fight."

Shu Wei sat, speechless. This man was mesmerizing. He wasn't sure he caught the meaning of all this rather raffish man had to offer, but he felt a stirring in his gut. He was deeply moved.

Twain rose and plunged his hands into a bag at his side. "Here, take this book. Take your time with it. Might give you an idea or two about life. My signature's in there with today's date. Gotta go—best of luck to you."

Shu Wei ran his thumb over the slightly embossed title, *Adventures of Huckleberry Finn*. Two boys in coveralls and broad-brimmed straw hats—one standing, one kneeling—were staring out pensively over a body of water. The erect one that looked to be older was chewing on a reed or stalk of grass. What were these boys thinking in their trance? Their lives appeared to be simple ones, uncluttered with fear and the unavoidable onslaught of an adult's messy complications.

To acquire a quick taste, he flipped the book open to a page. Tom Sawyer and Huckleberry Finn were having a heated discussion.

When Shu Wei looked up, the older man with the rumpled suit had paused in the doorway, hair askew, looking back at him for a moment.

CHAPTER THIRTY FOUR

The Hospital

After hearing about the raid at *The News*, Shu Lan-lan grew restive, paranoid again. Small noises jarred her. The girls at the Home were once again noticing her jitters, which by now had seeped into their fragile world.

On the third day after the raid a man dressed in a flowery clown outfit appeared in the lobby of the Home handing out peanuts from his colorful cart. A timely distraction. He was demonstrating a noise-making papier-mâché animal figure to two entranced children when Shu Lan-lan walked in. One of the girls, Minnie Tong, or "Tea Rose," as she was known, spotted Shu Lan-lan and pranced over to greet her.

At twelve years, Tea Rose had the grace and composure of someone much older. The corners of her mouth were perpetually upturned. Today she sported an ornamental hairpiece that graced a coiled bun on the right side of her head. Her blouse was brightly embroidered in butterflies and flowers, a product of the sewing class.

"What's the big occasion?" Shu Lan-lan asked, straining to be cheery. "Are you getting married today?"

Tea Rose gave Shu Lan-lan a playful nudge with her elbow and said, "No, no! Surely you must remember it's my birthday.

We're having a party in the reading room and we're waiting for you."

"Oh goodness! My mind has been a fog lately. Forgive me. I most certainly will join you."

One half of the chapel was decorated for the party. Twenty girls sat cross-legged on a large oval rug in the center of the room. Puffy *bo lo bao*, pineapple buns, were stacked in a pyramid on a side table. On the upper ones, candles stood jauntily between the crisscross scorings in the crusts. Small gifts of red envelopes, some decorated with cartoon characters, some with the calligraphic letters of the giver, lay next to homemade wrist bracelets and hair braids. One girl with paper streamers wound through her braids poured green tea from a steaming kettle into small ceramic bowls. Another started to blow out a vigorous rendition of "Happy Birthday," western style, on her *xun,* a clay ocarina.

When the girls were in the midst of another Chinese folk song, Shu Lan-lan heard the shuffle of footsteps behind her. Mother Grace leaned over and tapped her on the shoulder. Shu Lan-lan lurched upward, startled at the contact.

"Can I see you in my office please?" urged Mother Grace.

Thinking the worst, Shu Lan-lan stood up excitedly and grazed the table with the plate of buns, causing them to wobble crazily. The girls' heads swung around in unison, their eyes questioning.

Shu Lan-lan's first thought was that something had happened to her brother. Or, maybe she would be reprimanded for being lax in performing her duties at the Home. Slouching into Grace's office, she inhaled deeply.

Shu Lan-lan slipped into a low sofa as Mother Grace settled into a wingback chair behind her desk. One wall was filled with portraits and framed pictures of former and current residents—all survivors of one kind or another. Another wall next to the windows held larger plaques proclaiming statements of gratitude of relatives, social institutions, and the mayor. A large vase of bugle lilies and cornflowers brightened her otherwise colorless desk, piled high with uneven stacks of folders.

"I'm afraid I have some bad news," Grace began. "Our dear Bo Cai attempted suicide last night." Shu Lan-lan gasped, slapping a hand to her mouth.

"One of our night wardens was making her rounds and she heard some whimpering coming from one of the closets. She discovered Bo Cai, still holding a knife, sitting in a pool of blood. Mrs. Blakewell was able to wrap some cloths around the wounds and personally transport her to the County Hospital. She had to use my name to get her admitted as an emergency patient. You know they normally don't accept Chinese. Fortunately she has survived and will recover. One of the girls said Bo Cai had seen the article in *The Golden Hills' News* and was quite distraught. She kept saying 'Why did they do this to me?'

"The girls don't know—fortunately this happened while they were asleep. I will have to tell them that she has just gone to visit a relative. I'm not sure if you should tell Shu Wei. Wu Kang Ho said that it was not your brother's choice to run the article."

Shu Lan-lan sat, wringing her hands into a twisted mass of knuckles. Needles of pain crept into her wrist. Small bubbles of moisture spilled from her eyes and slid in rivulets down her cheeks.

"I am terribly sorry," Shu Lan-lan sputtered. "Bo Cai has been battered by forces beyond her control in so many ways. I will pray for her. Some of the girls are better at coping than others. I have suggested to several that their dark memories are best stowed in the dusty attics of their minds. Others simply get consumed by ghosts and wander in and out of reality. Many put on a lively exterior but can barely get out of bed in the morning."

"There will be a small group from the Home going to the hospital tomorrow. You're free to join us if you'd like. It will not be easy."

"I know that my brother would want to come along, but it seems best that he not learn of this until later."

"My feeling as well, Shu Lan-lan," said Grace, discretely dabbing at an errant tear. "I have suggested to Wu Kang Ho that this be kept from the rest of the staff at *The News* as well for now. They have their hands full as it is."

The next day, a contingent from the Home, including two aides, Shu Lan-lan, Mother Grace, and Freddie, one of the stocky doorkeepers, climbed aboard two horse drawn carriages.

The City and County Hospital was a two-story wooden building on Potrero Avenue in the Mission District. The building was showing its age. It had been cited by the local health officials as unsanitary and unsafe, setting the stage for replacement in the next couple of years. Inside, the gray painted hallways seemed to have been inspired by the fog that was swirling outside. Smells of disinfectant and bleach wafted about them. Only the rattling of metallic bed pans and trays broke the pervasive silence. Officious nurses scrambled about in their "feverproof" gowns cinched at the waist.

"How may I help you?" A matronly woman with a fury of gray hair held beneath a jaunty white cap, greeted them. Her voice was strained and harsh. Her folded arms rested on her ample bosom. Defiance. Authority. The message was clear.

Eyeing her name tag, Mother Grace ventured, "If you would be so kind Nurse Blackwood, we are from the Occidental Home and would like to pay a visit to one of your patients, Bo Cai."

"The patient is not takin' visitors. Besides, your numbers would put a fright into her. I know about your Home. You preach all the good gospel, takin' in Chinese girls and all. Then we're supposed to fix 'em up when they're broke. I've seen a lotta broke ones, believe me. Woulda been better off stayin' with their owners."

"You have a right to your opinion certainly Nurse Blackwood," Grace countered. "But these girls also have rights. They are to receive medical care in their time of need."

"Don't talk to me about their rights," harumphed the nurse. "We just go by the rules here. Lucky she's got a bed."

"I'm afraid you'll have to deal with Sergeant Growman who is just outside if you don't honor our request," bluffed Grace. Freddie edged closer to the nurse as if to emphasize the point.

A scarlet curtain of ire slowly progressed from her neck to her temples.

"You're stretchin' my tolerance, missie," spat Nurse Blackwood. "I'm gonna have to check with my superior. Now, settle yourselves in these chairs 'til I get back."

The nurse turned on her heels and pranced down a long dimly lit corridor. Glancing back quickly, she abruptly turned into a room and disappeared.

Shu Lan-lan's mind wandered back to the immigration station when they first arrived. It seemed to her that western medicine wasn't about caring. She missed the gentle ministrations of the *xuán hú jì shì*, the herbal dispensary back home.

Several minutes later, Nurse Blackwood returned, agitated. A sheen of moisture glazed her forehead. Her eyes wandered, looking past her visitors. Shu Lan-lan sensed something clearly had added to her already unbalanced demeanor.

"Awright," squawked the nurse. "You're cleared to visit. I'll getcha when your time's up—fifteen minutes. You'll need to wear these badges. Clean your hands in those bathrooms over there."

Lathering her hands in the sink, Mother Grace said in a low voice to Shu Lan-lan, "This is truly an unsettling place today. Something seems odd. I have been here many times before and people were generally more cheery."

"Maybe Nurse Blackwood has had a long shift," suggested Shu Lan-lan. "Or maybe they're short-handed."

"No, I think there's something else going on. I just have a feeling."

The group marched down the long corridor, passing two long-faced nurses who shuffled about in a trancelike meander, voices a whisper. Nurse Blackwood strode ahead purposefully, nodding grimly at a frail black man idly swishing a gray mop side to side. A stout woman pushed a squeaky cart stacked high with soiled linens. Chemical odors floated from dark stale-smelling cubicles. Gusts of overheated air escaped vents in walls with pockmarked plaster. Ceiling globes cast more shadow than light.

Standing to one side, Nurse Blackwood pushed open one side of the paneled pair of doors to the ward. "Your girl is straight ahead," she blurted. "Remember, I'm comin' to getcha in fifteen. Don't go disturbin' the rest of the girls."

The Chinese ward held eight girls in beds placed evenly along a curved wall that faced onto a courtyard. Grimy windows with yellowed shades denied all but a hint of the fading afternoon light. Two ceiling fans stuttered their way through the thick damp air. A pitcher, a battered enamel pan, and a flickering kerosene lamp were the token accessories at each bedside. A shroud of silence bathed the room, broken occasionally by low moans.

Bo Cai lay motionless, a drained drip bag hanging from a rusty metal frame on a stand. A small blanket of gauze dangled from one side of her neck exposing a dusky wound. Wrappings on her wrists had matted reddish streaks. *A prisoner again!* Shu Lan-lan thought.

Mother Grace leaned in and soothed back strands of loose damp hair from Bo Cai's ashen face. The others kept their distance. "We are so sorry, Bo Cai," offered Grace. "A few of us have come to wish you a speedy recovery. We know that you will be back with us very soon."

One of the Home's aides handed Shu Lan-lan a small vase filled with white champagne roses. As Shu Lan-lan cheerily presented them to Bo Cai, Grace grabbed her wrist firmly and said, "Wait. Stop. Something's not right."

An ooze of bubbly vomit dribbled from one side of Bo Cai's mouth. Her eyelids drooped lazily. She was slurring her speech. "Man come. Make Bo Cai sick. Must get better. Wa-water, dizzy," she mumbled.

"Nurse! Nurse!" bellowed Grace. "This girl has been poisoned!"

Shu Lan-lan and the others stood frozen in fear. They had never seen Grace this agitated, even on some of the tougher rescue runs.

"Shu Lan-lan, quick," urged Grace, "find Nurse Blackwood. Our girl is in big trouble."

Shu Lan-lan's insides were tumbling. It took several seconds for her to process what was happening. She bolted for the passageway at the side of the room and wrestled back the heavy curtain.

"A-y-y-e-e-e!" Shu Lan-lan's curdling scream caromed off the walls.

Freddie sprinted to the passageway, the source of Shu Lan-lan's blood-curdling scream. A man with a long bladed knife was trained on Nurse Blackwood who sat, trembling in a chair. Shoving Shu Lan-lan behind him, Freddie pulled a thick woven leather strap from his coat pocket. In an instant, the strap snagged the knife with such a force that it yanked it from the man's hand toward Freddie. It fell harmlessly in front of the burly doorkeeper. Two other men draped in black hoods appeared from behind the first. They taunted Freddie, knives waving threateningly. Then they were gone. Vanished down the side corridor to the rear alley.

"Oh, oh my," moaned Grace. "Nurse! Someone!"

Slowly, several nurses peered into the ward, one shaking and mumbling, "Dear Jesus, Lord above, our Savior."

"Do something!" ordered Grace. My girl is dying!"

Shu Lan-lan raced to Bo Cai's bed and tried consoling her. "The bad people are gone now, Bo Cai. We are helping you."

A tall slender nurse brusquely pushed Shu Lan-lan aside, removed Bo Cai's old intravenous drip bag, and hooked up a new one. The nurse, feeling for a pulse, said, "This one will need Doctor Flanagan. She's slipping fast."

General pandemonium prevailed in the ward. "Anyone know what kind of poison they used? What's the antidote? Where's the doctor? Bring over that IV! What's her breath like? Run a toxicity test."

It seemed to Shu Lan-lan that whoever did this had it well planned out. How could poison, or whatever it was, be administered without anyone noticing? It became clear when she and Grace went to console Nurse Blackwood who was still sitting on the same chair in a state of shock.

Trembling, the nurse gushed, "I saw the brainless orderly let in a man at the back door. He told me he knew him. Our staff is not to do that, the dumb cluck. Then, two more of them, all in black hoods with eyeholes cut out, came stormin' in behind him and threatened the lives of staff in reception. It only got worse. Another group came in behind them and made their way through the hospital, showin' their knives and tellin' everyone to stay where they were.

"They told us we must make things look normal and let some people move around—under threat of death of course. We had to listen, you see? Your group came in just after that. Your timin' couldn't have been worse.

"Our orderly said it was the Hap Tran Tong. He's done some gambling business with them and recognized rings on two of the hoodlums' fingers, rings with the Hap Tran Tong's insignia. One of the three that first came in had a scar on his left hand and a large ring with two serpents on his right hand. He walked with a limp. His face was covered so . . . so I never got a good look at the monster." Nurse Blackwood lowered her head. "It all happened so fast. That scummy group has been causin' problems in here before. And our security people are like pussy cats. Just here to take home a paycheck."

The nurses in the Chinese ward were now joined by two doctors and other staff. When Shu Lan-lan returned to the ward the other girls had pulled their bedding around their shoulders, eyes glazed with fear. Some trembled. Some had turned their faces into their pillows to escape the chaotic scene.

Two familiar caps bobbed among the group. Sergeant Growman and a deputy had arrived. They were in an animated discussion with the head nurse and the hospital director.

"Grace, I'm horribly sorry for all of this," said the sergeant. "We are pretty certain who's responsible. They will not get away with it."

"Sergeant, can you give us any update on the status on Bo Cai?"

The sergeant paused and the buttons on his uniform rose as his chest heaved up and down. "Your dear Bo Cai didn't make it. We think it was arsenic. I'm so sorry Grace and Shu Lan-lan."

Grace gasped. "JesusMaryandJoseph. May the good Lord bring her peace at last. The girl had a black destiny. Shu Lan-lan, don't you or your brother bring guilt on yourselves. I know that Shu Wei will feel that the article on Bo Cai brought this on. The Tong was no doubt agitated about her implicating them in her story. But, please tell him to always remember good often comes with the bad. Fan Ching tells me that that article has already drawn new readers to *The Golden Hills' News* and caused lots of discussion in tea houses and coffee houses."

"Tell you what," interjected Sergeant Growman, "I need to write up a report on this back at the station but first, I can take you both to *The Call* offices. I know you'd like to see your brother, Shu Lan-lan. You and Grace will be able to give him a first-hand accounting of this dreadful incident. I would advise, however, that *The News* hold off on publishing a story on this for a few days, while we're organizing our raids and paperwork.

On the way out of the hospital, Grace said, "Let's stop in here first, Shu Lan-lan. I think it would be nice to say a few words on behalf of Bo Cai."

The small chapel off the main entrance was modest, crisp in its decor: wood paneling and a small oval window of patterned colored glass. To Shu Lan-lan it seemed the nicest room in the hospital. Her thoughts drifted back to the chapel on the ship.

To her surprise, someone had hung a simple felt banner in one corner decorated with a white crane in flight, depicting longevity, and paired stalks of bamboo, a symbol to the Chinese representing old age and modesty. She settled in one of four short wooden pews while Grace kneeled on cushions that lay just below a simple brass cross at the front. Shu Lan-lan unconsciously lowered her head. Her mind a jumble of thoughts—mostly about the unending cruelty and mystery of this world, mixed with a determination to carry on. Determination. A word that once had clear meaning to her. But lately she questioned her own will to bring clarity to events in her life and to work with them and move on.

Shu Lan-lan knew she needed to see Shu Wei. The past seemed to be mirrored in the present. Fire. Death. This news would shake him. Also, she was apprehensive about reuniting with him. It had been weeks. The rift seemed to have hardened her; she had grown calloused in attempting to sort out his motives and aspirations. But that all melted away when she got to the *Call* offices. After hesitating, for what seemed like forever, she slowly drifted over to him. Shu Wei rose from the work table and the two stood, looking, searching each other's eyes. Their embrace was the first since they were reunited at the immigration center.

"Dear sister," said Shu Wei, "I am well aware that we have been drifting away from each other for too long. It is no secret that I am the guilty party. Of that, I need no reminding. Given the proper time and place I will, in detail, explain everything. If things keep going as they are, it will be very soon."

"These are very familiar words, indeed," said Shu Lan-lan. "I have heard many different versions of them. But, I trust you and believe in you. Once, in my English class in Sanhou, I heard the phrase, "All things come to those who wait.""

Shu Wei pulled Shu Lan-lan to him briefly again and released her, brushing the underside of her chin with a finger.

"Now, forgive me sister," he said, but I must help get a newspaper out."

Shu Lan-lan nodded.

Grace and the others in the room looked at one another and smiled.

CHAPTER THIRTY FIVE

Barbershop

By the end of the week *The Golden Hills' News* ran the story of the death of Bo Cai at the County Hospital, counter to Sergeant Growman's advice. They felt it was too important of a story to hold back. Interviews were held with hospital officials, Grace Caldwell, and Shu Lan-lan. Since the figures who held hospital personnel captive were masked, no one could corroborate the exact identity of the invaders. But concrete references by the orderly led Fan Ching and Perrier to imply, in the article, that it most likely had been the work of the Hap Tran Tong.

Two days later, early on a misty evening, Shu Wei, hunching, crept along Waverly Place. Time to head to Long Bin's Apparel and Dry Goods store to invest in an umbrella. It would provide additional camouflage.

Waverly Place was known as Fifteen Cent Street due to the cost of a haircut at the many barber shops. The barbers followed the custom of putting out a wash pan on a wooden rack outside their doors to indicate that they were open for business. Shu Wei inhaled the sweet aromas of talc and sesame poultices, mixed with a mist which had developed into a driving rain. Before he could buy his umbrella, he sought refuge under an awning of a shop where men were getting their foreheads shaved and their hair cleaned, braided, and oiled. Queues were constantly groomed to keep options open, should a man want to return to his homeland. A disrespect for the practice would go against the edict of the Manchu Qing Dynasty and jeopardize their freedom.

As Shu Wei tugged at his cap to further protect himself from the rain, a familiar caped figure walked by, with a limp. The man went a few paces past him and stopped, before turning back and confronting Shu Wei. Yong Qiang stood, staring at him with fiery opalescent eyes. The remains of a cigar, like a tiny sheaf of tortured wheat, bounced at the side of his mouth. His jaw muscles tightened. Shu Wei pressed backward, trying to find a deeper refuge among the men beside him. Yong Qiang's hand snapped up and yanked the cap from Shu Wei's head. With his other hand, he pawed at something in his coat pocket. The rain, driven into Shu Wei's face, blurred his vision, adding to a rising sense of helplessness.

"You rotten weasel! You coward!" growled Yong Qiang, "I should have known better than to trust you. A skunk has more brains. You knew our deal. You deliver, or your life is over. Instead, you double-crossed me."

Sensing a potentially disastrous situation, the men around Shu Wei quickly lurched off into the drenching downpour. Now alone with the madman, he frantically considered his options. He wished he had a weapon, but he harbored a genuine distaste for them. He was now sure that what Yong Qiang was holding was a gun inside his pocket.

"B-but I don't know wha-what you're talking about," insisted Shu Wei. "I did . . . did everything you told me to do."

"Shutup, you *nǎozhǒng*, you useless fool," foamed Yong Qiang as he grabbed Shu Wei by his coat. I would do you in right now except I have much more important business. But, trust me, you are all but a *sǐ guǐ*—a dead demon. *Comprende?*"

With that, Yong Qiang released his hold on Shu Wei and stormed off down the street.

Shu Wei's legs had turned to rubber. He somehow managed to coax his feet into action. He hadn't gotten more than ten steps when he heard several loud explosions followed by high-pitched screams, echoing off the brick facades across the street. Not daring to look back, he sprinted past a growing crowd of the curious. What seemed like half of Chinatown streamed past him as bold souls craned their necks to get a view and ran deliberately toward the commotion.

He was still visibly shaken when, just before dawn the next day, he met Brian in a passageway at the rear of his temporary lodgings. Brian had brought a new wardrobe for Shu Wei: a dark gray pea coat with wider lapels for obscuring his face, a matching gray hat that he could pull low over his ears and forehead.

"This one's better than the last, Brian. More coverage for my face."

"Good. Now come on, we've got ta get over ta *The News* offices. Things are movin' pretty fast around here. I . . . ."

"Just so you know, I almost couldn't join you today. A little problem with a man with a gun."

Brian's head whipped around. He grabbed Shu Wei's shoulders. Shu Wei felt the pinch. "Bloody hell! How? What? Wait, just tell me when we're off the streets."

The two wound their way along several back alleys off Sacramento Street to a stable fronting Brooklyn Place where a carriage awaited them for the trip to *The Call* building. Several horses pawed the straw floor in acknowledgement of their visitors, their nostrils sending plumes of vapor into the chilled morning air. Brian and Shu Wei climbed the mounting step of one of the buggies and settled in.

Reaching *The Call* building, Shu Wei finally breathed deeply. A safe haven, at least for now. When they arrived at the third floor, they found Fan Ching, Mei Huang, Jake Bradley, and Perrier huddled around the latest issue of *The Call*, intently scouring the front page.

"Well, you fellows are missing out on a big story," said Fan Ching. "*The Call* beat us to the punch on this one. Maybe you've already heard that one of two leaders of the Hap Tran Tong wiped out the other one last night. It all happened in a barber shop on Waverly Place. Yong Qiang took out Jun Min. I believe these are the two key names in the book you found. Yong Qiang managed to get away before the police arrived."

Shu Wei steadied himself against a chair. He felt nauseated, suddenly realizing just how close he had come to death. He surmised that Jun Min was Yong Qiang's 'much more important business.' Apparently Yong Qiang had chosen not to spend the money to engage a powerful New York lawyer. He had simpler methods. Trembling, Shu Wei turned to Brian. "That's my little story I was about to tell you. But I didn't know all the details until now." Gripping the chair with both hands, he continued to address the group. "Last night I sought refuge from the storm beneath an awning on Waverly Place. Yong Qiang himself came by and spotted me. He had a gun and . . . and may have used it on me had he not had a job to do down the street. That "job" was at the barber shop."

Fan Ching helped lower Shu Wei into a chair. "The gods have spared you," he said. "For that we are all grateful. More than grateful, we are ecstatic."

Mei Huang stood, walked over and vigorously massaged Shu Wei's neck and shoulders. He didn't protest. "At least we are rid of one heinous criminal," she said. "I expect our friend Yong Qiang will go underground somewhere for a while. I know that's of little comfort to you, but the police are now fully engaged. We are working with them to bring the entire Hap Tran Tong to justice. We understand that factions inside the Tong are warring with each other. In the meantime, Grace

Caldwell has decided to go ahead with the girls' concert at Old
St. Mary's—with a police escort, of course. We don't want the
Tong to think they rule this neighborhood. Strength in numbers. The Chinatown community is supporting a march to the
church. Our news group will be joining Grace and the girls in
the lead group. I have a feeling our next story is just around the
corner."

CHAPTER THIRTY SIX

A Concert

During the next several days the girls at the Home were deep in preparation for the concert at Old Saint Mary's Cathedral that Grace had arranged. Margaret Culbertson, the music director for the Home, had siphoned every bit of talent from the twenty girls in their two practices a day for the past eight weeks. They were now the Occidental Girls Choir. When they heard they would be in a parade through Chinatown their excitement was almost unbearable.

The girls milled about in the entry hall of the Home. Mother Grace was going over the procedures for this rare excursion into the community. Shu Lan-lan's sewing squad had put together new outfits for the girls, and one of the supporters of the Home purchased several bolts of piece-dyed white taffeta for the dresses. Each girl stood beaming on a discarded bottle crate while the fabric was shaped, pinned, pinched, pulled, bunched, straightened, and finally hemmed. A red satin bow was affixed at each girl's waist at the small of the back.

Hair had been arranged and braided, faces scrubbed, and shoes polished. Shu Wei thought the girls looked like a flock of angels. He was in charge of transporting two large vases of flowers that were to adorn the chancel on each side.

The girls, along with Grace and some of her staff, eight policemen, and a contingent from *The Golden Hills' News* assembled near the Home at Stockton and Sacramento. Slowly, the ranks were filled with locals from Chinatown and beyond: merchants, residents, representatives from the mayor's office, and the just plain curious.

It was a mild evening with a fresh breeze. The sky still glowed—a mass of interlaced streaks of amber and dark violet. Lights were rapidly appearing, igniting the scene like an earth-bound constellation. Suddenly it was dark. The parade was to snake around Chinatown and end up at the church. Fan Ching, Mei Huang, and Shu Wei were squeezed into one carriage. As far as Shu Wei was concerned, the closeness to Mei Huang was just fine. Jake Bradley, Brian O'Grady, and Perrier Banier occupied another open carriage. Shu Wei and Mei Huang gripped a banner announcing "*The Golden Hills' News.*" Two more carriages held Grace, two of her aides, and two doorkeepers, all displaying their typically stern countenances. Their banner, announcing the "Occidental Mission Home for Girls," drew measured applause as the carriage occupants gave queenly waves to bystanders.

The girls in the chorus walked just in front of the carriages and were instructed to grip a pigtail or queue of the girl in front as they made their way in groups of five. Shu Lan-lan said it looked like a procession of albino circus elephants. The other girls from the Home walked just behind. The girls' crisp white outfits were in stark contrast to the grittiness of the streets. A trio of musicians preceded them, one playing the *erhu,* a two-stringed fiddle, and two playing *xiaos*, end-blown flutes. Others joined in with their clashing cymbals and tom-toms. Their sounds pinged off adjacent buildings.

Tourists and locals alike stopped to admire the breezy looking caravan. Commerce was temporarily suspended in each block as shoppers and shopkeepers alike poured onto the sidewalks. Having seen the bright posters announcing the event several days ago, many began to join in and some even brought paper lanterns of various colors held high on wooden sticks. Children waved lighted joss sticks. A mass of brightly colored pinwheels gave the appearance of a blur of butterflies. Even the policemen seemed to have shined their buttons and badges for the occasion. Onlookers from balconies waved their hellos, handkerchiefs flapping like dove wings.

Grace leaned over to one of the aides and said, "I'm counting on our Sergeant Growman and his men to lead us safely to our destination. Nothing would surprise me from the Hap Tran Tong."

The aide replied, "Did you bring your ax, Madam?"

"I did indeed. I have stashed it beneath the seat. All I have to do is raise the seat cushion. But, with the good Lord's blessings, I won't have to use it."

"Amen to that," said the aide.

Shu Wei was entertaining similar thoughts in his carriage. He knew that if Yong Qiang were still around, he was capable of mass mayhem. They had just passed the Pekin Two Knife Man whom some called the Sword Dancer. Shu Wei had heard he was part of the Hap Tran Tong. His muscular frame thrust and stabbed the air with two sabers in a kind of martial arts dance in the street. His nickname was *Daniu*, or Big Ox, because of his strength. He made no move to follow them.

Shu Wei's mind was put at ease, at least for a time, when the contingent finally arrived at Old Saint Mary's. The church had the distinction of announcing Chinatown at its southern edge to the waves of tourists and locals from the city's business district. Grace explained to no one in particular, "The facade's red brick and iron work made it all the way round Cape Horn." She added that the granite trim pieces and other embellishments had appropriately been brought from China. "If you look at the plaque just below the large dial of the tower you can make out a saying that some insist came from Confucius. But it is actually a scriptural warning from the Bible: 'Son, Observe the Time, and Fly from Evil.' It has strong meaning at this moment, don't you think?"

The bobbing white mass of girls climbed the front steps and headed into the main entry portal. "Now ya will be gettin' a whiff of my religion," said O'Grady as he helped Shu Wei from the carriage. "Like I said before, I'm not the most loyal Irish Catholic, but there's a touch of it still in me."

Entering the church Shu Wei was intrigued as he gazed at the simple but well-appointed interior. Bursts of violet, tangerine, and rose light fell across the polished floors from the windows along the side aisles. Lingering vestiges of incense wafted from the previous service. Large multi-branched silver candelabras held sturdy red candle columns. Wide oval ceramic vessels held eruptions of camellias and hibiscus. Tourists ambled by the fonts near the entry, intrigued by the sight of the choral group now assembling on the risers at the far end near the altar. An elderly couple, hunched with the weight of time, navigated the central aisle by lurching from one row of seating to the next.

Locals were identified by their simple dress, while Nob Hill faithfuls arranged themselves in clusters on the long benches, broad hats carving up the air as they leaned this way and that to converse with one another. Heads swiveled to witness the entry of the remaining girls from the Occidental Home. Sergeant Growman's contingent removed their caps and found their way to seats toward the front, sides, and rear. A surprise visitor, George Brownhill, the General Manager of the Palace Hotel, sat near the rear in a crisp suit ornamented with a cranberry-colored ascot.

Margaret Culbertson reshuffled a few girls, who, in their nervous stupor, had forgotten their proper places. An important part of her job was to bring order to the jittery youths who seldom were out in public.

Mrs. Culbertson was of robust Scottish stock, her face almost as square as her shoulders with a pink glow highlighting her cheeks. Her charcoal gray hair was intertwined with strands of white and pulled into a giant donut shape that appeared capable of pulling her over backwards. A corsage of carnations nested on her large bosom. Her stern countenance and discipline belied her easy manner. The girls respected and admired her, a fact which Mother Grace had acknowledged as the principal reason for their improvement—and their increasing number of invitations.

Mother Grace stood to give her introduction to the night's event. The buzz in the crowd ebbed. Eyes were drawn forward. Mrs. Culbertson drew herself upright and clasped her hands in front of her.

"Our Occidental Girls Choir is delighted to be performing at St. Mary's tonight," announced Grace. "Mrs. Margaret Culbertson will be conducting. The first three pieces are Chinese folk songs. The first two, "Eight Fiery Horses" and "The Jasmine Flower" will be sung in both Chinese and English. The third, "A Snail and a Black-naped Oriole" will be sung only in Chinese. We hope you enjoy them."

Mrs. Culbertson raised her arms into a ready command as her eyes scanned from left to right, making certain the girls would all come in together. She dropped her arms a half-beat to signify the start and then began the sinuous arcing that drew the voices into a fluid whole. Her hands dropped, palms down, to signify a quieting and flapped vigorously to increase the energy. The voices had a silky resonance. The dominant treble range of the group swept across the church's ceiling and landed in the laps of the audience. As the prepubescent singers' voices grew in intensity, some in a higher register brought a sparkling tonal balance. Shu Wei felt a flood of goosebumps on his arms as his head gently swayed with the music. The choral sounds consumed the space around him and it seemed as if his own ribcage resonated with them.

Following five more songs, vigorous clapping brought three encores. The evening had been a success. The girls had made their own statement in the community. However, as the Monsignor, dressed in a purple-trimmed black cassock and purple sash, was clasping hands with the departing crowd, an event of an entirely different kind was unfolding a few short blocks away.

CHAPTER THIRTY SEVEN

Confrontation

While the girls were still gathering themselves at Old Saint Mary's Cathedral after their concert, Yoh Wang sat dejectedly on her bed, wiping her feverish brow with a cool cloth. She and two other girls were sick and had stayed behind on the second floor in the care of one of the aides at the Occidental Home. Two kitchen workers on the lower level toiled over the large vats of soup in preparation for the evening's dinner. Another was running a stringy mop in ever-widening circles over the worn tiled floor of the anteroom next to the kitchen. Little Ming, the cinnamon-colored Siamese cat, the mascot of the Home, patrolled her territory with a particular wariness. Her motions were jerky, nervous, as though sensing trouble; her back was arched, her fur bristling. The woman with the mop eyed the cat and shook her head as though judging a tempestuous child. The single doorkeeper had left his post at the front door to rustle a snack in the pantry.

Yong Qiang had seen the notices advertising the concert all over Chinatown. He knew that the Occidental Home would be largely vacant during the event. Now that his partner Jun Min had been exterminated, he was the Supreme Master of the Hap Tran Tong. Those who witnessed the slaying at the barber shop on Waverly Place were reluctant to name the perpetrator. They were well aware of the consequences should they do so. So, Yong Qiang remained free, for now, to conduct business as usual. His current business was the destruction of the Occidental Home.

Yong Qiang had worked out a detailed plan of attack. It had to be quick and efficient. Anything of value from top to bottom in the interior would be destroyed before setting the place afire. If anyone got in the way, they were to be dealt with in whatever manner appropriate. Yong Qiang urged his men to 'wash their bodies, use the puppy,' the very terms he had explained to Shu Wei that meant 'kill with the pistol.'

Ten of Yong Qiang's Tong members spread out around the two sides of the building, putting up ladders. One climbed to the second floor and launched a grappling hook around a chimney, pulling himself hand-over-hand. His assignment was to enter one of the dormers. Another eight Tong members stood, backs to the building, knives at the ready to ensure no one interfered. Two of the men lugged large cans of kerosene to the two exposed sides of the building. Yong Qiang, noticing the lack of doorkeepers, was reveling in his luck. As he ascended the steps off Sacramento Street, he unsheathed his dagger.

Yoh Wang, the girl on the second floor, heard a scratching noise on the exterior of the building and a loud thud on the roof. The noises were muffled with the passing of a cable car, its wheels grinding and its bell clanging. One of the kitchen workers thought she heard a loud clunk at the service entrance at the rear, off Joice Street. Ming the cat dove under a prep table in the kitchen.

The sound of breaking glass brought audible cries from those left inside. The few girls remaining in the Home gathered—as planned in case of an emergency—in a far corner of the second floor. They huddled, trembling, in a closet. Axes slashed at the service door off the kitchen, sending large splintered shards in all directions. The two kitchen workers grabbed the nearest utensil or pan. They retreated to the broom closet, holding on to one another in a panicked embrace.

Yong Qiang and two of his men battered down the front door. The one on the roof had pulled himself up to one of the dormer windows. More sounds of broken glass. Another Tong member entered the other dormer. Parts of splintered window frames cascaded to the sidewalk below. Several Tong members followed, nimbly climbing onto the attic floor. Several had already broken their way onto the second floor. Two stood by on the ground floor, ready to douse the building with kerosene. By this time, onlookers had gathered on the far side of Sacramento Street. At first, they thought the building was being renovated. But, slowly they came to realize the darkness of the affair unfolding before their eyes. Some wept. Others shouted out their condemnations.

What Yong Qiang hadn't known or counted on was the contingent of fifteen policemen inside the home. Or another battalion waiting a mere block away with shields and weapons. Or three large wagons around another corner capable of providing immediate arraignment.

Two evenings ago, Shu Wei, on one of his back alley trips home from *The News,* had overheard two bearded men speaking of the planned Tong raid. He was certain he heard the name Yong Qiang in the discussion. At the time he thought, *Oh no, this is even worse than the disaster in Sanhou. It brought nothing but anguish to me and my family, but here it could involve many more innocent people. I must tell Mother Grace.* When Mother Grace and Shu Wei met with the police, it seemed like the perfect time to orchestrate a counter-raid, a sting.

Yong Qiang and most of his men moved quickly inside through the entry lobby toward the front parlor on the main floor. It was then that several blue-coated officers converged on the Tong members from all sides—some from the chapel, some from the kitchen, some from behind curtains. Realizing they were cornered, the Hap Tran Tong slowly backed toward the entrance foyer.

Another wave of police, led by Sergeant Growman, rushed to the scene in their patrol wagon from their position a block away. The Tong lookouts on the sidewalk fired random shots that gave off a muffled pop when they hit the wooden sides of the wagon. The police stood their ground behind the wagon and fired back. Using their new call box system from the wagon, Growman's men requested reinforcements from another precinct. Just then Yong Qiang and his group of marauders came bursting back out through the front door of the Home. Now caught in a crossfire between the policemen inside the Home and behind the wagon, they sensed the hopelessness of their situation, put their hands up, and sat down in an anguished heap.

Some gunfire was heard on the upper floors, but that too was short-lived. The element of surprise was too much for the Tong. The police had strategically crouched behind counters, beds, and furniture, catching the intruders off guard. Only two or three Tong members attempted to fire on the officers, now equipped with the recently-issued Colt New Police revolvers and protective vests. The cry went out: "Drop your weapons, now! Put your hands behind your necks. You are under arrest."

Slurs poured from the Tong in a torrent: "*gāo bízis!* High Noses! *hóng máo guǐzis!* Red fur devils,*"* but they complied.

One policeman had been stationed on the second floor to protect the girls and the aide in their closet sanctuary. Another policeman knelt, gun drawn, near the janitor closet where the kitchen workers sought refuge.

The main casualties were on the first floor and the street. Several Tong members lay in a bloody pile on the sidewalk, limbs splayed in different directions. Some slumped, lifelessly against the building, some lay face down. Others were gripping an arm, a leg. Two policemen received superficial wounds and were being cared for by medical workers who had arrived with the other precinct's wagon. In all, a force of thirty-two policemen were either actively handcuffing Tong members or rounding up weapons and assessing the status of the wounded—the largest all time show of force ever by the police in the city.

A streetlight spread its amber cast on a silvery pile of daggers, pistols, and swords collected from the Tong. A captain of the force was affixing lengths of rope around sawhorses to cordon off the area. Sacramento and Joice Streets were closed entirely. Sheets now covered the deceased on the sidewalks, lumpy snowdrifts with accents of burgundy and scarlet. The wagon horses scuffed at the brick pavement and snorted impatiently. The small crowd had now grown to over a hundred bystanders. Staccatos of "Oohs," "Aahs," and "Yays" bore through the thick night air.

The carriages carrying the Occidental Home concert contingent were just heading west up Sacramento Street. The girls in their white outfits were dancing and singing beside *The News* carriage, filled with the euphoric aftertaste of a successful evening. Some attending the concert had joined, good heartedly, in the short journey back to the Occidental Home. The horses suddenly slowed and reared up, showing their frothy tongues. In the next block, a large gathering of people, carriages, and bright lights halted the reverie of this group of returning merrymakers. Something of great significance was clearly taking place.

CHAPTER THIRTY EIGHT

Redemption

Grace and Shu Wei had already anticipated the commotion that confronted them in front of the Occidental Home. The others drew back in disbelief that the Home seemed to be the focus of such turmoil.

"What in the great Buddha's name is happening here?" said Shu Lan-lan. "Why are all these policemen here? And medical people? And why are there broken windows in our Home?"

The carriages came to an abrupt stop just short of the milling mob of onlookers. Biting smells of gunpowder and peppery medicinal fluids floated in the air. The crowd's buzz oscillated in intensity, rising with the loading of a body into the medical cart or a handcuffing. Emphatic voices spiked above the rest. Urgent. Disciplined. "Over here Frank! Bring the stretcher." "Move it. We need to clear the area." "Stand back folks!"

Grace and Shu Wei had jumped from their buggy before it had come to a rest. They broke through the crowd and lifted the rope restraint. Sergeant Growman spotted the two and shepherded them off to one side. Hopping up and down like a swarm of oversized sprites, the girls from the Home tried desperately to manage views.

"Well, the mouse, or should I say rat, took the cheese," the Sergeant said. "Everything worked perfectly. Of course, we knew there'd be some damage. But we kept it to a minimum. Your people inside were never in harm's way. Can't quite say the same for our officers, but at least we got out with only a few minor injuries. Important thing is, we caught our main man, Yong Qiang, and have shut down the Hap Tran Tong operations. Course, we have some clean up to do back at their headquarters, if you know what I mean."

"We owe you a great deal Sergeant," offered Grace, "These people were a scourge in our community. And an increasing threat to the Home, as you know. Our planning paid off. But, of course, without the heads-up from our friend Shu Wei here this might have had a very different ending." Grace wrapped her lanky arm around Shu Wei's shoulders and gave him a robust hug.

Shu Wei stood, inhaling the sights and noxious smells before him. He was more than stunned. He was overwhelmed that there was a point of finality to his efforts. Not only could he stop hiding and running but he could entertain long lost thoughts of not only revenge, but redemption. Revenge on those who had conspired to steal his family's very soul. And redemption. Redemption of that precious commodity, family honor. He noticed the crumpled form of one of the detainees, limping, as policemen escorted him to a patrol wagon. A glint of opal light launched from a large ring on his right hand. Yong Qiang. Small pearls of tears began to form in Shu Wei's eyes. The simmering rage in him abated. He watched as his nemesis was detained and fitted into a pair of handcuffs, while a warmth coursed through him like nothing he'd experienced.

Someone tugged at Shu Wei's sleeves. He was so absorbed in his thoughts that he hardly noticed. When he did, he saw the upturned face of his sister. "Is that him? The man you're looking at?" she asked. Shu Lan-lan wrapped her arm around her brother's waist. He could tell she was trembling. Words froze on his tongue. All Shu Wei could do was nod affirmatively.

Mei Huang, Perrier, Brian, and Fan Ching encircled the two. A flurry of hugs ensued. Some in the group were unabashedly teary. Some embraced for what seemed an eternity. Soon the girls from the Home came along asking their innocent questions about what had happened here.

The Monsignor from Old Saint Mary's had already heard about the incident at the Home and had raced over the short three blocks to see for himself. He and Grace were in a tight huddle.

"Grace, you and your girls have seen tremendous joy and now, sadness—all on one night," the Monsignor said. "When I heard about this encounter I was shocked but buoyed by the eradication of one of the most vicious bunch of hoodlums in our community. It was high time that our police joined in the fight. Let me offer our church as refuge while proper repairs are being made to your Home. We have many cots in our basement, access to plenty of food, and our blessed congregation will no doubt rise up and give whatever other assistance is necessary."

"Monsignor, you are indeed as kind and benevolent of a person as exists in all corners of our world. I should very much like to take you up on your offer. I trust the repairs can be made in good time. Once the police let us, we will retrieve some things of value and sentimentality. Dolls and stuffed animals, as you might suspect, can make the nights more tolerable. And we do have a pretty good store of food that we're happy to transport to the church. You are indeed a lifesaver. By the way, we might even have the girls put on a concert or two while they're there."

CHAPTER THIRY NINE

Confession

Two days later, Shu Wei finally sat Shu Lan-lan down in their room at Wu Kang Ho's store and told her of the events in Sanhou.

"My heart has born the weight of my deed in Sanhou for what seems like forever," Shu Wei began. "And I know, my dear sister, that you have thought I have been overly mysterious and unfairly secretive about the whole affair. Trust me, I did not act out of some mean impulse to hide matters critical to the family. I only wanted . . ." Shu Wei's throat constricted, he continued. "You see, as I was performing my duties as Town Scribe near the town square, I couldn't help overhear a conversation—you know me—between two men. They were speaking behind a vine-covered shelter just next to where I was sitting. One spoke of the plan to direct a good portion of the town's taxes for their own benefit. The worst thing was one of the men I knew to be Huang Nuo, the town treasurer! Another was plotting to kill the Town Tax Collector so their plot would be secure.

"So, I began taking notes on the conversation, thinking that this should not be kept from the public. All at once the other man stopped speaking and, having seen me through the vines, asked what I was writing about. He stripped my notebook from me and started yelling when he saw what I was re-cording, causing nearby townspeople to turn their heads out of curiosity. I knew that I was in trouble. Little did I know it would turn out so badly.

"I was riddled with shame. My honor had been instantly destroyed. I thought if I kept it to myself, I could spare my family further humiliation. Of course, I was stupid to think that. I was in a panic. The longer I said nothing, the harder it was to confess my unfortunate deeds. When the fire happened, I knew things were totally out of control. But, once again, I still thought I could save things by myself, even then. It was clearly too late. Things escalated further at the inquisition at the town square. All life went out of me when I saw my father accused of things he didn't do. He was an honorable man. And I had caused this . . . this madness!

"Once I realized Yong Qiang had followed us on our way to San Francisco, my brain ceased to function. He threatened my life on that ship, telling me I would die if I told anyone of our conversation. He said he had big things in mind for me. Of course, that was also the time our poor father was suffering, from his injuries and grief around what had happened to his family, his business, and his honor. On that ship, I was certain that our father's life was taken by his own hands. He had cer-tainly tried before. I . . ."

With the mention of 'his own hands' Shu Lan-lan's eyes clouded. She let out a stream of air that startled Shu Wei. "Shu Wei, please do not think such thoughts. I now can see your in-tentions were good and I'm sorry you carried such a load with you. You should now recognize the dangers of keeping things to oneself. All that while, my feelings were badly injured and will take a while to repair. As you know I was born under the sign of the snake—I have a great compassion to help others when I'm allowed. I felt there was nothing I could do or say, even when I reached out."

"I am so, so sorry. I was selfish and naive."

"Well, at least we can say that things turned out pretty well—except for our poor father," said Shu Lan-lan. "He would be happy for us. We have both gained from our experiences in our new land and can build on them."

Shu Lan-lan leaned into her brother and pulled him close. He felt the warmth of her embrace. Stroking her ebony hair, he laid his head against hers.

"So now, I want us to have a special moment together, just the two of us," urged Shu Lan-lan. "Come outside with me."

Shu Lan-lan grabbed a steaming pot of black tea and poured two cups, handing one to Shu Wei. She took his hand and led him to the backyard of the store. "Take a seat."

Shu Lan-lan placed two cushions next to the ring of stones around the still-struggling mulberry tree, scaring off a small, bony bird. They both settled in, cross-legged.

"In honor of our father and mother," began Shu Lan-lan, "who now grace the night sky, I have placed two new special rocks around our tree. These are meant to call to the spirits in tribute to those we have lost. Now I will also use them to be-seech the gods to honor those good friends we have gained. I was going to place them long before this, but the time never seemed right. I felt you had grown away from me, and yet I wanted to do it with you. So now, when we look out our win-dow, this tree and those rocks will hold more meaning than ever."

Uncrossing his legs, Shu Wei pulled himself to his knees and reached over to his sister, holding her, oblivious to the fine beads of rain that had started to fall. A baptism for the new rocks.

CHAPTER FORTY

Fame

Six days after the Tong arrests at the Home and after everyone at *The Golden Hills' News* had a chance to regain control of their battered senses, they met at their newly renovated offices. Thanks to the efforts of Brian and Jake, repairs had been made where the worst damage had occurred from the Tong's raid. The scent of fresh paint conjured up a feeling of renewal. The Mergenthaler was once again giving off its characteristic 'kerchunk, kerchunk' and throwing off oily threads. When Shu Wei walked in, heads were intently bowed around the oak editing table. Fan Ching, Mei Huang, Brian, and Jake all sat in deep concentration, ignoring their visitor. They remained silent until Shu Wei finally couldn't stand it any longer.

"Hello, anybody home?" Shu Wei asked. "I said . . ."

Mei Huang responded, "Please, don't bother us, we're expecting someone important."

"Okay, I'll bite," said Shu Wei. "Who would that be?"

The group jumped up simultaneously and shouted, "You, silly!"

"Whew, for a minute I thought I was at the wrong newspaper," Shu Wei countered.

"Well, Shu Wei," said Fan Ching jokingly, "time to get our hands dirty and do some real work now, don't you think? We've got some stories to put out."

Shu Wei and Mei Huang glanced at each other with knowing smiles. "I guess you're right," responded Shu Wei. We've kind of been flaking off lately."

"I think the phrase is "slacking off," advised Mei Huang.

"I was just seeing if your editing hat was on straight," responded Shu Wei. Mei Huang, Fan Ching, Brian, and Jake broke out in unrestrained laughter—laughter that had been sorely missed around the office for some time.

Over the next few weeks, a flurry of stories ran in *The Golden Hills' News*. The heinous activities of the Hap Tran Tong were exposed in all their horror: money laundering; illegal enterprises of prostitution, gambling, and smuggling of young girls; trafficking in opium; blackmailing; and homicidal acts. The book that Shu Wei discovered in the passageway provided more than enough evidence. Three straight editions detailed the story of the death of Bo Cai at the hospital. Later articles covered Marie Banier's life and the amazing coincidence of Shu Wei and his sister's discoveries on Wu Kang Ho's property. Perrier, and his eventual involvement with *The News*, followed as a part of Mei Huang's local interest series.

When Evelyn Parkford was told of Claude Parkford's confession to hiring the killer of Marie Banier, she collapsed in a heap. It was deemed a mild heart attack. She was expected to make a full recovery. The day that story broke in *The News*, a mysterious fire consumed most of the Globe Hotel. As Claude was being handcuffed for arraignment in Marie's murder, traces of kerosene were detected on his clothing. One more bizarre twist in the saga of the Globe, one more potential charge against a psychopath.

Mei Huang put together an absorbing story on the life of Shu Wei and Shu Lan-lan. All issues were sold out in six hours.

Presses were now running day and night at *The News*. Daily circulation had skyrocketed. Fan Ching was even able to buy another press—with some help from Perrier.

In the meantime, the police probe of the Hap Tran Tong grew to an international scale. The trail of criminal activities went back to Sanhou where Shu Wei first encountered the vile Yong Qiang. Authorities there made a sweep of the local branch of the Tong and arrested twelve, eight of whom held office in the town.

The writings of Shu Wei and Mei Huang were lauded at every turn. They were the new stars of investigative reporting. Brian was mentioned as a third collaborator. But it was Shu Wei's resolve and work that got the strongest praise. 'Shining example,' 'man of the hour,' 'idol,' even 'hero'—words and phrases that were included within editorials in the local papers. The news about Marie Banier was picked up by the Paris newspaper *Le Matin* and the *London Daily News*. Not bad for a lowly Town Scribe from a small town in China.

CHAPTER FORTY ONE

Celebration

At the beginning of December, a grand gala was held at the Palace Hotel in downtown San Francisco. Mayor Phelan had arranged a dinner and concert, jointly sponsored by the San Francisco Chamber of Commerce and the Chinese Six Companies to honor the commitment and service of *The Golden Hills' News,* the Occidental Home for Girls, and the Chinatown Police Force. As a reform mayor, he said it was his special privilege to celebrate the work of institutions working for a better and safer community.

Several carriages were dispatched to transport the staff from *The News* and a group from the Occidental Home. The Occidental contingent was in a buoyant mood. Their spirits remained high after the shutdown of the Tong and the return to normalcy. Shu Lan-lan and Brian O'Grady had recently formed a new alliance once she had mustered the conviction to forgive him. Brian was now an aide to Shu Lan-lan's sewing program: setting up the day's patterns, cleaning up the studio, and making sure supplies were replenished.

When they finally reached the seven-story Palace at New Montgomery and Market Streets the girls from the Home were spellbound by its grandeur. The surrounding low buildings— some consisting of crude sheds—only enhanced its dramatic presence. Evergreen swags were draped at the roof level of the hotel. This time, Shu Lan-lan had added scalloped neck collars and fresh twigs of holly to the girls' queues—details aimed at a holiday audience.

Entering the main entrance from New Montgomery, the clattering from the carriages on the cobbles echoed off the walls of the Grand Court. Necks strained upward to catch glimpses of the arcaded galleries rimming each floor. The Court was bursting with a tropical garden filled with exotic plants, statuary, and fountains.

Having climbed from the carriages, Grace Caldwell and Margaret Culbertson ushered the choir through the Ladies Reception Room. Murmurs of disdain came from some of the women in the room. Some tossed their fur stoles about their shoulders as if this act might protect them from this intrusion of low lifes. Mrs. Culbertson was prepared: she had the girls break into a shortened version of the English carol, "I Saw Three Ships." This seemed to erase the scowls from faces in the room. Some even forced out feeble smiles.

The group crossed the marble floor of the Reception Room and entered the carpeted elevator lobby. Some of the girls balked at first, when told that they would be riding in completely enclosed boxes run by water. Their fears were dampened when they saw the lavish interiors of the elevators, all covered in some of the most elegant wood paneling they had ever seen. Vertical sheets of mirrors on two sides caused an outbreak of giggles as some worked their faces into fantastical contortions.

When the elevator doors opened onto the third floor they were just outside the South Parlor. A sign announced the evening's program: "The Occidental Girls Choir, 7 PM." A large cluster of chairs for the audience sat on a glistening parquet floor. An ebony grand piano stood at one end of the room with a large glass vase holding a profusion of flowers mixed with stems of bulrush. Nearby, several rows of chairs for the performers had been set up on three risers.

The room was abuzz. The first two rows of seats in the audience had been filled by girls from the Home who chattered and bobbed excitedly. *The Golden Hills' News* staff occupied the third row of seats. Shu Wei had settled into a seat between Mei Huang and his sister. Helping Mei Huang with her sweater, he held her gaze for a long moment. She briefly gripped his arm for a few seconds. Shu Lan-lan, wearing a bright red and yellow dress with an orange corsage, had her arm looped through her brother's. Brian entered, doing a controlled jig and sporting a vested suit and bright green tie. Doffing his beret in salute, he sat on the end next to Perrier Banier, who exchanged hearty greetings in French. Fan Ching spoke to him in Chinese. Jake Bradley stood and hugged the Irishman warmly.

In the fourth row, Wu Kang Ho and Li Po Tun were in animated discussion with Quincy Baron, dapper as usual with fob and high collar. Evelyn Parkford sparkled in a glittery gown and pearlescent beads.

Grace Caldwell, with her flowing gown, puffy sleeves at the shoulders, and colorful feathered hat, pranced her way to the middle of the first row. The girls on either side of her nuzzled her sides. Mrs. Blakewell had baked special holiday cookies which lay in a tin under her seat. On her lap was a colorful post-concert bouquet meant for Mrs. Culbertson and her singers. Sergeant Growman stood stiffly along one of the side walls with two of his deputies. Two curious children were inspecting his sheathed baton.

Mr. Brownhill, the manager of the hotel, called for quiet and spoke.

"Good evening ladies and gentlemen. I have the honor of introducing our musical program for the evening. When I heard their magical voices at the Old Saint Mary's Cathedral I was convinced that it would be a treat to bring them to this hotel. So, without further delay, let's welcome the Occidental Girls Choir."

Handkerchief tucked judiciously in her frilled cuff, Mrs. Culbertson brought her arms high and drew them abruptly downward as the choir began an energized version of "Jingle Bells." Shu Lan-lan had acquired some old leather straps from a barber. Her sewing group sewed small bells on cut-up sections of these which they proudly shook. Smiles flowered on a good many audience members' faces; some heads bobbed in time with the spirited melody.

Mrs. Culbertson had been careful to create a program rich in Asian and Western numbers. The Chinese folk song "Clear Moon, Quiet Winds" was followed by "Dong-Dong-Kui" and "The Anthem of Joy," a Hunan tribal folk song. A vigorous "Hark! The Herald Angels Sing" prompted some to sing along. Mrs. Culbertson introduced "The Jubilant Torch Festival" as a version of one that was traced to the legendary wrestler *Atilaba*, who drove away a plague of locusts using torches made from pine trees.

A merchant friend of Grace's had just received a shipment of some newly-invented flashlights. Each girl held up one of these small lighted fiber tubes with brass end caps and lenses. Using them as imitation torches, they alternately held them beneath their chins and waved them in figure eights. The concert was rounded out with "Snow White Flower Blossoms," a delicate but captivating folk song originating from the Va Tribe in the Yunnan province.

After the final piece, a crescendo of hand-clapping and bravos brought more curious heads to peer into the room from the adjoining hallway. The choir members hugged one another unabashedly. Shu Wei and Mei Huang slid their arms behind one another.

When the clapping had calmed, Mr. Brownhill said, "And now I'd like everyone to adjourn to the Green Room where we will continue our program."

A large audience had already gathered in the Green Room. This time a large dais with fresh cut flowers had been set up across the long side of a room with sweeping swags of green cloth ornamenting the walls. A gallery of framed pictures of notable former guests, from presidents to international dignitaries imparted gravitas, substance.

Once the girls from the Home shuffled in and joined those already seated, Mr. Brownhill stepped to the microphone. "Now if you'll all take your seats please. We are indeed privileged tonight to enjoy the company of our esteemed mayor, Mr. James D. Phelan. He was the guiding light behind organizing tonight's program and we thank him for taking time from his busy schedule to acknowledge our honorees. I should add that the hotel has decided to make this inaugural event an annual feature of our community outreach program."

The mayor, a rather taciturn thickset man with an oval face, shrouded by a tightly trimmed mustache and beard, rose deliberately from his position at the center of a long table. The mayor smoothed his vest, fiddled with his cuffs, glanced around the room and began.

"First, let me say I am honored to be a part of this event. We are here to celebrate those who are dedicated to the principles of justice and decency. Most of the children you see before you have already lived lives well beyond their ages. They stand here as examples of survivors—survivors of degradation and abuse. We honor these girls for their stamina under conditions that no human should have to endure. Tonight, we also honor their liberator and guiding light, Grace Caldwell. She has worked tirelessly and fearlessly to rescue and shelter those who would otherwise have had a dismal future."

The entire room erupted in steady drumbeats of applause. Shu Wei had found his way to the aisle and circled the room, capturing the moment with his camera.

"So, Grace, we honor you for all you do," the Mayor continued. "And to Shu Lan-lan, Mrs. Culbertson, and the rest of the staff at the Occidental Home, I can also say, wow, what a back-up team! Today we heard the angelic voices of the Occidental Girls Choir. I had never heard them before but I think it speaks volumes as to what spirit Grace and her team has instilled in these young women. Please come forward, Grace."

Grace Caldwell strode to the center with her usual purposeful vigor and accepted her plaque. "Let me thank the mayor but let me also say that I am accepting this award on behalf of Bo Cai, a girl that should have been here today. I know that she is now living peacefully in God's favor." A standing ovation followed.

"Next, let me acknowledge our fine police department in Chinatown," the mayor added. "Without their cooperation in the pursuit of ending the corrupt and vile enterprises of the Hap Tran Tong, we wouldn't be sitting together here today. Their aid in the rescue of endangered girls and in the arrest of homicidal psychopaths has been unwavering and unselfish in risk of life and limb. With that I give this award to my good friend Frank Growman." Frank shuffled over, head down, and took his plaque.

"And now, last but certainly not least, our next award goes to *The Golden Hills' News*. Where do I start? I guess I have always underestimated the power of the news. Fan Ching and his people have scoured the corners of our community to bring us stories that present a truthful picture of the dark and the virtuous in our society. Without their tenacious resolve, we and the general public would remain behind a cloud—a cloud that often hides from us the lowest enterprises of humankind.

"Let me specifically point out a key player in all of this. Someone who has come a long way under very difficult and dangerous circumstances. Shu Wei, please stand." Shu Wei couldn't believe his ears. It took some nudging from Mei Huang before he unraveled his body from his chair.

"As a junior member of *The News* he has, over the months, quickly and brilliantly transformed himself into one of the finest investigative reporters in the area. With the support of his partner, Mei Huang, he has steadfastly pursued stories while under both emotional and physical duress. The value of his pen is not to be underestimated. We all look forward to hearing more from both of them in the future. And, a big huzzah to the third member of that team, Brian O'Grady. Brian too, has charted new paths from difficult and wayward days.

"Finally, due to the tenacity of Fan Ching who refused to let his newspaper die and who believed in his team, we say a great big thanks. We also know you had the good fortune to partner with Perrier Banier at a timely point. To Perrier, we send our strongest condolences for the loss of your mother and our admiration for your commitment to *The News*. And lastly, Jake, from what I have come to know, you are the indispensable workhorse that keeps the presses oiled and running—without which we wouldn't be holding this in our hands." Phelan held aloft the current edition of *The News*. "Now, I'd like Fan Ching and Shu Wei to come forward to receive this plaque."

Fan Ching rose, smoothing out his elegant tunic with colorful beaded edgings. He searched for Shu Wei's elbow and guided him toward the mayor.

Still trembling, Shu Wei carried the plaque to his seat. He didn't make it. Mei Huang wrapped her arms around him and firmly kissed him on the cheek, bringing the biggest applause of the evening. They stood, arms around each other, smiling broadly. "Looks like we have a mandate," Mei Huang whispered to Shu Wei. "Where should our little team go next?

Wait, you don't need to answer that. Let's go get something at the hotel bar—maybe something even stronger than black tea."

Just then Fan Ching handed Shu Wei a buff-colored envelope and said, "This just came to our office yesterday. I forgot to tell you."

Shu Wei glanced over at Mei Huang while he worked the envelope open with his forefinger and gingerly removed its contents. It read:

> Master Shu Wei, Esq.
>
> You should recall our earlier meeting at The Call. I have recently come across news that you have drawn good swords against a villainous herd of outcasts and thieves. It is my great and good pleasure to hear of such a positive outcome. From my bully pulpit, where I famously give counsel to the virtuous as to the degenerates—as much as one can distinguish one from the other today—you are to be commended for mature acts twice your age. And, good lord, your skills with your newspaper reporting has the shine of precious gems. Now, as my future is on the wane just as yours is taking flight, allow me to dispense some of Twain's Maxims:
>
> To waste words is weakening to an article—don't waste words.
>
> Always do right. This will gratify some people and astonish the rest.
>
> Keep away from people who try to belittle your ambitions; small people always do that, but the really great make you feel that you, too, can become great.
>
> The difference between the right word and the almost right word is the difference between lightning and a lightning bug.

Don't part with your illusions. When they are gone you may still exist, but you have ceased to live.

Your good and continuing friend, *Mark Twain*

Shu Wei folded the paper back up and put it in his pocket. Shu Lan-lan joined her brother and leaned in to give him a strong sisterly embrace.

Acknowledgments

Where to start. Over a decade has gone by since this project started so I'll inevitably leave out someone who contributed in some way. If so, my apologies. First, author, novelist, and travel writer Linda Watanabe McFerrin (founder of Left Coast Writers) took my "story" and helped me make it into a "novel" through months of rewrites and editing. Her Writers Workshop was bloody for me but invaluable. Joy Brown did heroic work as copy editor. Ronald Kidd, author of many successful young adult books, offered timely advice on the intricacies of weaving a story that would appeal to this genre.

My good friend, the late Jerry Veverka, Cynde Wood, and my daughter Margot all weighed in with very perceptive comments. The folks at the San Francisco History Center of the San Francisco Public Library willingly guided me to reference materials that were invaluable. In a like manner, the Chinese Historical Society of America in San Francisco's Chinatown provided inspiration through their many excellent exhibits of historical artifacts and images. FoundSF.org's digital library was a font of resources.

Last, but certainly far from least, I want to thank my dear wife, Peggy, who has had to endure years of my moanings and frustrations while I sweated over numerous drafts and concepts. The value of her moral support, editing instincts, and critical eye has been incalculable.

A Word on Sources

I include here a very brief list of sources to give the reader the option of digging deeper into a given area of historical interest.

Bamford, Mary E. *TI: A Story of San Francisco's Chinatown*, Chicago: David C. Cook Publishing Company, 1899

Chen, Yong. *Chinese San Francisco: 1850—1943, A Trans-Pacific Community*, Stanford, California, Stanford University Press, 2000

Choy, Philip P. *San Francisco Chinatown: A Guide to Its History & Architecture*, San Francisco, City Lights

Clayborn, Hannah. *Historic Photos of the Chinese in California*, Nashville, Tennessee, Turner Publishing Company, 2009

Donaldina Cameron story (Grace Caldwell in the story): https://cameronhouse.org/

Genthe, Arnold. *Genthe's Photographs of San Francisco's Old Chinatown*, Selection and Text by John Kuo Wei Tchen, New York: Dover Publications, 1984

Hua, Vanessa. "Cherishing Chinatown," article in San Francisco Chronicle, May 13, 2003

Lee, Anthony W. *Picturing Chinatown: Art and Orientalism in San Francisco*, Berkeley, California, University of California Press, 2001

Olmstead, Nancy for Mission Creek Conservancy, *A History of San Francisco's Mission Bay,* 2nd ed. expanded, 2010, San Francisco

Various historic newspaper articles: Library of Congress online digital collections: www.loc.gov/collections/

_____. *City of Victoria; A Selection of the Museum's Historical Photographs.* Hong Kong: The Urban Council of Hong Kong, 1994

_____Wikipedia, several sources, including *Four Great Classical Novels*

_____Pathfinder library catalog, Bancroft Library, University of California, Berkeley

www.ingramcontent.com/pod-product-compliance
Lightning Source LLC
Chambersburg PA
CBHW020957120726
47905CB00009B/2740